What people are saying abou...

HOW SWEET THE SOUND

"With poetic prose, lyrical descriptions, and sensory details that bring the reader deep into every scene, Amy K. Sorrells has delivered a lush, modern telling of the age-old story of Tamar. But that's not all. With a full cast of colorful characters and juxtaposed first-person narratives woven throughout, this story dives into the Gulf Coast culture of pecan orchards and debutante balls, exposing layers of family secrets and sins. In the end comes redemption, grace, forgiveness, and faith, but not without a few scars carried by those who manage to survive the wrath of hardened hearts. Bravo!"

Julie Cantrell, *New York Times* bestselling author
of *Into the Free* and *When Mountains Move*

"*How Sweet the Sound* is one of those books you want to savor slowly, like sips of sweet tea on a hot Southern day. Achingly beautiful prose married with honest, raw redemption make this book a perfect selection for your next book club."

Mary DeMuth, author of fifteen
books, including *The Muir House*

"Meeting these characters and stepping into their worlds forever changed the contour of my heart. Sorrells's words effortlessly rise from the page with a cadence that is remarkably brave and wildly beautiful."

Toni Birdsong, author of *More than a Bucket List*

"Filled with brokenness and redemption, grit and grace, *How Sweet the Sound* is a heartrending coming-of-age debut about God's ability to heal the hurting and restore the damaged. Sorrells deftly reminds us that no matter how dark the night, hope is never lost. Not if we have eyes to see."

Katie Ganshert, author of *Wildflowers from Winter* and *Wishing on Willows*

"A stirring tale of loss and redemption. Amy Sorrells will break your heart and piece it back twice its size."

Billy Coffey, author of *When Mockingbirds Sing*

"A daring and enchanted story, Amy K. Sorrells's *How Sweet the Sound* beckons readers to a land of pecan groves, bay breezes, and graveyard secrets rising up like the dead on judgment day."

Karen Spears Zacharias, author of *Mother of Rain*

"Amy Sorrells weaves an engaging tale of heart-wrenching family tragedy in stunningly beautiful, lyrical prose. If you are a fan of women's fiction, don't miss this fresh, new voice."

Jordyn Redwood, author of the Bloodline Trilogy

"*How Sweet the Sound* takes on the hard things of life. Author Amy Sorrells writes with tenderness, grace, and the heartbroken voice of experience."

Lori Borgman, columnist for *McClatchy-Tribune*,
author of *The Death of Common Sense*,
and national speaker

"Can love heal the pain and hurt of lies and deep secrets held across generations? This heartwarming and heart-wrenching story by Amy K. Sorrells takes us into the depths of this question as one family fights back from a disaster that shattered hopes and dreams. Amy K. Sorrells takes us on a powerful journey of love and redemption, a journey the reader will not soon forget."

Henry McLaughlin, award-winning
author of *Journey to Riverbend*

"Amy K. Sorrells has a lyrical voice that immediately draws you into the complex lives of captivating characters and a powerful tale that will leave you breathless. This is one of those stories that will continue to live on in a reader's mind long after turning the last page. It is hard to believe that *How Sweet the Sound* is a debut novel."

Tina Ann Forkner, author of *Rose House*

"What a powerful story. This book reveals and heals through the power of love. I'm a better person for having read this tender-but-truthful coming-of-age tale."

Janalyn Voigt, literary judge and
author of *DawnSinger*

"*How Sweet the Sound* brings to light the wrecking torment of a sin-filled past and the aftermath of fear that paralyzes a family's ability to cope with the present. Through the lives of a Southern family, we see how deeply hurt people hurt even those they love. While it's a story of one family, it's also a look at the world in which we live. Sorrells vividly exposes sin's path to destruction, but leaves us with a beautiful reminder of how hope is restored when grace arrives to cover the brokenness."

Tami Heim, president and CEO of
Christian Leadership Alliance

"Sorrells has created a story of hope and redemption set in an Alabaman pecan orchard. Rich with Scripture, folk music, Creole phrases, pecan orchards, and Southern ways, Sorrells weaves a tale of generational sex abuse. I've never see a fiction book depict the devastation and healing process for survivors in such a candid and accurate way."

Lucille Zimmerman, counselor,
teacher, and author of *Renewed*

"Evocative, brutal, yet redemptive, *How Sweet the Sound* forces you to think long and hard about difficult subjects and pain, but it leaves you with the hope of grace and mercy. Thanks, Amy, for taking me there."

Dave Rodriguez, senior pastor of
Grace Church, Noblesville, IN

"Amy Sorrells reminds us of the pain that many families face when some of the members want to keep secrets so the family name will be protected. Hurricane Frederic, pecan harvesting, jubilees, and cotillions reminded us of both the painful and enjoyable times we've had growing together as a successful farm family. We pray Amy's book will help those who have experienced similar pain."

Mona Barfield and Sandra Bishop, B&B Pecan Company, Fairhope, AL, since 1956

"A colorful, compelling novel—just what you'd expect a story of the South to be. It is alternatively explosive and introspective, but always engaging."

Richard J. Roth, senior associate dean of Northwestern University in Qatar

"A beautiful story of God's redeeming power to make all things new! Amy Sorrells takes her readers on a journey confronting the spiraling darkness of generational sin and experiencing healing and freedom when the light of Truth shines."

Carmen D'Arcy Stanczykiewicz, worship arts and programming pastor at Traders Point Christian Church

"I have been a voracious reader ever since I learned to read and have enjoyed many memorable books for many different reasons. *How Sweet the Sound* reads with the sweetest honesty and unpretentious beauty. The word *unsophisticated* comes to mind, and I mean that in the best possible way—sophistication is a veneer we hide behind. I'm not sure I can find the words right now to express all this book has made me feel, because even though I am done with it, I don't think it is nearly done with me."

Carolyn O'Brien, Page & Palette Bookstore, Fairhope, AL

"This beautifully well-written book offers hope and healing from tragedy and brokenness. The believable characters come alive in this remarkable book."

Birdie Gunyon Meyer, RN, MA,
coordinator of the Perinatal Mood Disorders
Program at Indiana University Health

"There are certain books you enjoy reading until the last page, place them back on the bookshelf, and move on with your life. Then there are those you want to savor—with storylines and characters that work their way into your heart and hold fast. *How Sweet the Sound* is a book in the latter category. You'll catch yourself wondering how Anniston, Comfort, and the others are getting on in life long after you've turned the last page, and you'll find yourself hoping you'll meet them again soon. Amy Sorrells's debut novel exceeded all my expectations. I can't wait to see what she has in store next."

Kathy "Katdish" Richards, blogger,
humorist, and Internet tornado

"*How Sweet the Sound* offers a glimpse into the trauma and devastation of incest and abuse that impacts so many lives. Amy Sorrells's insight brings the reader into a front-row seat to reveal the far-reaching effect that sexual abuse has on not just the victim, but the family and the community. This is a poignant story that will captivate and enlighten."

Anita M. Carpenter, CEO of Indiana
Coalition against Sexual Assualt, national
speaker, and advocate for social justice

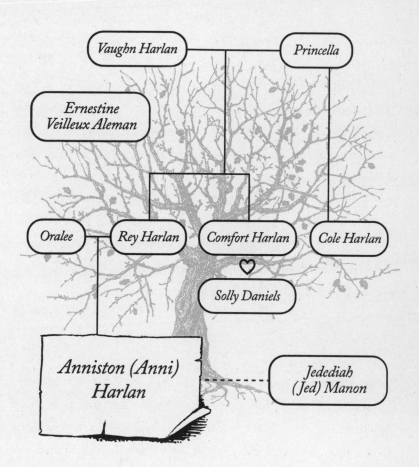

HOW

SWEET

THE

SOUND

HOW

SWEET

THE

SOUND

A NOVEL

Amy K. Sorrells

David C Cook®
transforming lives together

HOW SWEET THE SOUND
Published by David C Cook
4050 Lee Vance View
Colorado Springs, CO 80918 U.S.A.

David C Cook Distribution Canada
55 Woodslee Avenue, Paris, Ontario, Canada N3L 3E5

David C Cook U.K., Kingsway Communications
Eastbourne, East Sussex BN23 6NT, England

The graphic circle C logo is a registered trademark of David C Cook.

Luke 2:25–26, 28–32 in chapter 10 and 2 Corinthians 1:6 in chapter 41 are
taken from the Holy Bible, New International Version©, NIV®. Copyright
© 1973, 2011 by Biblica, Inc.™ Used by permission of Zondervan. All
rights reserved worldwide. www.zondervan.com; Psalm 147:3 in chapter 16
is taken from the King James Version of the Bible. (Public Domain.).

The website addresses recommended throughout this book are offered as a
resource to you. These websites are not intended in any way to be or imply an
endorsement on the part of David C Cook, nor do we vouch for their content.

This story is a work of fiction. Characters and events are the product of the author's
imagination. Any resemblance to any person, living or dead, is coincidental.

LCCN 2013949575
ISBN 978-1-4347-0544-0
eISBN 978-0-7814-1125-7

© 2014 Amy Sorrells
The Author is represented by and this book is published in association with the
literary agency of WordServe Literary Group, Ltd., www.wordserveliterary.com.

The Team: John Blase, Nicci Hubert, Amy Konyndyk,
Nick Lee, Tonya Osterhouse, Karen Athen
Cover Design: FaceOut Studios, Tim Green
Cover Photo: Shutterstock

Printed in the United States of America
First Edition 2014

1 2 3 4 5 6 7 8 9 10

122013

ACKNOWLEDGMENTS

You hold this book in your hands because of a grand mix of people who took a chance on me, and an even grander mix of folks who prayed for me—and for you, the reader.

I'd like to thank a few of them.

To Judy Mikalonis, who believed in me enough to invite me to Mount Hermon Christian Writers Conference in 2009, and to Rachel Williams and all her staff, who nurture writers under the dappled canopy of the great redwoods every year. Saying yes changed my life forever.

To my writing prayer team, who've stuck with me since 2009, even when I offered them chances to jump off this wild and crazy writing train: Mike ("my Gandalf"), Trish, Birdie, Alyssa, Serena, Tami, Glenn, Billie, John, Greg, Christie, Mike, Kara, Carol Lee ("Mrs. C."), Tera, Ana, Eileen, Amy, Ann, Anne, Cyndy, Debbie, and my "random" Mount Hermon roomie and "twin," Sherri. Love you all and grateful beyond measure for your support. Any hearts moved by the words in this manuscript are in large part because of the prayers you poured over this sojourn.

To Pastor Dave and Penny, who shepherded me when I was Anni's age, who loved and supported me when they learned I was a lot like Comfort, and who, along with Pastor Tim, were gracious enough to read the crappy first versions of this book. To my Wednesday-morning girls: Susan, Mary Susan, Cornelia, Melinda ("Samson"), Lisa, Susan, Cara, Jennifer, Heather, Susan, Anne, Amanda, Sarah, and Amy—I couldn't and wouldn't dare do life without you! And to all my friends and family at Grace Community Church for always pointing me back where I belong: at the foot of the cross and in the arms of my Savior, Jesus Christ.

To my hospital coworkers for your enthusiasm and encouragement for "my other life" as a writer and for always making me laugh. It's a privilege to work alongside you all.

To Kathy "Katdish" Richards, Billy Coffey, Karen Spears Zacharias, Mary DeMuth, Barbara Scott, and Rachelle Gardner for being some of the first folks to believe I could make a go of this.

To my agent, Sarah Freese, and to Greg Johnson and all the good folks at WordServe Literary—I adore you, you are incredible, and I'm not worthy!

To John Blase for taking a chance on me and to Don Pape, Ingrid Beck, and everyone on the David C Cook team. Your faith and professionalism inspire me to do and be so much more.

To Amy Konyndyk and the design team for creating a breathtaking cover I can only hope the insides are worthy of.

To my editor Nicci Jordan Hubert. You scare the living daylights out of me. Thank you for being so thoroughly tough on me and for giving me the permission I need to go to the hard places.

And to my copy editor, Tonya Osterhouse—it's the little things that make the biggest difference, and you are the reason this novel shines.

To my precious sons, Tucker, Charlie, and Isaac, for putting up with me wearing pajamas all day and wearing curlers in the carpool lines, and for giving up your Minecraft time so I can be on my computer all day. For teaching me what no child signs up to teach his parent: what it's like to live fearlessly and unscarred. And for allowing me to relearn how to love life through your wondering hearts and eyes. God is already changing the world because of each of your brave and beautiful hearts.

To my husband, Scott, who loves me in spite of everything and still. Who puts me on airplanes when I'm too afraid to go. And who says to me multiple times a day, "You are beautiful." Someday, because of you, I will believe that.

And first and foremost, to Jesus Christ, who has, does, and will always make all things new. In Him I move, breathe, write, and owe my entire being.

To the silent ones.

Marine experts say that the jubilee is caused by an
upward movement of oxygen-poor bottom water
forcing bottom-type fish and crustaceans ashore.
Auburn University Marine Extension and Research Center

Behold and see
What a great heap of grief lay hid in me,
And how the red wild sparkles dimly burn
Through the ashen greyness ...
"V"

E. B. Browning

She carries within her a tree of silence
born from seeds of pain sewn long ago.
Its roots are now thick as a man's arm.
To tear them out would collapse her,
her body's posture built on the scaffolding
of things as they should not have been.
So she walks as if retreating, leaning back
not in fear but at a slight angle where
the sun and dark have finally found rest.
John Blase

LATE 1979

Kay koule tronpe soley men li pa tronpe lapli.
"A leaking roof may fool sunny weather, but cannot fool the rain."

CHAPTER 1

Anniston

I thought I'd lived through everything by the time I was thirteen.

Hurricane Frederic nearly wiped the southern part of Alabama off the map that fall, and half of our family's pecan orchards along with it. Daddy said we were lucky—that the Miller pecan farm down the road lost everything. The Puss 'n Boots Cat Food factory supplied our whole town of Bay Spring with ice and water for nearly a week until the power and phones came back on along the coast of Mobile Bay. Anyone who could hold a hammer or start up a chain saw spent weeks cutting up all the uprooted trees and azaleas, pounding down new shingles, and cleaning up all that God, in His infinite fury, blew through our land. Like most folks who lived along the coast, we'd find a way to build back up—if we weren't fooled into thinking the passing calm of the eye meant the storm was over.

If I'd only known this about Hurricane Frederic—that the drudging months leading up to Thanksgiving would be the only peace we'd see for some time. Weren't no weathermen or prophets with megaphones standing on top of the Piggly Wiggly Saturday mornings to shout warnings of storms and second comings to us.

The only warning was the twitch of my grandmother's eye.

"Happy Thanksgiving!" Mama, Daddy, and I said in unison.

Princella pulled the front door open to let us in, kissing us each coolly on the cheek as we passed. Her graying hair was twisted into a tight, smooth bun on top of her head, and a purple suede pantsuit hung on her too-thin frame.

"Thank you. Oralee, Ernestine will help y'all take that food on to the kitchen."

"How are you, Mother?" Daddy had grouched around the house all morning as we readied ourselves to go to the big house.

"Why, I'm fine. Thank you, Rey. Your father is in his den." Princella nodded toward the book-lined room to the left of the foyer.

I followed Daddy. Though I loved peeling potatoes and painting butter on yeast rolls as they came steaming out of the oven, I didn't feel like being around Princella, who preferred I call her by her proper name, saying she felt too young to be called *Grandma*. I couldn't figure her out. Then again, who could? Mama called her an enigma. I called her old and bitter.

The thick, wide shoulders of my granddaddy, Vaughn, filled every inch of the leather chair behind his desk. Wire-rimmed spectacles sat on the tip of his nose, and he rubbed his neatly trimmed moustache as he concentrated on the thick ledger open in front of him. As soon as he saw Daddy, he got up and threw his arms around him hard, patting him on the back. "Good to see you, Rey."

"You, too, Daddy."

"And how's Miss Anniston today?"

"Fine, sir." The sun caught on the silver bevels of a sword sitting on Vaughn's big wood desk, sending shards of light dancing across the walls and ceiling.

"Wow, I haven't seen that in a long time." Daddy gently picked up the sword and let his fingers glide along the blade, down to the tip and back again. Carvings of horses and soldiers wrapped around the thick handle.

"My granddaddy gave me that sword. Belonged to his granddaddy, Gabriel Harlan, from before the War." Vaughn picked up the case, the name *Harlan* inscribed deep into the worn, cracked leather. "I intended to wait until later, but I might as well give it to you now."

Surprise spread across Daddy's face, ruddy from all the days working outside in the orchards, but softened by the kindness in his eyes, which were heavy with the love I saw when he read to me each night, even still, before bedtime. "I always thought this belonged to Cole next."

Vaughn stood up and peered out the window overlooking the orchards. "Granddaddy helped Gabriel plant most of these. Helped him plant the trees, babying them until they pulled in a crop. While they waited for the trees to yield enough to live off of, Gabriel oystered and fished and worked for lumber companies, making an honest living and providing for everyone—including the freed slaves—who lived on this land. One of only a few abolitionists back then, he paid his black workers a fair wage, sometimes choosing them over white workers who needed a job, and at the expense of ridicule and putting his family in danger. He retired from the Confederate Army before the War, so he never fought in it. Granddaddy told stories about how Gabriel wouldn't have fought in that war if he'd died refusing, because he hated slavery so." He turned to face Daddy. "He stood up for what was right and for the weak. Raised me to do the same. And that's how I believe I've raised you."

"Daddy—"

Vaughn held his hand up, and to my surprise, a tear rolled down the side of his face as he kept talking. "Been thinking a lot about this family lately, how I done you and your sister, Comfort, a disservice over the years by feeling sorry for Cole. Listening to your mother when she said I was too harsh with him, when harsh was what he needed. I felt sorry for him, I suppose, not having his real daddy around. I never listened to you or your sister, or anyone for that matter, who voiced concern about his choices and actions. And now I see those actions have taken a toll on all of you, and I'm sorry for that. I brought him in and raised him as my own—and I would do it again—but you and Comfort … You're my flesh and blood."

He took the sword from Daddy's hands and slid it into the leather case. "When my daddy gave Gabriel's sword to me, he said it stood for peace, not war. That it should be given to the firstborn son, a son raised to believe in freedom. Someone who will fight injustice with courage and truth."

Quiet fell over the room, except for the ticktock of the grandfather clock in the hallway.

"Take it, son. Will you?"

"What's going on in here?" Princella's unexpected voice struck us like a whip across our bare backs. "What are you doing, Vaughn? That's Cole's sword."

Vaughn walked right up close to Princella until he stood about an inch from her face. "Something I shoulda done a long time ago."

"Hey, everybody!"

My aunt, Comfort, and her long-time boyfriend, Solly, burst through the study door, giggling like a couple of kids my age. But their faces fell when they saw Princella and Vaughn standing there in obvious disagreement.

"I'm—I'm sorry. Were we interrupting?"

Princella turned sharp and stomped out of the room.

"Sorry, Solly. You're fine," Vaughn said. "Please come in."

"Welcome to the festivities," Daddy simpered.

"Comfort!" I ran and hugged her despite the tension I felt in the air.

"Hey, darlin'," Comfort said in a tempered voice, hugging me back. Despite my affection for T-shirts, boy shorts, and flip-flops, her outfit, as usual, was to die for. Beneath a striped, fringed poncho, she wore flared white trousers, a bright-orange halter top, and orange plastic platform shoes that matched. Her hair was done up in a high bun tied up with a matching orange-and-white scarf that trailed down her back.

"What about me? Don't I get a hug from my girl?" Solly, a burly fellow with curly dark hair that fell over his ears and glasses, caught Daddy's eye as he yanked me into a bear hug. He looked handsome as ever, dressed in what appeared to be a brand-new pair of jeans, a plaid, button-down western shirt, a black cowboy hat, and black boots.

Thank goodness they came when they did. If Princella wanted to be in a snit, fine. But with Comfort and Solly there to brighten the mood, maybe she wouldn't ruin the whole of Thanksgiving Day.

Bo nan bouch, men pè dan.
"Kiss the mouth, but fear the teeth."

CHAPTER 2

Anniston

The mess during everyone's arrivals redeemed itself over the sizzle of fried turkey, yeast rolls melting in our mouths, and the crunch of crawfish-pecan dressing. The sweet potato soufflé settled as Vaughn finished carving the turkey.

"Rey, would you do us the honor?"

"Amen," we said in unison after Daddy finished thanking God for blessings past and yet to come.

"Somebody pass the giblets," Vaughn said with a gleam in his eye.

"Saved some just for you." Princella winked at him, one of her few ways of showing affection, as she passed the bowl of steaming bird innards. How anyone ever ate those, I never could understand.

"Princella, your cranberry mold is beautifully done. It must've taken you forever to get it to set like that." Mama took a bite of the scarlet jelly.

"Thank you for noticing, Oralee. It did take quite awhile."

"And the silver. I've never seen it shine so," said Comfort.

"I can't tell you how many times I've dreamed of your yeast rolls since last year, Mama," said Daddy.

Princella smiled at them both, all the while holding her neck up high, stiff, and hawk-like, perched over the rest of us as if we were the meal. Thankfully, the centerpiece, a vase stuffed to overflowing with every shade of rose you could imagine—reds, pinks, peaches, yellows from Princella's garden—nearly hid me as I pushed pieces of turkey around my plate.

Princella and I had a complicated relationship, not the warm-milk-and-cookies type most of my friends had with their grandmothers. On the rare occasions I spent the day with her, I caught glimpses of kindness, even sympathy, especially as she tended her rose gardens or brought food to church shut-ins. But most days, she acted matter-of-fact and strict in matters of fashion, manners, and social standing—especially when it came to my life.

The back door opened and shut with a boom that rattled the crystal, and my uncle, Cole, barged into the room. Princella stood up so fast she nearly knocked her plate off the table. "Welcome home, son!"

"Mama." He held her by the shoulders, kissed her on the forehead, then stood back and glared at the rest of us. The outline of his thick chest muscles pushed against the *Alabama Southern* on the front of his T-shirt, and his face was a mess of unshaven stubble. Though he coached football at Alabama Southern, Cole often moved back and forth without notice, never settling here or there.

"Nice of y'all to wait for me," he said.

"I'm so sorry, hon—"

Ernestine, our family's Haitian nanny and house help for the past thirty-five years, interrupted. "Don't you give your mama a hard time now. We can't ever be sure of when you'll show your face around here. You surely know that."

"All I surely know is that I'd appreciate a tall glass of bourbon." He sneered. Never was one to put up with correction from anyone.

Ernestine, who sat on my right, started to get up, but the lengths of her flowing, Caribbean-style dress caught on the leg of the chair.

"It's okay, Ernestine. You sit. I'll get it," said Mama, glowering at Cole.

"On the rocks."

I watched as Ernestine's rough, ebony hands adjusted the napkin on her lap. She'd worked for our family ever since Daddy was a boy, raising him, raising Comfort, and half raising me. Whenever Mama worked, Daddy brought me here with him, and even now after school, Ernestine minded me. Up until I grew too big to sit on her lap, she'd held me with her dark brown arms. Eyes rich and sweet like chocolate chips, she listened to my every dream and fear. On rainy days, she brought out her squeezebox and handed me the *frottoir*, and we made music and danced up a storm under the protection of the giant, pillared front porch, singing and laughing like crazy at the lightning, and drowning out the pounding of the thunder. She taught me how to braid friendship bracelets, lines of color knit together in a tight string of love. She taught me the Bible and how to pray on my knees. She was my best—and close to my only—friend.

"So." Princella sat back down, straightening her napkin on her lap. "How long will you be staying?"

Cole pulled out the empty seat next to her and winked. "Long enough to get good and full of your cookin', Mama."

Princella's whole face looked brighter. Meanwhile, the rest of us ate our meal in silence. Those of us close to Cole knew to keep our mouths shut when he came around. The whole town had worshipped him ever since he'd grown old enough to hold his head up with a football helmet attached. Kenny Stabler picked him for an understudy in youth leagues. He led Bay Spring High School to the highest-ranked season finish ever, second only to a big school out of Birmingham in the state championship. Got himself a full ride to Alabama Southern with the promise afterward of coaching for them. But when he was home … Well, he was unpredictable.

"Now? Do you think?" Solly whispered to Comfort.

Comfort blushed and nodded as she grabbed his hand under the table.

Solly set down his fork and cleared his throat. "I have an announcement to make. Comfort and I do. Vaughn?"

Vaughn gave him a crooked grin and nodded.

"Last night, I asked Vaughn's permission for Comfort's hand in marriage."

"And he has my approval." Vaughn beamed.

"And after proposing properly to Comfort"—he kissed her on the temple—"she agreed to be my wife."

Together, Solly and Comfort brought their linked hands up onto the table, and sure enough, a small diamond on her ring finger caught the light from the dining room chandelier.

I squealed, and Mama, eyes welling, about crawled over the table to hug Comfort.

"Oh, Comfort, I'm so happy for y'all!" she said.

Princella gave a thin smile and set her spoon down a bit harder than she should have. "Well, then. Congratulations. But I do hope the ceremony will be … private."

"What do you mean, Mama?" Comfort's face faded from pink to the color of the mashed potatoes.

"She means," Cole said, wiping his mouth with the pressed linen napkin, "we don't need to invite the whole town to see a whore get married."

Mama's fingers tightened around her fork and knife.

Solly's and Daddy's jaws clenched.

Comfort's chair squeaked as she pushed back from the table. "Excuse me—I—"

"Wait." Vaughn's voice cracked across the table like a gunshot. Then, softly, he spoke to Comfort. "Please, darlin'. Please wait." Then he scowled down the table at Princella. "Enough."

"What on earth do you mean?" she replied.

"We will let them celebrate, and we will support whatever and however they choose to do so."

"Of course. I don't want to draw the whole town's attention to it. That's all."

Cole sniggered, and Solly woulda come across the table at him had his arms not been around a trembling Comfort.

Daddy pounded his fist onto the table, ice rattled in the glasses, and our plates jumped. "She's your daughter. My sister. We will all support them, with or without you two." He pointed a finger at Cole. "And as for you, the only reason anyone thinks poorly of Comfort is because of you and the heinous things you've said about her over the years. Things I'm not gonna let you get away with anymore."

"Whatever, John Boy."

Princella's chair squeaked across the floor next. Cole laughed and threw the rest of his bourbon down his throat. The ticktock of the grandfather clock grew loud in my ears.

Ou konnen ki sa ou genyen, men ou
pa konnen ki sa ki ap vini an.
"You know what you've got, but you don't know what's coming."

CHAPTER 3

Anniston

"What is that banging at this time of night? Anniston? You okay?"
Mama hollered from her bedroom across the hall.

The noise had already jolted me awake. Sounded like someone ramming a post against the front door, they banged so hard. I
stumbled out of bed, one of Daddy's old Tulane T-shirts hanging
down to my knees, and met Mama in the hall. Her pretty brown
hair fell in tousled pieces around her face. Daddy, dressed only in
his boxer shorts, rounded the corner to the front room and flipped
on the porch light. Molly, my white retriever, barked like crazy,
scratching at the threshold as Daddy turned the lock and opened
the door.

"Rey? Who is it?" Mama pulled her thick, pink bathrobe tighter around her slender self.

"Dear God, it's Comfort. And she's hurt. Oralee, call an ambulance." Daddy yanked the door open, and Comfort stood on our front doorstep, shivering. Her face was swollen, her dress torn at the shoulder and splattered with blood.

"Tell the operator to send an ambulance," Mama instructed me. Then she ran to Comfort, who fell into her and Daddy's arms.

I made the call from the phone in the kitchen, and the operator's flat and solid voice steadied my shaking hands as I held the phone against my ear and asked her to please send help.

Back in the living room, Mama led Comfort to the couch and looked over her wounds. "Grab a couple towels and a washcloth from the bathroom, would you please, Anni?"

"Who did this to you?" Daddy and Mama were both kneeling in front of her when I came back from the bathroom and placed a damp washcloth into Comfort's limp hand. Her eyes, hollow and unseeing, fixed on an empty space on the wall above the television. She wrapped her thin arms around herself and slowly rocked back and forth, humming a tune that sounded familiar but that I could not place. I sat next to her and used another damp cloth to try to wash clumps of dried blood from her hair, its golden waves reaching nearly down to her waist. Right now, Comfort didn't look anything like the former homecoming queen and newly engaged woman she was.

Mama brushed a wad of matted hair away from Comfort's face. "You're safe now, sweetie. Can you tell us who hurt you?"

Sirens screamed in the distance. The sound of crashing metal jarred our attention back to the front door as my uncle Cole ripped open the storm door. He exploded into the room, bringing freezing cold air and the strong stench of alcohol in with him. His Alabama Southern football jersey fell half out of the waist of his jeans, and the knee of one of his pant legs was torn open. His face glowed purple with fury as he leaned over Mama and Daddy, and stuck his finger in Comfort's face.

"Think you can run away from me, you piece of filth?"

Daddy jumped up, his frame thick and strong from working the pecan orchards dusk to dawn—pruning the trees, fighting off critters and disease, planting and moving new trees and saplings. He put his hand on Cole's shoulder, squeezed hard, and got up real close to his face. "You better back off right now, brother. Can't you see she's hurt?"

"I see plenty. And you're the one who'd better back off." Cole shoved Daddy's arm off him.

I let out a yelp when Cole lifted the gun he held at his side and pointed it at Daddy's chest. Comfort did, too, and got up and ran to Mama and Daddy's bedroom, Mama following after her and grabbing me along the way.

"Did you do this to her? *Did you?*" Daddy yelled. "And get that gun outta my face."

Cole turned toward the bedroom, close behind us. Mama tried to step between him and Comfort, but she couldn't stop him. He was one of the biggest men in this corner of the state.

Those sirens were taking forever.

Cole grabbed Comfort's already-swollen arm and threw her on the bed. "You want it again, sis? Do you?"

"Stop it! Stop it, Cole!" Mama shrieked.

Now, I'd heard a shotgun fire before—even shot one myself when Daddy took me out to hunt wild turkey and other game allowed to roam the orchards. But I'd never heard one in the confined space of a bedroom. The blast deafened me, the sudden force of it causing me to brace myself against the wall. I clamored to the safety of Mama and Daddy's closet nearby. The door hung open, as if in awe of the scene playing out in slow motion before us.

Cole grabbed the side of his chest and fell backward, away from the bed, letting go of Comfort but still hanging on to his gun, which he raised and pointed at Daddy, who stood in the bedroom doorway, aiming his shotgun at Cole's head.

Daddy dropped the shotgun and fell to the floor the near instant the bullet fired out of Cole's gun, and the sparkle of life in his eyes left him, floating like stars into the sky from his eyes. I learned then that blood truly is thicker than water, especially when it's full of pain thick as molasses, pushing through fragile veins, puddling onto the floor like an oil stain in the center of an empty Piggly Wiggly parking lot.

"We're gonna need backup, Wes. And the coroner."

A paramedic named Joe, who worked with Mama at the Bay Spring Memorial Hospital Emergency Department, talked out of the corner of his mouth into his walkie-talkie. Another paramedic pulled sheets over Cole and Daddy. A third tended to Comfort in the bedroom. No one noticed me leaning against the closet door, watching as the two puddles of blood spread into the gray carpet like the pain overwhelming my heart.

"Anniston? Anni?" I hadn't seen Mama come back into the room. She crouched before me, and I collapsed into her arms and sobbed. The smell of her freshly showered hair and skin did little to ease the sting of gun smoke still burning my nose. She pressed my face into the crook of her shoulder, shielding my eyes from the sight of Daddy and Cole's covered bodies, as we followed Comfort—now on a stretcher—and the other paramedics out of the house. Cold snaps weren't unusual in late November, and our breaths formed fragile plumes as we exhaled.

By the time we reached the hospital, Princella and Vaughn were already waiting there. Vaughn, dressed in his trademark overalls and collared flannel shirt, tried to keep his arm around a fidgeting Princella. His cheeks looked hollowed out, making his red, swollen eyes too big for his face. Too frightened.

Princella pushed him away.

"What have you done to my son?" Princella wailed at Comfort, who, from the ambulance stretcher, stared past her with hollow eyes.

"Ma'am, please let us through," Joe, the paramedic, pleaded.

"*Sons*, Princella. You have—" Mama caught herself, tears pouring down her cheeks. "*Had* two of them. They're *both* gone."

More police cars squealed into the parking lot.

A cold, misty rain swirled around us as the doors to the emergency room slammed open, and I felt caught, like I was in one of those glass snow globes, shook up with no place to go. Evil trickled down soft all around us, landing in a blanket that would cover up the sins of the fathers until spring came along, shaking us up all over again.

Chak venn afekte kè a.
"Every vein affects the heart."

CHAPTER 4

Anniston

Spanish moss hung from the great arms of the oak tree like a curtain, waiting patient but sure to close upon the innocent parts of my life. The lacy billows hung thick from years of soaking in ocean air, and they hid the cloudless sky above. Mama nudged me with her elbow to pay attention and to face the scene before me where two caskets waited to drop simultaneously into cold black holes dug out of burned, red Alabama clay.

Preacher Beckett from the Bay Spring Presbyterian Church wore his black Sunday preaching robe. He tugged at the tongue of his white collar, which peeked out at the center of his neck. In the days since Daddy and Cole died, a hot wind had blown in from the Gulf of Mexico, which caused a stream of sweat to trickle down the side of Preacher Beckett's smooth-shaven face.

Sweat rolled down the back of the black wool dress Princella had picked out for me. I rubbed the scratchy cloth between my fingers, still bothered about having no choice in what to wear this day.

"A daughter wears black to her daddy's funeral, Anniston." Princella had scrolled through hanger after hanger of my favorite T-shirts until she found the dreaded black wool dress in the back of my closet earlier that morning.

"Here." She shoved the dress at me and dodged stacks of sealed-up moving boxes as she left me in the center of my bedroom. Pretty amazing how thirteen years of my life were packed away in a matter of days.

Luckily, she hadn't said anything about my shoes, so I stood in the middle of that cemetery, my Chuck Taylor All Stars the only splash of white in a sea of drab, gray townsfolk. The mayor of Bay Spring, Hiram Lawson, stood across from us, a reminder of our status in the community. He'd been so proud of the national attention given to the Harlan pecan orchards and their over-whelming sales, he'd commissioned the Harlan company logo painted on the local water tower. So no matter where I went in town—or in life, for that matter—things reminded me of my place in the world.

Too bad Hiram Lawson didn't know what I knew, that being a Harlan wasn't all it was cracked up to be. Sure, I sat in press-box seats at Alabama Southern football games, took cotillion lessons with sweaty-palmed boys, and got hairdos at the finest salon in Magnolia County as soon as my hair grew enough to fit around a curler. But none of that meant a lick considering the place we found ourselves in this day.

Instead of the singing of a hymn or the soft strum of a guitar, the throaty hum of mowers circling the pecan trees accompanied the ceremony. Acres of rolling hills stretched as far as I could see, stiff rows of trees standing at attention, branches raised as if to salute the two dead men. The small graveyard where we stood was the dot on the exclamation point of land that generations of Harlans before us worked and tended, side by side and in peace. That is, until the events that led up to this day.

I did not listen as the preacher spoke. Instead, I wondered how it came to pass that two brothers—one of them my daddy— were dead. I wondered which came first—the hate or the crime? I wondered if Cain always hated Abel, or if the hate that caused brother to kill brother happened in a flash of evil. Mostly, I wondered what I would do after the red clay covered my daddy and if any of us would ever recover.

After the preacher said the twenty-third Psalm and closed his Bible, the caretaker lowered the caskets. Folks lined up to throw dirt or flowers on top. Princella and Vaughn sat on one side of the graves in a row of velvet-draped chairs, and Mama, Ernestine, and I sat in the front row across from them as we all waited for the crowds to pass. None of us said a word, and I was glad for the quiet. Glad the noise from the past week had disappeared, for this moment at least. Glad for Mama's soft, white hand wrapped around my left one, and Ernestine's ebony, calloused fingers holding tight to my right. Not a one of us let go, even as we walked from the cemetery to Aunt Comfort's house next door to pick up the empty grocery basket on her front porch.

Comfort had stayed home from the funeral, even though she lived right next to the cemetery. No one could blame her. Problem was, she hadn't come out since the shooting, almost an entire week ago, and it didn't look hopeful that she'd come out anytime soon. After the sirens stopped screaming and the detectives stopped coming around, she came home from the hospital and shut herself inside her cottage on the edge of the Harlan property, and she wouldn't come out for nothing.

We walked along the rocky wall separating the cemetery from Comfort's yard, Solly following close behind. Spindly pecan seedlings poked up in places where the wall crumbled. Wisteria hung in mournful clumps from the pergola covering the back patio. Fiery mums stuffed the flower boxes under Comfort's front windows, uncomfortably bright but well-intentioned gifts from church folks. Kudzu wrapped around the corners of the taupe stucco walls, purple shutters, and white porch railings, softening the edges like the pictures in my copy of *A Child's Garden of Verses*. We took turns knocking on the door, and I picked up the empty basket as we waited for an answer. The more persistent our knocks, the more persistent the silence. Mama said it's 'cause of what Cole did to her on top of the pain of him and Daddy killing each other. Even so, I couldn't understand why she wouldn't come out at all.

"Comfort, darlin', won't you please open the door?" Solly begged.

"Just keep fillin' dat basket up is what we'll do!" Ernestine shouted at the door in her singsong, Haitian accent. Then she shook her head and lumbered down the steps. "She'll have to come out sometime."

I wasn't so sure. For the second time this week, we'd left a basket of food, cards, and flowers for her. And for the second time, she'd taken the basket after we left, returning it empty to the front porch.

Empty except for a yellow-edged note card tucked into the folds of the basket's weave.

Nobody else noticed it.

I quick stuck it in my pocket and kept the message a secret.

Sak vid pa kanp.
"An empty sack can't stand up."

CHAPTER 5

Comfort

You do that, Ernestine! I want to holler back at the four of them, out there waiting for me to open the door, but I have no voice.

No face.

No body anymore.

Familiar lumps of my bleached, duck-canvas-covered couch embrace me, and I pull my legs up closer to my heart. The footsteps of the people closest to me—Solly; my niece, Anniston; my sister-in-law, Oralee; and Ernestine—creak down and away from the sun-worn, wood porch steps. Tears threaten to spill from my eyes, but I won't cry. Can't cry. If I do, I might never stop.

I pull the leather-bound scrapbook off the whitewashed, antique coffee table beside me and open the cover to a full-page photo of

Solly and me. In the photo, he holds me close and our legs crisscross as we sit, tucked safe in the corner of a sugar-soft sand dune, surrounded by sea grass that is bordered by rickety sand-trap fencing. Waves of azure ocean play behind us in the background.

I blow a strand of hair away from my face.

"Your hair's pretty enough to weave angel wings," Solly always says. He always did like my hair, even when he pulled it when he sat behind me in second grade. I'd come home that day and cried to Princella about it, but she'd only said, without looking at me, that it was probably because the boy liked me.

Some things never change. Mama still doesn't look at me. And Solly still likes me. Loves me. So much he asked me to marry him next summer. I hold the diamond ring against my lips as I turn page after page of happy vacation pictures that seem impossible, though they were taken only a few months earlier on the beach. Before Hurricane Frederic. Before this past week.

I run my fingers over a photo Solly took of me kneeling to pick up shells. Every time we go to the beach, I bring home a bucketful of them. Whole shells, half shells, broken shells. I never throw broken shells back in the ocean. Each fractured angle eventually finds a place alongside another in the mosaic furniture and frames I make and use to fill this cottage home in which Solly and I are supposed to live together.

Neither Solly nor I have much, but Daddy had the house built for me when I finished beauty school last spring. Shortly after, Qarla, owner of the Curly Q Hair and Nail Salon, hired me full-time.

Daddy. If ever a man's heart was too big, it was his. He'd made a commitment to Mama when he'd brought her home with him from college one day, and he would not break that commitment. She'd arrived on the Harlan plantation all those years ago pregnant with Cole, an illegitimate child, and with nowhere else to go. People in these parts—especially society people—don't get divorced. Problem is, all that devotion eats away at the soul's ability to see evil creeping in. And once a person's blind to evil, nothing can stop it, leaving generation after generation to stumble around in its darkness.

Lucky for Mama, Daddy always wore blinders when it came to her.

If she was any bit alive before Cole and Rey died, six feet of clay and silt covered it now. Everyone knew she grieved for Cole, not Rey. And certainly she did not grieve for what I'd been through. Who could say for sure what makes a mother choose one child over another, or even over two? And yet, it is difficult to remember a day when Mama acted happy for anything having to do with me and Rey.

Rey came along only two years after Cole, and I came along a lonesome eleven years after that, both of us unexpected children—if not unwanted—who shot pains of childbirth through Mama like cannonballs announcing the mistake of our arrivals. Ernestine said Vaughn wanted to celebrate, but Mama would not entertain even the notion of showers for either of us. No tables covered with petit fours. No bowls of pastel, melt-in-your-mouth mints to greet guests. No birth announcements. No lace-covered bassinets. No room in her world, already established and centered around Cole, for either of us. She'd hired Ernestine as soon as she could to raise us.

Princella had her reasons.

At least that's what Ernestine always says. We still don't know what they are exactly, just accept them like the inevitable yearly growth and harvest of our pecan-laden hills.

And so Rey learned to go to Ernestine instead of Mama for all his needs. By the time I came along, it went without saying that I should do the same. Daddy helped when he could, setting us on his knee in the evenings, telling us stories from the Bible, taking us to church. But every other minute of the day, he wandered and worked the rolling hills of pecan trees, straight lines of them, like soldiers at arms, surrounding and guarding the secrets within our great, white house. The orchards were the only place he could escape from the choice he'd made to save Mama from ruin by whisking her off to the safety of the Harlan plantation like a refugee escaping a dark desert of sin.

I flip to another page in the album and focus on the way Solly's hand rests on the small of my back. Even in photos, his hand sends hot chills up my spine. I've never wanted a man so.

Another photo captures him kissing the top of my head. Anyone who doesn't know us would have thought we were on our honeymoon, the way we interlaced our fingers, how he brushed wisps of hair away from my face and tucked loose strands up under my floppy hat, how his eyes searched mine in a way that gave away his feverish longing for all of me, too.

Now we have nothing.

Cole stole all of that and more.

Stole Rey, too.

I shut the album, knowing part of me is to blame.

But then again, how could any of us have known such fast-moving thunderclouds loomed beyond our carefully pruned lives?

That the darkness I felt in my heart whenever Cole came around would swallow us like a storm surge?

Were each of us so blinded by pious allegiance to our family that we overlooked such impending wickedness? We'd basked in the sunny eye of our own hurricane too long, and when the waves came, billows of pain and pride careened over the top of me, breaking me and slamming me to the gritty ocean floor, somersaulting me like a weightless piece of driftwood and leaving me in a filthy, foamy mess.

Sin settled in the boughs of the Harlan family years ago, and now the boughs were breaking.

In the bathroom, I tack an empty, old pecan sack over the mirror to cover every glimpse of my reflection.

I do the same with the mirror above the dresser in my bedroom.

I always did hate mirrors.

A salty breeze from Mobile Bay brushes a lace curtain into the room at the same time the phone rings, and fear seizes through me. Happens all the time now, the way I startle at every sound, every shadow, every out-of-the-ordinary smell.

I don't want to answer the phone. I know it is Solly. It hurts too much to hear his voice, his assurances, his pleas to help.

I pick up the receiver and hold it to my ear, but I don't speak.

"Comfort. Honey. Say something." Solly sounds exhausted.

A single, scalding tear runs down my face.

"Tell me how I can help. I'll do anything. Take you away from here. Take care of you, like I've always promised. Like we're still going to promise each other before the entire world next summer at our wedding. For better or for worse. I'm yours, even now."

"There isn't going to be a wedding."

"Comfort—"

I hang up before I can hear his pleas. They tear my heart into slivers of burlap, splitting at the edges, impossible to sew back together without unraveling even more.

He is asking me for things Cole destroyed.

Parts no longer mine to give.

Knock all you want to, Ernestine.

I couldn't ever come out again.

Kay piti, ou prann nat ou anba bra ou.
"[When] the house is small, you hold your bedding under your arm."

CHAPTER 6

Anniston

I sat on my bare mattress and traced the outline of Comfort's handwriting on the note card she'd left us the day of the funeral.

Behold and see
What a great heap of grief lay hid in me....
Stand further off then! Go.
-E. B. Browning

Mrs. Nowlan, my English teacher, taught us how Elizabeth Barrett Browning never came out of her house. How she never saw the places she wrote about but managed to paint pictures of green hills and dark valleys as if she roamed them every day. She even managed to knock the socks off Robert Browning before they ever met in person.

Maybe Comfort wanted me to understand the poem meant she wouldn't come out again, either. Or maybe people felt too prickly to her now. Maybe she needed a rest, like the pecan trees all around us, dormant and naked.

I folded the note card and tucked it in the secret compartment at the bottom of my musical ballerina jewelry box, which I put, along with a few last stray stuffed animals and a purple-and-gold Bay Spring High School felt banner, into the moving box. Molly's coal-black eyes seemed to sadden as she watched me tape the box shut. She curled herself into a ball on my floor and sighed.

Mama and Ernestine's voices carried from where they packed in the kitchen.

"It'll only be for a little while, until I can get my feet back under me," said Mama.

I wondered if she was trying to convince herself or the rest of us of the wisdom of this move as I joined them in the room where we had eaten so many family dinners—Daddy, all but his fresh-washed hands filthy with dirt from the orchards, and Mama, the blue of her nursing scrubs matching the blue of her eyes, laughing as we talked about our days. Now, the avocado-green stove and refrigerator looked sad against the empty white cupboards and faded yellow linoleum floor.

"Vaughn said he'd help us find another place in town soon. And Princella won't bother us much. She has all her social obligations. Ernestine will be there and you can stay in Comfort's old room. She'd like knowing you're in there."

"*Oui*, child. It'll be good to have you awhile." Ernestine handed me a plate from Mama and Daddy's set of wedding china to wrap in packing paper.

I supposed this day counted as special an occasion as any worthy enough to bring out the fancy dishes, which were etched with delicate, pink flowers and rimmed in gold. Just a week after the funeral, the movers were coming that afternoon to put most of our things in storage and move the rest into Princella and Vaughn's. Always the practical one, Vaughn offered for us to live there, knowing how hard it would be to stay another night in the house where Daddy and Cole shot each other to death. Blood doesn't come out of carpet that easy.

I didn't argue with Mama about the move. Sadness made my chest feel too heavy to make a fuss, and I didn't want to burden Mama with any sass. Besides, I didn't want to stay any longer in the place where Daddy and Cole had died, either. Ernestine, she had a way of making things better, so living with her might help us for a while. And most of the time, Princella really did leave us alone. Still, if I was wary of anything, it was about living under the same roof as her.

The only other thing that might be good about living there was the beauty of the orchards. Those hills held plenty of work to keep us busy.

"Maybe it'll be nice staying there," I said.

"Mmm-hmm. You might find it to be." Ernestine grabbed a couple more cups out of the cabinet and started singing as she wrapped.

There is a balm in Gilead
to make the wounded whole
there is a balm in Gilead
to heal the sin-sick soul.

Tears spilled down Mama's face as Ernestine sang, and I wondered if there could be a balm this side of heaven strong enough to heal this big of a mess. What part of this could ever be whole again? What part of Mama? What part of Comfort? What part of me?

And what about Princella? She was already broke up in pieces before. Surely there wasn't anything in creation balmy enough to heal her.

Before long, all the breakables were wrapped and stacked in moving boxes. I pulled an old, fleece-lined, flannel shirt of Daddy's tighter around me, bones chilling at the thought of him buried deep in the dark, winter ground. Mama wore one of his shirts, too, still woody-smelling from the pecan harvest. Together, we turned and took one last look at the house where I'd grown up. Reminded me of a house straight out of the pages of *Anne of Green Gables*. Painted the color of beach sand with shutters as blue as the deepest part of a wisteria petal, its window boxes bulged with pansies in the spring, but they were empty now. Ivy grew nonstop, hugging the sides of the house and climbing across roof corners. One of the prettiest homes in Bay Spring proper, Daddy always said.

Molly and I sat next to Mama as she drove our maroon station wagon behind the moving truck, which bumped along in front of us as we followed it toward the highway running alongside Mobile Bay. Ernestine, her light blue El Camino piled full of overstuffed boxes and the flailing legs of upturned chairs, drove in front of us.

Soon, we would turn east, away from town and into the heart of Alabama, where silt and clay roads crisscrossed green fields. And soon it would be Christmas, when farmers of most every crop worried about the possibility of a deep freeze ruining the hope of summer fruit and cotton. Daddy never worried so much about the cold. He said pecans hibernated more deeply than other trees. Said the trees know better than to let their leaves unfurl until late spring.

Mama turned into the Piggly Wiggly parking lot, stuck front and center amidst a gaggle of other stores. I imagined that smiling pig waving good-bye to anyone leaving town and greeting those coming to visit.

"Let's get something good for dinner. And a few more things for Comfort."

Toddlers stuffed into the seats of grocery carts—and some hanging over the sides of them—reached for low-hanging candy, sugary cereals, and cookies as their mamas struggled to stick to the items on their lists. School was in session, though Mama let me miss again since we were all grieving, so it felt strange that no kids my age were around. The Piggly Wiggly served as the prime hangout spot for those of us old enough to make and spend a dime or two on candy, teen magazines, or soda.

Mama placed an order at the meat counter, and I turned the corner into the snack aisle as the chatter of a couple of women caught my ear.

"Heard she asked for it. That's what Trina said."

"She must've. I can't imagine Cole doing something as awful as that."

"And that Rey, he always was a hothead. Shoulda been teaching his whore of a sister to keep her legs shut, is what he shoulda been doing."

I backed up, nearly knocking over an entire display of Little Debbie Snacks. I'd always thought Cole was a good-for-nothin', and Mama said as much, but I never knew folks thought Comfort was that way, even if Princella and Cole had said those things about her at the Thanksgiving table.

Whore.

Cole had used that word for her that night. But she'd been steady with Solly since junior high. They went to all the dances together. They were engaged. How could anyone think Comfort brought this on herself?

"Anything you need while we're here, hon?" Mama's fingers barely stuck out the bottom of the sleeves of Daddy's shirt as she put her arm around me, and I jumped at her unexpected voice.

"Flowers? Can we get Comfort some flowers?"

"That's a wonderful idea. Why don't you go pick out something from next door?"

By next door, Mama meant the Proper Petal, the florist and landscaping business where Solly worked. A cedar arch entwined with purple wisteria haloed the entrance to Bay Spring's most popular florist and nursery, which provided everything from landscaping supplies to bouquets and boutonnieres for the town's life-and-death events.

A big display of azalea and jade, roots sticking through the slats of their green plastic pots, surrounded the entrance. I nudged the door open, and my eyes adjusted to the dark. Spades, hand rakes, glass gazing balls, and wooden stakes with names of fancy herbs painted on them filled wooden crates fashioned into display shelves. The air smelled like unsweetened chocolate, heavy and rich with a hint of magnolia sweet. Wind chimes of all shapes and colors hung from the ceiling. An orange, striped cat hopped over my foot and slinked around the cash register table. I ran my fingers across the top of a purple, glass gazing ball.

"Best not touch the fragile things, unless you have enough in your pocket to buy something if it drops and breaks."

The raspy voice startled me, and I almost knocked the ball off its stand. I turned toward the voice to see the man, hands pushed down tight in the bottoms of the pockets of his green apron.

"Sorry I scared you, Anni. Wouldn't want you to break somethin'."

"Solly!" I scolded him. "Scaring a person like that's one way to make sure something gets dropped."

"What brings you here, sweetie?" He scribbled something on a notepad behind the register. Sadness hung from his face like a tired old coat on a hook.

"We're following the moving trucks out of town, and Mama stopped next door to get some groceries for dinner. I asked if I could get Comfort some flowers to drop off with another basketful of food and things for her. Any ideas?"

Solly walked out from behind the counter and leaned against it. Wrinkles I'd never noticed before cut into the skin around his eyes, reddened with worry and pain. He rubbed his chin with his fingers and thought hard about it.

"Come out here."

He led me out the back door to where rows and rows of potted plants waited—trees with their roots balled up in burlap bags, plastic flats full of flowers spilling over the sides of them, and domed greenhouses filled to overflowing with more.

"She always has liked pink," Solly said over his shoulder. He seemed inches shorter, shrunk by sadness as he ambled slowly through the rows of shrubs and plants.

"What about those?" We passed a display of hydrangeas, huge puffs of pink, blue, and white, like mounds of cotton candy.

Solly shook his head as we passed, then stopped when we got to a section with pots full of tall purple, pink, and white flowers with yellow centers.

"Asters?" I read the name off the price tag, disappointed. Surely he'd point out something fancier than a wildflower anybody could pick on the side of the road.

He didn't notice my hesitation. "The best sort of flower to get someone mourning is one they can plant. Something that'll live and that grows there naturally. Something you don't have to fight to get growing and keep alive. These asters don't care where they grow. Don't even mind clay and rock, which is why you see them on roadsides. They're happy with other plants, and they don't kill off and choke out their neighbors. They don't mind the hot Alabama sun, either."

"I don't know …"

"They smell good, and butterflies love 'em. Once you have a bunch of 'em growing, you'll have butterflies everywhere."

"Butterflies would be nice."

"And if you like history, asters have a history. In France especially, after the World Wars, mourners placed bouquets of asters on the tops of the graves of soldiers."

"Why?"

"Asters mean you wish a story ended different."

Perfect.

Jamais di: "Fontaine, mo va jamais boi to dolo."
"Never say, 'Spring, I will never drink your water.'"

CHAPTER 7

Comfort

Only after Oralee and Anni put the basket on my porch and I hear them leave do I open the front door. The breeze carries the scent of the ocean, floating in and filling my entryway. Today, the basket holds toothpaste, a new toothbrush, bread, lunch meat, eggs, and milk. A note falls out of a pot of pink asters.

Dear Comfort,
I love you.
Please come out soon.

Anni

Dear, sweet Anni. How can I?

And how can you know the hulking shadows of fear and pain in my head I wade past every day in order to get out of bed? Shadows that push the incline of my heart away from Solly, Oralee, and anyone, even as they reach toward me.

I remember learning to swim, how I thought if I grabbed at the top of the water, I could pull myself up for air. How I learned that water leaves the hands empty, and the hope of air siphons away.

As each day passes, fear, like a reaper's bony fingers, crawls deeper into my heart. I don't answer the door or the phone. I keep the shades drawn tight. And the knot within my belly grows, like a fetus, fed and nurtured by a cord of despair.

I accept their packages of food, though graham crackers and milk are my three meals a day. I can't handle more than their familiar, unchanging taste.

Come out soon, Anni wrote.

And in the shadows of evening, I do. But only to dig a hole and plant the asters, praying they don't die. I welcome darkness as it seeps over the horizon, shame traveling with it like an incoming fog, overwhelming me.

I lock the door back up and go back to hating myself in my most hidden places. Places Cole took from me with his whiskey-drenched hands and tobacco-stained mouth. Monsters linger again outside my front door as I crouch and make myself small—so very small—upon the cold, tile floor of my bathroom. Pain pushes graham cracker and milk back up toward my throat.

Comfort.

The voice comes from a place deeper than those in which I hide.

Comfort.

The voice nudges at the fear, and for a moment, I answer: *Abba? Yes, child.*

I shudder, wondering how even He could be with me now. The God of my youth. The smiling face of Jesus I couldn't wait to see on the Sunday school wall each week, who called His father *"Abba,"* "Daddy."

I pull my knees into my chest even closer, at once afraid of what He will say next and afraid He will not say more.

I am here.

A tear rolls from my face onto the tile before I reply: *But for how long?*

Bèt nan fòm pòv ap mòde.
"Animals in poor shape will bite."

CHAPTER 8

Anniston

Daddy let me drive the tractor, which sometimes we used to pull a wagon of supplies, as soon as I turned seven. Sun shone on our windburned faces on those long, winter afternoons as we zipped the bright, John Deere-green of the four-wheel-drive utility vehicle around the trees. Groups of wild turkeys barely outran us as I drove up and down the hills.

We slowed down only long enough to gauge the measure of sky through the gnarled and lanky branches. If we couldn't see enough blue when we looked up, we would make a note to thin the branches in that row. Around the trunk of every tree, clumps of Bermuda grass as tall as my hips called for a whacking. Handfuls of cattle—which Daddy referred to as Granddaddy's "bad, hobby-farming habit"—huddled in groups scattered throughout the orchards. But despite smelling bad and getting in the way, the cows helped eat the grass and kept crows and deer from nibbling at the trees. Red-tailed hawks hung over our heads, wings stretched wide and floating on the wind, nests high and safe in the branches of the tallest trees. Squirrel nests, on the other hand, we blasted out with a shotgun. They were one of the worst varmints around for getting into the trees and eating away the crops.

Even as Mama drove the packed station wagon toward Princella and Vaughn's glaring white mansion, these memories felt like a thick, homemade afghan around my shoulders. Though I often complained about going along with him on days Mama worked at the hospital, these orchards were as much a part of me as my daddy … a place to run and dream, to plant and tend, to cut back and fertilize, like I'd done at his side my whole life. Here in these hills, I'd make sure Daddy lived on within me. I'd find him strong and safe in the most distant of fields where I could run until I had no breath left, and then lie down in the green pastures, like in Psalm 23, and be restored.

The sparse branches of the sleepy orchards sent a spooky chill through me as we drove up the long driveway. Especially against the cloudy gray sky, the orchards—carefully and purposefully planted rows of them—looked as if they bowed with the weight of sorrow. I tried to focus on the coming work the winter orchards would bring.

"Mow the grass by the creek down near the pond, Anni," Daddy'd remind me, the single dimple on his right cheek deep and cheery, "or the weeds'll grow up over and hide it. Somebody'd forget it's there and drive that tractor right into it and sink."

That's the thing about the orchards. They were always changing. Always something to cut back so as not to hide the important parts. Always something that doesn't get noticed, unless you take your time to be still and walk slow among the rows.

"Not everybody notices the details in life, but the details are what make or break a pecan crop. Knowing the difference between a hawk and a squirrel nest. Seeing the starts of a webworm nest and pulling it off the branches. Being able to tell when branches grow toward each other too much before buds show on the ends of branches, and knowing when they need to be cut back before they sap the strength out of their neighboring trees," Daddy'd said.

One year, Daddy showed me how a whole row of younger trees close to the creek leaned away from the bigger, older row alongside it. "If that leaning gets too bad, we'll have to cut all the young ones back."

Daddy's lectures stuck with me, mostly because he repeated them every year. He taught me all kinds of odd things, like how each tree should be at least fifty feet from the next, and how even though you'd watched a perfect one grow all your life, sometimes you had to cut it down for the health of the whole crop. I knew how to use a chain saw, the jarring growl of it slicing through the thick of a trunk. And I knew how to haul away the cut pieces of tree for a bonfire or to sell to someone offering the right price. I knew how to drill holes in fresh-cut stumps and pour trunk killer all over what was left of the former tree, making sure it wouldn't grow back again.

After Mama parked the car, the afternoon school bus squeaked to a stop at the end of the driveway. Kids from my school spilled out, and the Bailey brothers from next door chased the girls like usual.

Without seeing it, I recited to myself the sign above all the school-bus windshields that read, "Passengers are not permitted to stand forward of white line while bus is in motion." The line always reminded me of the Freedom Riders. Daddy named me after the town where those men and women all nearly died: Anniston, Alabama. Back in that town on Mother's Day, 1961, the Freedom Riders weren't doing anything wrong except fighting for folks who couldn't fight for themselves. They wanted to show how whites and blacks deserved equal rights. A huge mob of disagreeing townsfolk threw firebombs at the bus, and when it started burning, tried to hold the bus doors shut to burn the Riders to death. Hot flames must've licked and stung the necks of those folks as the inside of their bus threatened to become an inferno. They must've pressed their faces hard against the windows, their expressions like silent screams on Halloween masks, half a dozen of them crammed into the front stairwell of the bus, begging someone to open the door before the fire turned them to ashes. On the other side of the glass doors, a dozen men pushed back, their faces twisted with hate. The Freedom Riders managed to escape, but then the mob beat them, as if nearly burning them to death wasn't enough meanness to dish out.

Daddy always said I should live like a Freedom Rider, willing to step across some lines to set folks free. I wondered if this was one of those times he was talking about as we moved box after box into my grandparents' home.

The throaty cry of the mourning doves in the magnolias woke me Sunday morning, and the haze of quiet sunlight floated into the room like a slow dance between dreaming and waking up for the day. Slow dances reminded me that in spite of Daddy and Cole shooting each other to death, in spite of Christmas coming, and in spite of the general mess of all we'd lost, Princella had not forgotten about the upcoming Bay Spring Junior Cotillion. She was in charge of the annual event, which was only a few months away, so I suppose she couldn't help herself from nagging me about a date. Last night, as we ate another donated casserole, she reminded me I needed to find a date. The conversation pricked the back of my mind like a pebble caught in my shoe from recess.

I wondered if someone from church group would be okay to take, but thinking about those few boys embarrassed the heck out of me. To start with, Grady Bingham ruled the Bay Spring Junior High football team. He cared more about grass stains on his cleats than an old dance, let alone attending a dance with me. Besides, my family did nothing to give me any kind of affinity for football players.

Tommy Sharp might've been a possibility, but I'd known him since kindergarten, which meant I also knew he used to chew on pencils and eat paste.

I considered Eddie Prince, but I didn't want to be stuck alone with him, seeing as how it was rumored he'd planted a first kiss on at least a dozen of my female classmates.

"Anni, you want waffles or eggs for breakfast, child?"

I groaned at the sound of Ernestine's voice outside the bedroom door and shivered at the prospect of sticking my feet outside the warm covers. "Eggs, I guess. Thanks, Ernestine."

By the time I came down the winding staircase to the dining room, fine china and serving bowls full of steaming eggs, grits, sausage, and biscuits filled the table. Glass carafes of orange juice, tomato juice, and water sat next to a silver pitcher, steam from fresh black coffee rising from its spout.

"Anniston." Princella already sat at one end of the table.

Vaughn walked up beside me and patted me on the back, then took a seat at the opposite end of the table. The room felt thick, like an apology waiting to happen that everyone knew would never occur.

"Morning, ma'am," I said.

"Did you sleep well?"

"Yes, ma'am, thank you."

She sprinkled salt and pepper on her eggs. "Say, have you thought about any of those boys in your Sunday school class?"

"Ma'am?" Playing dumb rarely worked with her, but I couldn't believe she was bringing it up again.

"Surely there's one there you could ask to the dance. Do any of them stand out to you as at least a possibility?" Princella had a way with words that could make Jesus Himself feel guilty for not committing a sin.

"I don't know, ma'am. Not really."

She clicked her tongue in irritation, then rang a small bell in front of her plate. Ernestine appeared through the swinging door that led to the kitchen, carrying a tray with cream and sweetener. "Come sit down with us now. Everything looks delicious. You've outdone yourself this morning, Ernestine."

"Nothing is too much for my girls." Her smile warmed me.

Princella's face grew pinched when Mama took a seat next to me. Dressed in sweatpants and the same T-shirt she'd worn during the move, she wore her hair pulled up and twisted like a bird's nest on top of her head. We ate our meal in silence from then on. The tension between Mama and Princella thickened the air, making it feel hard to breathe.

Finally, Ernestine broke the silence. "Do you need me to go to the storage unit with you this morning, Oralee?"

"I think I'll wait until I unpack these boxes. I'm sure I'll have more to take over there before the day's done."

Princella set her fork down with a clank. "I hope so. We have room for you all, but not that much room."

"I know. I'm sorry, Princella. I couldn't sort through it as much as I would've liked. I'll get it out of your hair by the end of the day."

"You'll take your time, is what you'll do." Vaughn's voice boomed across the table, and yet he smiled at Mama kindly. Then he spoke to Princella. "We've all been through enough. We will treat each other with kindness and grace."

"Of course we will." She wiped her mouth. "Excuse me. I have to be at church early. I'll be driving separate, unless you're ready, dear."

"You go on ahead. I'll ride with the girls here." Vaughan nodded toward me and Mama, then toward Ernestine.

We all let our breaths out at the same time after we heard her climb the stairs to her room.

"I'll find a place as soon as possible, Vaughn. Really. I don't want us to be a burden."

"Woman's got bigger burdens than you are to her, Oralee."

"But we're reminders of everything that happened."

"No more than the sky is a reminder that we live on earth. Working through this whole thing with Cole and Rey has more to do with her coming to terms with her own past than with you living here. She'll have to work that out on her own. Besides, you, Anni, Comfort—you three girls are all I got left. You girls living here is my choice, and this is my house and my land. Maybe I never said that before, but I'm saying it now."

Princella, carrying a box full of poinsettias, clip-clopped past the dining room where we sat and pulled open the double front doors without looking at any of us.

"Good-bye, love," Vaughn called out to her.

The slam of the door was her reply.

Jijman Bondye a vini sou yon bourik.
"God's judgment comes on a donkey."

CHAPTER 9

Anniston

The first Sunday of December was filled with church and the Bay Spring Sugarplum Parade, the annual kickoff of the Christmas season. My church, Bay Spring Presbyterian, sat across the street from the Bay Spring Resort Hotel. For this reason, the church caretaker, Ed, prided himself on concocting eyebrow-raising, sometimes funny, and always convicting phrases for the church sign. He firmly believed tourists should go to church on Sundays, too, despite being hundreds of miles away from their homes. This week, still in the off-tourist season, Ed went pretty easy on the town: "All we want for Christmas is your presence."

Mama and I gussied up into the best church clothes we could, considering we had to dig them out of packing boxes. I felt the stares of many folks as we slid, along with Ernestine, into the back pew, ends covered in evergreen branches tied up with big, red velvet bows. At least the extra lights and smells of the season helped hide the hangdog state of our hearts. Princella and Vaughn walked past us to their usual spot in the front row.

The sign near the pulpit listed hymns 57, 8, and 212, in that order and to be sung upon Preacher Beckett's cue. I only had to stay for morning announcements and the first hymn since anyone in high school or younger scattered to their Sunday school rooms for a lesson and a snack, which almost always consisted of Voortman sandwich cookies and Thelma Cunningham's homemade lemonade. She'd bring eggnog on Sundays in December, if we were lucky.

Felt awful strange sitting in church again, this being the first time since Daddy and Cole's funeral. Mama had wanted a separate service for Daddy, but she had nothing left inside her to argue with Princella, who insisted the brothers be honored and laid to rest together. I forced myself to pay attention when Preacher Beckett mentioned "the Harlan family" as he read down his list of prayer needs, praises, and financial news. As he motioned to Mrs. Reed, the organist, to begin hymn number 57, "Joy to the World," the floorboards creaked, indicating a latecomer.

Solly.

I glanced at him as I made my way to the back of the church for Sunday school. He searched my face for any news about Comfort and bowed his head when my face told him I had none.

Mama and I went along with tradition that evening, despite not having Daddy with us. We nabbed our seats at 6:30 p.m. on the library steps to watch the parade, which stepped off at 7:00 p.m. sharp from Town Hall around the corner. Floats and bands lined up and stopped traffic for two miles down the highway. Twirlers flipped and flung their batons behind the grand marshal of this year's parade, Milo Sterns, a command sergeant major who'd won three purple hearts in Vietnam. A scruffy mix of veterans followed behind him, including Daddy's old friend Larry, an oysterman who kept his skiff in the slot next to Daddy's fishing boat.

Throngs of Boy Scout troops dressed up like elves pulled a flatbed full of their overpriced Christmas trees behind them. Princella's ladies' group—the Daughters of the Confederacy Auxiliary—hosted their own float, upon which all the well-to-do Bay Spring women dressed in red velvet, fur-trimmed dresses that made them look like elves, too, except the one crowned Sugarplum Queen. White taffeta and poufs of netting and sequins made her look like a sugarplum, all right. And I couldn't help but scrunch up my nose when I saw Princella's friends waving as they passed.

"At least she had the decency not to be a part of that," Mama said, referring to Princella's decision not to ride on the float this year. Instead, and to our surprise, she'd said she had a headache and couldn't bear the crowds.

"Amen," said Ernestine, who'd joined us on the steps.

The Bay Spring High School marching band all wore Santa hats and played "Silver Bells" and "Sleigh Ride." Every cheerleader of every age in the Bay Spring area followed the high school squad, which carried a banner stretching from one side of the street to the other with *Merry Christmas* written in red and green poster paint. A drill team, stiff and proud, strode by from the local all-boy military academy. Horses whose manes and tails were braided with red and green ribbons clopped along carrying riders from the Thurmont Plantation Walking Horse Club. The United Methodist carolers, dressed in old-fashioned costumes, sang "God Rest Ye Merry Gentlemen." The Devil's Disciples motorcycle gang showed up fifty strong and all dressed in Santa suits.

In the middle of all the glitter and noise, a rickety float from the Weeks Bay Christian Church passed, nearly squashed between the Shriners on their thirteen-passenger bicycles and the Loxley Amateur Bagpipe Band. The float featured Mary and Joseph, live sheep, and a live donkey nibbling on hay falling out of a chicken wire basket. The baby Jesus was plastic, of course, and that's all there was to His part of the parade, probably because the main point of the parade was to usher in Santa. And usher him in they did, with a float decked out with a blinding number of Christmas lights; a real, life-sized gingerbread house; real reindeer from the Miller's pecan farm; and real midgets who evidently didn't take offense to dressing up like elves to throw buckets of candy at the crowds.

As soon as Mr. Claus and his crew passed, we moved along, amoeba style, with the crowds toward Center Park, where tables draped in green and red fabric were topped with homemade casseroles, finger foods, and every kind of Christmas cookie you could imagine. I searched for Ernestine's basketful of pecan cinnamon rolls, grabbed one, and tucked myself back into the huddle of Mama and Ernestine and their friends.

"Do you want to sit on Santa's lap?" Mama's eyes, wet with sadness, told me she knew the answer before she asked.

I shook my head no. What use would it be? We had no mantel of our own to set the photograph of me and Santa on. I had no adoring father to make me giggle as my too-long legs dangled off the lap of the fat man with the glued-on beard. So what if the picture donations went to fund youth mission trips. I had my own mission to get through.

Maybe Mama and I thought sticking with the traditions of years past would help us get through the sting of losing all that'd just been ushered out of our lives. But instead, it only pointed out how different we were now. How Cole had blown away more than my daddy. He'd blown away our lives.

Wont pi lou pase yon sak sèl.
"Shame is heavier than a bag of salt."

CHAPTER 10

Comfort

The radio crackles and pops as I turn the knob, searching for something decent to listen to from one of the many churches sending out live waves of salvation to empty, homebound hearts.

I suppose I qualify as that. The empty heart, definitely. The homebound part, pretty much, although I managed to drag myself to the Piggly Wiggly in the early morning hours when the only folks who shopped were those too old to recognize me or too young and busy shushing fussy infants to notice. Sammy, the hauntingly pretty, young cashier, she noticed me. Greeted me by name too.

"—now let's listen as Preacher Faust brings us a word from the Summerdale Baptist Church."

I leave the dial there, more to fill up the stifling silence than to glean anything from what the man says. The rest of the family is in town kicking off Christmas, and though I've chosen these walls around myself, I long for memories of good Christmases past: Daddy holding me on his shoulders to get the first glimpse of Santa; Solly holding my hand for the first time in eighth grade as we sat on the Bay Spring live nativity float. He was Joseph; I was Mary. The manger holding the plastic baby Jesus hid our sweaty hands as we clutched them together beneath the straw.

"Now there was a man in Jerusalem called Simeon, who was righteous and devout. He was waiting for the consolation of Israel, and the Holy Spirit was on him. It had been revealed to him by the Holy Spirit that he would not die before he had seen the Lord's Messiah." Preacher Faust reads the scripture in the raggedy voice and cadenced way of an aging priest.

Even as I am resting upon you.

The voice comes not from the airwaves, but from the near constant, pounding pain in the back of my head.

But Simeon was a good man, Abba.

And you are a good woman.

"Simeon took him in his arms and praised God, saying: 'Sovereign Lord, as you have promised, you may now dismiss your servant in peace …,'" the preacher drones on.

I will bring you peace.

Peace? How can anyone—how can You—bring peace to me?

"'For my eyes have seen your salvation, which you have prepared in the sight of all nations: a light for revelation to the Gentiles, and the glory of your people Israel.'"

My light will reveal hope to you, My child.

I dismiss the prodding, still small voice. I even laugh out loud at the ludicracy of the conversation.

Peace and light are nice thoughts, Abba, but they are as tangible to me as the star that hung over Bethlehem too long ago.

LATE FEBRUARY, 1980

Bonjou se paspò ou.
"Hello *is your passport.*"

CHAPTER 11

Anniston

That Christmas faded like all the other Christmases. One Friday afternoon in late February, long after we boxed the decorations away, and weeks after I'd started back at school, I tossed my backpack on the counter as Molly hopped and skipped at my feet.

Princella stood at the kitchen sink washing dishes. "How was your day, Anniston?" She smiled on occasion, this being one of them, but for the most part, Lord, if her moods didn't change like the weather. One minute she was all storm and thunder. The next she was all sunshine and blue sky.

"Fine, ma'am." I grabbed a peach out of the green, salt-glazed bowl on the counter, and followed Princella's gaze out the window above the sink, which faced her rose garden. The bushes were each cropped close to the near-frozen earth. "Gonna add any new kinds of roses this spring?"

Even if we couldn't talk about anything else, I knew I could talk to Princella about her roses. She loved them, after all. Collected as many types as she could, traveling all over the area to find new varieties to bring home. She really did have the prettiest rose garden in the whole bay area.

She sighed and studied the sleepy winter garden. "I think I might stick with the ones I have this year. See if I can't treat the ones I have as good as I can."

She kept staring out the window, and I wondered if she might really be talking about me and Mama on account of her losing two sons, but one could never tell for sure if Princella meant something nice or not.

Mama brought her plate to the sink. "Anni, honey, you've been cooped up and helping inside enough this winter. Ernestine and I can handle the rest of the kitchen. You're starting to look pale. Go on outside and help Vaughn. He's out there picking up sticks or something in the orchards. He'll give you something to do." Mama smiled at me, her eyes turned down at the corners from a sadness that wouldn't leave her.

"If he doesn't, I'm sure I'll find something to do out there, Mama."

I changed clothes upstairs in Comfort's room, which I now called mine. For the most part, I'd adjusted to staying there. Wasn't hard. Her bookshelves overflowed with Agatha Christie and *Little House on the Prairie* books, and her soft bed was encircled by four posts and the lace canopy I'd always dreamed of. Hers and Daddy's old room—where Mama slept—were joined by the bathroom where I stood, weaving my hair into a braid. Everything in the bathroom matched, from the pale blue tile down to the matching blue porcelain tub and toilet.

Besides Mama being in there, sleeping next door to Daddy's old room helped calm my heart on nights when the fear of dreams of banging and gunfire kept me from sleeping. The same wallpaper he'd picked out as a little boy, a patriotic plaid, covered the top of the walls, and woodwork painted navy blue covered the bottom. Model airplanes of all kinds hung from the ceiling on fishing line. A teddy bear with fur rubbed off its paws and a missing eye sat against the pillow on the corduroy bedspread. Fishing rods and a stack of college textbooks about agriculture peeked out from an opening in the sliding closet doors. Old high school yearbooks lined a short stack of bookshelves, and an aging guitar sulked in the corner. He'd left it here in favor of the new one Mama'd bought him as a wedding gift years ago.

Across the hall, Cole's room loomed, door shut tight since before me and Mama moved in. But I remember it from before. Football and baseball trophies lined shelves; posters and sports pennants pinned on all the walls. The posters always bothered me. Posters of girls in bathing suits, girls on cars, girls on beaches. Girls with not nearly enough clothes on their glistening bodies.

Downstairs, I pulled on a stocking cap and wrapped Daddy's lined, flannel shirt around me before heading outside with Molly to find Vaughn. A blue jay circled above us as we walked toward the pole barn where Vaughn kept all the machines and equipment.

"Blue jays and crows are bad," I remembered Daddy saying. "But squirrels are of the devil."

One year, fox squirrels ate over two hundred pounds off old Mr. Bailey's orchards next door. Squirrels, they didn't care what stage the nuts were at. They ate mature nuts, nut buds, even the bark off the trees. While shotguns worked best to get rid of the critters, Vaughn would just as soon catch them in the act using squirrel traps.

When we reached the workshop, Vaughn stood fiddling with wood squirrel traps. "Tomfool varmints. Don't let their cute little noses and beady button eyes fool ya."

He handed me a spring trap, a hammer, and a leather apron full of nails. I knew from years past precisely what to do. My job was to hammer the trap onto the tree, about four feet off the ground. Then we'd load 'em up all year, until harvest, with peanut butter, nuts, or whatever attracted the squirrels any given day.

"Take the tractor and wagon and get around to as many trees as you can get to."

I put a couple dozen traps in the tractor wagon and drove off to the east part of the orchards, near where a wide creek dumped into the large pond on the far corner of the property. Once there, I grabbed a couple of traps and picked out two of the largest trees to start with—trees so large I knew they had to be either native to the land or planted by a Harlan around the time of the Civil War.

Molly barked, and then she let out a slow, low growl in her throat. She was not a barker—one of the reasons Mama and Daddy let me keep her a few years back. She'd been a stray, and workers from the orchards had found her limping, ribs showing and all, and brought her to Mama, on account of her nursing knowledge. Sure enough, with some help from the vet, we cleaned up her bloody front paw and her torn left ear. We combed through her fur, matted from the tips of her paws clear up her sides from the filth of roaming in mud and creek beds. Once we gave her a good bath and pulled the ticks off her ears and neck, a perfectly good white retriever appeared. After we fed her for a few weeks, we couldn't see her ribs anymore.

Like I said, Molly wasn't a barker, so when she did bark, I knew something was off. I followed the stare of her eyes to where they focused on a rustling close to the creek. It was too large and slow to be a deer, and my heart thudded in my throat. As I got closer, it turned out to be a boy who looked to be about my age. He crouched down and used a sifting pan on the edge of the creek. Then he stood and walked farther on down the creek. He hadn't seen me yet, so I had time to notice that he limped a bit when he walked.

"Hey." I figured I oughta let him know I was there, rather than both of us scaring each other. When he turned around, he threw a cigarette to the ground and squashed it with his work boot. He tilted his head toward the sky and puffed out a couple of smoke rings.

"Impressive." I waited for him to reply, but he kept silent. Maybe he *was* a new boy Vaughn hired. Actually, Daddy probably hired him before he died. That was his job. Vaughn kept track of the books.

I walked toward him, and soon noticed he had a crooked eye to match his crooked leg. Molly ran to him, sniffing him up and down and running circles around him. "Aren't you gonna say something?"

"Hi." He leaned down and scratched Molly around her neck and ears.

"I'm Anniston. Anniston *Harlan*." Maybe he'd catch on by my last name that I wasn't any old girl wandering through. But it didn't faze him. "Well?"

"Well what?"

"The polite thing to do would be to tell me who you are."

"I suppose it would." But he still didn't tell me. Just stood there looking at me some more and with a smart-aleck grin on his face.

"Fine." I turned away and started back toward the tractor and my business. I'd find out who he was on my own if he wasn't going to tell me.

"Name's Jed, short for Jedediah. Manon's my last name. Rey— Mr. Harlan—brought me on late last fall. I'll be working all spring and summer through harvest time, once it's time to start working the orchards again."

I spun back around and faced him. "*Rey* is dead."

"I know. Read about it in the papers. Awful thing to have happened."

"He was my daddy." I let that sink in him before I turned and walked back up the hill. "Now I've got to set these traps up."

I was almost back to the tractor when he ran up beside me. "Why don't you let me help you with that?"

"I can handle it. Grew up doing this."

"Now who's impolite?"

"Refusing help from a stranger is not rude, Jedediah."

"Jed."

"Fine. Jed."

"That your house up there by the road?" He pointed toward Comfort's house.

"No, that's my aunt's place. I live—I'm *staying*—in the house over there." I pointed toward my grandparents' home.

He raised his eyebrows as if I was suddenly fancy to him.

"It's not all it's cracked up to be, living here. Believe me."

"Rey—I mean … Your daddy, he didn't tell me he had a daughter."

"Probably didn't see a need to."

Jed kept his dirt-brown hair long enough for the wind to tousle, and a band of freckles covered his nose and cheeks. He wore a green army jacket and jeans that were almost too big, in a nice sort of way, even if he did have a bit of an attitude. I wasn't used to thinking a boy was cute, but this one stirred something warm up in my knees and worked its way toward my heart. I hoped he couldn't tell.

"Maybe not. Say, would your granddad mind if I search for fossils and critters down here? When I have days off? I've been picking around along this creek for a couple of weeks now, but I can leave if you think he'd mind."

"No, he won't mind. You coulda asked him, though. Where you from, anyway? You new around here? I've never seen you at school or around town before."

"I'm from Tuscaloosa. Got reassigned to a new foster family down here. I been in school. Maybe you just ain't noticed me before. What grade are you in?"

"Eighth."

"I'm a freshman. Besides, sometimes I don't feel up to going, so I don't."

"Must be more often than not that you don't." I wasn't so sure about this boy. "Where do y'all live?"

"In town. Behind the library. I live with John and Hettie Devine."

This time, my eyebrows raised. Main Street and the library were kept up and quaint for tourists, but a patch of run-down trailers filled the block behind.

"So you know the place."

"Ain't many places 'round here I don't know." I wrapped the leather tool belt around my waist and headed toward a line of trees. "I better start on these traps, if you don't mind."

"You sure I can't help?"

"Nah, I got it. Thanks, though."

"Have it your way." He pulled another cigarette out of his pocket, lit it up, and walked back to the creek.

While pounding traps into the trees, I kept my eye on Jed, who busied himself sifting through sand and studying rocks on the edge of the creek. After picking up a couple more traps out of the wagon, I walked down to the creek bank and sat down near him. "What'd you say you're looking for?"

"Fossils. Critters. Rocks. Geodes, in particular. You seen one?"

"I'm not sure I even know what one is."

"It's a special kind of rock, all bumpy and dirty and useless on the outside. But if you shake it, and it rattles, you know you've got yourself a geode. Crack it open on the hard ground, and it's full of sparkling crystals. You can find them in fields and near creek beds like this."

"Wow."

"Yeah. Here's one." He placed a bumpy rock a little larger than a golf ball in the palm of my hand. I held it to my ear and rattled it. When I handed it back, he threw it against a boulder, the crack of it loud as a firecracker echoing across the hills. He picked up the larger of the crumbled pieces. "See?"

Clear and pale yellow, golden crystals lined the inside of the hollow rock. Rays of the sun got all caught in the angles and glimmered like jewels.

"That's not all. I got fossils I've found in Tuscaloosa and northern parts of Alabama, and a few I've found here already. Look at this one."

He handed me a stone smoother than the first with what appeared to be a carving on it.

"Those lines there mean it's a cephalopod." Jed ran his finger along the ridged places on the stone.

"Looks like a dead bug."

"It's more like a snail or a squid than a bug. Cephalopod fossils are all over Alabama, because ocean used to cover the whole state. The fossils are old mollusks, like slugs or small octopus from over four hundred million years ago."

"How do you know so much about this stuff?"

"I live next to the library, remember? Just 'cause I skip school don't mean I'm not learning anything." He pulled another dark-red, dirty stone out of his orange box. "This here's a piece of hematite. It's used to make iron, and it's all over Alabama. State mineral, in fact. That's what makes the dirt so red. Find good pieces of it, you can shine 'em up and folks fashion them into beads and stuff. I'm hoping to find a variation of it called hematite rose, which has patterns swirling through it like rose petals. That's why they call it *hematite rose*, of course."

"'Course." I held the geode toward the sun, playing with the light bouncing around the diamond-like crystals.

"Take those geode pieces and the hematite home with you."

"You sure you don't mind parting with 'em?" Whoever invented the burnt-umber crayon must've copied it off of hematite; the red of it mixed in with the faded gray of the rock, which I would've thought nothing of before now.

"I'm sure. I have plenty back home, and I'm sure I'll find plenty more. They're all easy to find if you know what you're looking for. Take 'em." He grinned.

I turned away so he wouldn't notice me blushing. "Thanks."

I left him alone the rest of the afternoon, but the hematite and two halves of the broken geode felt warm in my pocket as I worked to put up the rest of the traps. I drove the tractor and wagon up to Comfort's house to pick up the empty basket from her front porch, and as I walked up the steps, I noticed the asters growing taller in a soft patch of soil nearby. In place of the basket, I left a note I scribbled on a piece of scrap paper I found in the wagon, then set half of the geode on top so the note wouldn't blow away.

Sot pase mòn yo, plis mòn.
"Beyond the mountains, more mountains."

CHAPTER 12

Comfort

Dear Comfort,
This geode reminded me of you.
Beautiful.
Love,

Anni

Beautiful.

That's what Solly called me. We'd sit on the front porch in separate rockers. Back and forth, to and fro, the curved wood would press and creak against the floorboards. On many visits, he'd reach for my hand, but since the incident, I hadn't let him see me at all, much less hold my hand. But still, he visits. And when he does, he still calls me beautiful.

I don't know if I'll ever believe that I am.

Folks around town used to say I'm beautiful too—even Shirley O'Day, the town's society reporter for the newspaper, when she did a write-up on me the time I won homecoming queen and prom queen in the same year. While I'd been more tolerant of such compliments before what happened at Thanksgiving, I was still surprised anytime I'd been crowned. When I won homecoming queen, Solly stood at my side and held my hand as we stood on the center of the cinder track. I leaned on him hard, feeling like I might pass out, when they called my name. Same thing when they crowned me prom queen, then county fair queen. Sure, Mama dressed me well. Nothing but the best clothes and shoes and makeup from New Orleans for me. But beautiful? That was something other girls could claim.

Especially now.

Anni meant well, leaving that geode, hollow insides sparkling like a tiara. But then, how could she understand the depths of my pain? How could anyone, really? Sadness deep in my chest threatens to explode. Sharp crystals cut against my cavernous heart. My soul rattled when Cole shook it, and even now my soul shivers, terrified of aftershocks and memories.

I throw the geode against the floor. Though shaped and formed by eternal forces, the craggy rock crumbles as if it were hand-blown glass, splitting into millions of shards when hurled against the floor. I skid to my knees, gathering the fragments, their knife-like edges piercing my skin. Maybe I can put the pieces back together again. Make it all whole again. But parts are missing. Others don't fit right, tiny chips lost forever beneath furniture or in cracks in the floorboards.

I wrap myself as tight as I can in the quilt Ernestine made me, and lie upon my bed, watching the yellowing lace curtains float back and forth against the open window. Maybe if I can pick out one of the songs of blessing she sang over me still lingering on the breeze, I'll still feel connected to myself. Maybe even to the world. Everything hurts so much I feel like I'm flying above a dream of myself. I strain to hear songs floating in the air, but instead I hear Abba again. I doubt it's Him at first, but still He comes, gentle, like a cool rag on a fevered forehead.

I know the desert. I've walked the wastelands, too, He says.

Someplace in the shadowland between wake and sleep, He sets a dream of Solly and Anni, Oralee and Ernestine on the horizon like a mirage I strain to melt into. My mind is wavy with contemplation and apprehension, twins fighting like Jacob and Esau for their father's blessing. But I can give neither the first rights they seek.

I dream I am running down Point Clear River, snakes slithering alongside me, legs too weak to leap from stone to stone to cross the rapids. Something worse than the snakes chases me, and I know if I do not escape the shadow gaining on me, I will not awaken. I fight the currents and sucking mud at the bottom of the river, and still the form gains on me until I fall over a waterfall, the light at the bottom offering peace and escape.

I fall.

And fall.

And fall.

And I wake before I reach the light.

Like every other of the hundreds of nights I've dreamed the same dream and awoken, I try to sleep and beg my mind to dream it again, praying for the courage to stay asleep and see what waits at the bottom.

Until, on this afternoon, I realize, the dream is real.

I have dreamed it since childhood.

Because Cole hurt me long before he killed Rey. Cole has been my nightmare, the shadow gaining on me, since I was very, very small. And like a mirrored lake held back, then released by a dam, memories flood through me, the surge of remembrance jolting me awake.

I sit up straight in my bed, my sheets a wet mess of sweat, the moon shining upon the truth of these memories buried since childhood. Buried since he stopped. And now, resurrected.

"You're such a pretty girl, Comfort. You're my girlfriend," Cole had said.

Back then, I believed him. And why not? I idolized him. The town idolized him. Throngs of folks in hot, metal bleachers screamed and cheered for him as he threw touchdowns and raced up and down green fields and crowds raised him up on their shoulders as a hero. My big brother, the town hero, the family cornerstone, called me his most special girl.

"This thing we do, this game, is sweet and secret, baby girl. Something good big brothers do for their sisters. Don't tell Mama. Especially don't tell Daddy."

And I hadn't.

One time, Mama burst into my room in the middle of Cole playing his secrets on me. She held a stack of laundry in front of her. She looked in my eyes. I remember she did. Deep and long, she looked straight into me.

Then she turned and walked out of the room, closing the door with a quiet click.

Later that day, I'd heard her talking to herself in her rose garden. "Better her than me," she whispered as she snipped the roses, her fingers bleeding from the thorns. "Better her than me."

She whispered that all the time, come to think of it. Even as she washed the floors, the one task she would not delegate to Ernestine.

As if she were the only one who could scrub away the secrets.

Santi bon Koute che.
"Smelling good is expensive."

CHAPTER 13

Anniston

I thought about Jed the whole way back from the orchards. Surely our paths would cross again if he worked the orchards all summer. But then what? I knew foster kids moved around a lot. I said a small prayer God would let him stay a long while.

Mama's dusty, maroon station wagon was still parked in our carport. She worked more nursing shifts now than ever—nights, days, weekends—whenever she could get overtime, even though Vaughn told her she didn't have to work at all. She said she wanted to be independent, to get us a place of our own without help.

Ernestine creaked the screen door open when she saw me climbing the front porch steps and presented me with a plate full of egg-salad sandwiches and a tall glass of milk. She kissed me on the forehead.

"*Bonswa*, Anni. You hungry after all that time in the orchards, yes?"

"Yes, ma'am. Thanks!"

With a sandwich in one hand, I tossed Daddy's shirt and my hat on the couch with the other and headed to Mama's bedroom. A mix of Aqua Net and shampoo floated through the air. She wore her spring-blue nursing uniform, which meant she worked that night after all.

"Hey, Anni. Your granddad find something for you to do?"

"Yep."

"Don't forget we're going to the Curly Q tomorrow morning for the haircut Princella arranged to get you ready for the Bay Spring Cotillion."

As much as I hated getting my hair cut, the Curly Q's reputation of being a treasure trove of town gossip made it a pretty cool place to hang out. The Q stood for *Qarla*, the owner of the place. Bubblegum-pink and shiny gold paint covered everything inside and out. Gold mirrors, pink velvet chairs trimmed in gold, gold chandeliers, gold ceiling fans, even gold-handled scissors. Sometimes, Qarla painted her fingernails gold and glued rhinestones on the tips of them. The woman couldn't get enough gold.

Princella organized the Bay Spring Cotillion, also known as the Daughters of the Confederacy Cotillion and Bay Spring Auxiliary Auction, every year, just like Vaughn's mama did and her mama before her. As such, Princella took it upon herself to make sure I looked pretty, even though wearing dresses and being fussed over appealed to me about as much as picking cotton with bare hands. To make matters worse, being thirteen required me to invite an official date. The thought of holding hands with a boy—even if we both wore gloves—made my stomach hurt. But Princella said I had to find an escort from an upstanding family. Mama said she didn't care what boy I took, so long as I took one. I doubted any would want to go with me, but Princella said any young man from the right kind of family would consider it an honor to go with the granddaughter of Princella and Vaughn Harlan to the biggest social event of the year for any young person who expected to make something of themselves when they grew up.

But finding a boy to take to the cotillion was the least of my worries.

First I had to make it through the Curly Q.

The following day, Mama—late from oversleeping after working most of the night—slammed the station wagon into a too-small parking space behind a car with a Louisiana license plate and in front of the Pen and Ink Bookstore, which was around the corner from the library. I peered around to see if I could catch a glimpse of the trailer Jed lived in, but they all looked the same.

Across the street, through the glass and gilded doors of the Curly Q, Princella sat with her arms crossed, perched on the edge of a pink velvet chair. She wore her silver mink coat, so long it nearly dragged on the floor. She wore it any day the temperature in Bay Spring fell below sixty degrees. Personally, I'd swelter in such a coat. But Princella, she loved wearing that coat around so much she never cared.

"See what Vaughn brought home for me?" Princella had said when she first showed us the coat one afternoon a couple of years ago.

"It's beautiful, Princella," Mama gushed. I could tell she didn't care for the coat when she turned her head toward me and winked, which I took as my cue to gush over it too.

"Must've taken a lot of animals dying to make that coat." I couldn't help wrinkling up my nose.

"Well, now, Anniston," Princella chided, "they raise minks like the ones they use for this coat at special farms, so they're supposed to be turned into coats someday. A coat like this doesn't hurt a thing in the wild. Anyway, I adore the silver, like the Alabama Southern Silver Tigers. It's perfect for wearing on those chilly football game days."

Perfect for showing off. Princella and Vaughn's pecan farm made them the biggest financial contributors in Magnolia County to Alabama Southern University. Ever since Cole got a full-ride scholarship there as starting quarterback, Princella and Vaughn threw money at the university like snowbirds throwing suntan oil on their lily-white bodies.

"Hello, Anniston. How's my favorite granddaughter today?" Princella's sugar-sweet voice grated in my ears as she wrapped her mink-clad arms around my neck. The fur tickled my nose so I almost sneezed. She always called me her favorite grandchild. Easy for her to say. I was the only one. The only daughter of her dead and buried son. A son she hasn't talked about. Hasn't even mentioned by name.

She ran her fingers through my hair and I shivered. "I'm fine, thank you, ma'am."

"What are we gonna have Qarla do with that mess of hair of yours today, sweetheart?"

"I think she just needs a trim," Mama said.

I prayed she wouldn't argue with Mama, but of course she did.

"Well, you're old enough we could add some color to your mousy brown, and how about some nice feathered layers like those Mandrell sisters? Feathered hair is supposed to be the rage. I saw Mandy Appleton the other day—you know, last year's homecoming queen—and she wears her hair feathered. She looks so beautiful. And the boys flock to her."

"Looks like a golden retriever." I stared at my new rainbow-and-smiley-faces shoelaces.

"What's that, Anniston?"

"I said Mandy looks golden and dreamy with that hair of hers, ma'am. I'd really like somethin' simple." I tried my best not to whine. Mama said to be gracious and grateful to Princella, even if she did things for the wrong reasons. I sank back in a pink wingback chair across the room, hoping she wouldn't talk much more to me.

Mandy Appleton.

What a laugh.

Mandy could fill a whole set of bleachers with friends. Drop-dead gorgeous, Mandy coulda passed as Brooke Shields's twin. Princella always talked about the prettiest, most popular girls in town and wanted me to be like them. But why did she care? Especially now, with Daddy and Cole gone? Why didn't she care about that? Buzzing around to all her social activities like nothing happened at Thanksgiving. Acting all cheery and bossy about a haircut when she wouldn't even bring up Daddy's name.

I picked up a giant magazine about hair that was filled with foreign languages and spiky-haired models with black lines painted across their eyelids. I wanted to cut my hair short and spiky, or maybe color it black like the crows in the pecan trees. Page after page of models stared back at me, their skin like porcelain and hair plastered in razor-sharp swaths across the sides of their faces.

Across the way, the table where Comfort worked doing ladies' nails sat neat and empty, and Mama got into it with Princella. "We certainly appreciate what you're doing here, but you've got to quit trying to turn Anni into Comfort."

I couldn't breathe for a second after Mama said Comfort's name.

"I don't know what you mean." Princella's eyes opened wide, and her cheeks turned rosy against the silver of the mink coat.

"You do know what I mean." Mama came forward in her chair, her whisper rough. "Even though Rey isn't here to defend his daughter, don't think I won't. Comfort was special by her own rights, and she only wanted to make you happy. Didn't get her too far, now did it?"

Well, that musta nearly knocked the wind outta Princella, because as fast as her cheeks turned rosy, they turned gray like the inside of a raw oyster.

"How dare you bring up what happened with Comfort here, Oralee, you—"

"Anni, I'm ready for you, sugar." Qarla saved me from the two of them in the nick of time as she leaned against the waist-high, gold room divider separating us from the working part of the salon. She led me to the back, where gold hair-washing stations lined up like statues at the King Tut exhibit in New Orleans. I lay back in the chair, and Qarla started washing. She massaged and kneaded my head until my eyes drooped with sleep.

Once we got back to the cutting chair, Qarla yakked away about her kids and her husband and the latest Bay Spring gossip. I tried to listen, but in the chair next to me sat a very pregnant Minnie Davies getting her hair wrapped up in tin foil. Minnie's neck turned splotchy red, and tears flowed down her face like rain against a window. I knew Minnie because she attended our church, and we brought her a casserole every time she had a baby. She had so many babies already, I didn't know what number this one made. Anyway, Minnie cried all over herself in the chair next to me, and I was too busy trying to figure out what she was crying about to listen to Qarla.

"I know whatever I do will come back to me, and I'm scared ... scared something will happen to my baby," Minnie said.

"What do you mean?" her hairdresser asked.

"Every time we do something bad, God punishes us by bringing something bad." Fear pulled on Minnie's cheeks and wrinkled up her forehead. "I haven't done anything bad to speak of, but what if I do? What if I do and don't mean to? And then my baby comes out deformed or simple-minded? That's what sin does, you know. Comes back to bite so God can teach us a lesson."

I wondered where Minnie got those ideas. Preacher Beckett never talked like that at church. Made me think of boys on the school bus, trying to get even with each other through punches. Life doesn't deliver punches for punches, though I wish it would. Life's more backward than anything. The folks who get punched always work hard to live life right, and the folks who deserve to get punched always give everyone around them a fat lip. And the good people who stand up for others? Well, folks either try to burn 'em up in buses like those Freedom Riders in Anniston, Alabama, or they end up dead like my daddy.

I wished Minnie would stop carrying on so loud, because through the mirror I saw Jed come into the salon. He caught my glance in the mirror and smiled at me with his crooked eyes. I bet his real mama didn't do anything bad to make him crooked. Sometimes babies just came out that way.

Jed walked past me and tossed a wad of cash at a woman sitting a few chairs down. Busy choosing roller sizes for a permanent wave, the woman barely acknowledged him, just kept smacking her gum and fingering through the box of curlers.

Could that be his foster mother?

I focused on Minnie's laments again. "I couldn't handle it if one of my babies came out with something wrong with them."

"Excuse me, ma'am, where's the bathroom?" Jed asked Qarla.

"In the back." Qarla nodded without missing a snip.

As Jed limped to the back of the salon, Minnie saw him in her mirror as he passed. Well, if her jaw didn't fall open far enough to catch a dozen flies! She dabbed her eyes with a handkerchief with one hand and rubbed her watermelon-size belly with the other.

"What's yours look like, Anni?"

I had no idea what Qarla had been talking about. "What?"

"Your dress for the cotillion. What's it look like?"

"Oh, my dress. It's okay for a dress, I guess. We found it at the Dillard's in Mobile. It's white with lace over the top of it and a big satin ribbon around the middle the same color as a robin's egg."

"Sounds perfect. And did you get your gloves and shoes, too?"

"Yeah."

"I remember your aunt's first cotillion when she took a boy. Solly, of course. Such a fuss your grandmother made about it. Comfort … she loved dressing up and she loved a party. We put giant curlers in her hair and pinned it up high and let the ringlets fall down her back. Such a princess, that Comfort."

If there was one thing I appreciated about a haircut with Qarla, she wasn't afraid to talk about anything. She talked about Comfort like it was no big deal to say her name out loud. I suppose it wasn't to her, since Comfort had worked for her all these years. So I went along with it like it was the most natural topic of discussion this side of Biloxi, Mississippi.

"Mmm-hmm," I agreed.

"Comfort was the talk of the town in junior high and high school. Every mother wanted their son to date her, and every boy with a set of workin' eyeballs wanted to. She broke all the hearts in Bay Spring when Solly scooped her up."

"Then you know about what happened to her?" I wondered how many people knew Comfort's side of Cole and Daddy's deaths, 'specially since she hadn't worked since then.

Qarla stopped smiling, and our eyes locked in the mirror in front of us. She bent down close to me and gently tucked my still-damp hair behind my ear. "Your aunt is a beautiful and brave woman. Always was, and still is. And your father, Rey, was a good man. I've always been afraid for you, how the tongues of this town twist stories around and what you'll hear, especially now that you're becoming a woman. But you trust Miss Qarla when I tell you Rey was a good man. And Comfort is a good woman."

My face blurred in the mirror, and I fixed my gaze on the soggy snippets of hair settling all over the lap of the pink waterproof apron wrapped around me.

Qarla went on. "Honey, poison got into your family through Princella and settled on your uncle Cole. A ginormous tragedy. Someone shoulda noticed Cole's problems after he went off to college, and someone shoulda protected Comfort, but Princella, she wore blinders when it came to that boy. Always did. Still does, too, which is why Comfort's in the state she's in today. It's not right when the victim becomes the criminal. Happens more often than not, though. Such a shame it's happening here."

Qarla shook her head with regret, and puddles of tears settled in the bottoms of her eyes. But she quick wiped them away and continued trimming my hair. I saw Mama in the mirror's reflection, her nose in a book. I strained to see Princella, but she must've left the salon to do some shopping.

As if she heard my mind worrying about what Princella would think if she heard this talk, Qarla stopped trimming for a second and bent down next to my ear again.

"And another thing, Anni. Your grandmother may be payin' me, but you're my customer, and I'm here to please your heart, not hers."

"I love my hair, Mama."

Her eyes focused on the road in front of us. We were nearly back home.

"It's definitely you, sweetheart."

Princella would hate it, of course. Qarla cut it clear up to my ears in a short bob and frosted the ends of it like the model in the magazine.

Mama stopped the car next to Comfort's house. "Go on and grab that empty basket as long as we're here."

I ran up to Comfort's house and grabbed the basket. Another yellow-edged index card fell out, and the wind tossed it across the porch. I caught it with my foot and read it on the way back to Mama's car:

there's no such thing as a generational curse

after all no father would wish

harm on his own child

only the failing of one generation to

stop the sin

break the cycle

shine light onto paths long shadowed

by shame

or ignorance

or both

Piti, piti, zwazo a ti kras bati nich li yo.
"Little by little, the bird builds its nest."

CHAPTER 14

Anniston

Ernestine pulled a pecan pie out of the oven as we walked into the house. "Your hair ... *Byen bèl*, Anni!"

"Thanks, Ernestine. I hope you can still braid it."

"*Oui*, child, I can braid anything long enough to hold between two fingers." All the girls in my class coveted Ernestine's plaits—even the ones who never talked to me otherwise. But Ernestine, she saved her braiding for me, smiling and humming "Jacob's Ladder" as she pulled the strands tight. Said that's her favorite song because of the reaching and climbing she's done to come up out of her miry life.

Comfort hummed that song the night Daddy died.

"Pie smells good." I snuck a couple of sugared pecans off the steaming top of the pie, tossed one into Molly's mouth, and another

113

into mine. Salty and sweet. She made the best pies around. Folks traveled from across the South to buy her pies at a booth she ran every year at the Moonlight and Magnolias Music Festival every August. Most of the Harlan pecans were sold to manufacturers and distributed that way or by catalog, but we kept some back for her to sell there, too, boxes of salted pecans, sugared pecans, pecan brittle, chocolate-covered pecans, pecan butter, and every other kind of pecan combination tied up in fancy packaging with *Harlan's Best* stamped on the side.

"Don't be picking at that, child. It's for after dinner." Grinning, she pulled a couple off the top for herself.

"Jambalaya for dinner?" A giant pot sat on the back burner, steam seeping out around the edges of the lid.

"Oui."

Princella walked into the kitchen, arms full of shopping bags from her favorite boutiques in town. "Anniston! Your hair!"

I shrank closer to Ernestine, bracing myself for a tongue-lashing.

"You look like a boy! How are we ever going to fix this? Didn't Qarla listen to anything I told her to do? I'll have to take you back myself and stay there this time."

"You'll do nothing of the sort." Mama walked in, just in time. She glared at Princella, seeming to be daring her to argue back.

Princella's face twisted like she wanted to say a whole slew of things, but her mouth stayed shut. Then … "Fine. Y'all have it your way."

"I really like it, ma'am." I right away wished I hadn't said anything, but something stirred inside me I couldn't keep back.

"Pull your shoulders back and quit slumping," Princella said as she came toward me. She grabbed my chin with her bony fingers, then turned my face from side to side. She let go, but the leftover grip of her fingers kept twisting into me. She sighed and stared out the window into the distance. "You're such a pretty girl. All I want for you and all I wanted for Comfort was to have a chance at a life I never did. A chance to deserve all this."

She turned toward us and spread her arms out wide. "You have no idea what I've been through. No idea about the life I've lived. No idea what it's taken me to finally feel worthy of this life here." She paced across the room, and Mama, Ernestine, and I looked at each other, shocked at the way her voice softened and sounded almost childlike. "Vaughn had everything. I had nothing. And even less after ... oh, never mind." She dug her fingers through her styled and stiffened hair. "All you need to know is Vaughn brought me here, and folks hated me. Hated me until I proved I was worthy of this society. This place. This home."

I'd figured she had to have a heart in there somewhere. But as always, she never let it show for long.

"Took a hell of a lot of work, but I did it." She sighed and paced toward me, eyes glaring through me like an arrow. "Hopefully your dress will distract from that awful hack job. I'll be asking Qarla for my money back."

She spun away from us, and we listened to her heavy plods up the stairs, where she would most likely stay shut in her room until dinner.

I couldn't help bursting into tears.

"*Rete tann, pitit.*" Ernestine tried to grab my hand, but I brushed her aside and ran into the front hall where I hollered up the stairs after Princella.

"I'll never be who you want!"

The house hushed, full of silence, and Princella emerged from her room at the top of the banistered landing. Her face was masklike. "I'm only tryin' to—"

"Tryin' to what? To make me a debutante? To keep folks from finding out what happened at Thanksgiving? Or are you so mad because you only really loved Cole, and now all you have left is us?" I felt Mama standing behind me. Good thing, since I felt like I might pass out, hardly believing I'd hollered at her so.

"That's not your business, Anniston." Princella looked at Mama. "I didn't love him more. He just—Oralee, tell her."

"Tell her what, Princella? Exactly what do you want me to tell my daughter about Cole?"

I didn't want to hear anything else she said, so I ran through the kitchen and out the mudroom, grabbing Daddy's shirt along the way. I hoisted my bike up from alongside the driveway where I'd set it last, and pedaled past Comfort's house, past the rows of pecan trees, past workers mowing and trimming. Out on the open road, the rows passed faster and faster, and my feet pushed on the pedals harder and harder until the bare, reaching branches of the orchards gave way to open fields and lazy oaks, interrupted by an occasional fresh peach and produce stand. The collar of my shirt squeezed my already-tight throat. But soon the pedaling smoothed my mood, and I drifted along nice and easy, feeling the cool breeze and smelling the sweet salt of the wintery sea and marshes. The hard ride helped my purple anger fade like the yellowing edge of the sky.

The dirt road turned to pavement near the outskirts of Bay Spring. I often rode to town for no particular reason, sitting for hours along the bay to watch barges of freight cars stacked up like Chiclets, shrimp boats with their skinny arms stretched up at the sky like folks in church singing praise songs, the lights of the oil drills winking in the distance, or fishermen tossing patient lines off the pier. I set my bike down on a stretch of lawn, then walked toward the docks and boat slips. Many were empty this time of year—sad holes left from seasonal residents storing their crafts in dry dock for the winter. Busiest place here this time of year was the Crab Shack Restaurant and Bar, built right in the middle of the pier. Daddy and I'd sit at the bar together after we were done fishing or sailing, him with his beer and me with my cherry co-cola. The bartender made sure to serve it with a paper umbrella and a shiny maraschino cherry.

I coulda made my way to Daddy's old boat slip blindfolded, I'd been there so many times. Daddy's old boat, *The Jubilee*, still bobbed and rocked there the same as always, as if waiting with glee for passengers.

"Sorry, old girl. Only came to see how you're doing. Can't take you out anymore."

Mama'd sold the boat with the house. No reason for us to keep her, she'd said. I suppose she was right. She didn't fish. And while she liked taking rides at sunset, we both knew it wouldn't be the same without Daddy.

The last time the three of us went out in *The Jubilee* was before the weather turned colder. Must've been sometime in October. Daddy dressed in a Hawaiian shirt, flip-flops, and scraggly cut-off shorts. We'd caught chub bait in estuary waters, then headed toward more open water to fish for the real stuff—red snapper, grouper, king mackerel, and amberjack. No telling which ones would bite until we got out there. Whatever we caught, we'd take home and barbecue.

"Hey, Larry," I said when I noticed the man sitting in the rickety oyster skiff in the slat next to *The Jubilee*. Daddy and I got to know Larry in spite of his quiet nature because of all the time we spent at the docks. Larry wore an old army jacket and a ball cap with a logo I recognized as the same as the ones on all the whiskey bottles in Princella's kitchen cupboard. His whiskers were scraggly, and his mustache hung well over his top lip. He stared at the ocean, rocking along with the rhythm of the water, his lips moving to some lost song only he could hear. His legs were skin and bones, and his jeans barely hung on to his hips.

He did not look up from the hooks and tackle he worked between his fingers. "Sorry about your daddy, Anni. Sure do miss him."

Tears pricked my eyes. "Me, too, Larry. Thanks."

"They're taking good care of her. Them folks who bought *The Jubilee*."

"Good to know."

I sat down Indian-style on the dock between Larry and *The Jubilee*, then turned around as footsteps closed in behind me.

"Come here often?"

"Jed. What are you doing here?" My cheeks warmed, and I hoped he didn't noticed.

"I come here whenever I can." He held a fishing rod and cooler in one hand and a tackle box and livewell bucket in the other. He nodded toward *The Jubilee*. "Pretty one, that one there."

"Yeah. Used to be Daddy's."

Jed frowned. "Must've seen some good times."

"Lots."

Jed set down his gear and sat cross-legged next to me, content to be silent along with me for a while. Seagulls dove across the sky above us, free and light without the burden of knowing sadness in their hearts. Daddy said they were scavengers, seagulls. Eating whatever folks left behind or stealing fish other birds like pelicans worked hard to capture. This reminded me of Cole, stealing from Comfort. Stealing from Mama. Stealing from me. I didn't bother to hide the tears now flowing down my face.

Jed untied a red bandana from around his wrist and handed it to me. "Wanna sink a few with me?"

The sparkle in his eyes was hard not to melt into, like the sun sinking into the arms of the ocean horizon. I wiped my eyes, then handed the bandana back to him.

"I'd love to."

"Say, what's your favorite thing you and your daddy ever caught?"

I thought of the giant fish, all shades of blue and teal, that Daddy stuffed and hung on the wall in his den. Now the beast was buried away in a storage unit.

"A blue marlin. He was so proud of that fish. Took three men to pull it in." I tilted my head toward Larry, still intent on his lures.

"She's not lyin'. What a time. I didn't think we'd ever get her in the boat."

"You were there?" Jed asked, unbelieving that scruffy old Larry might be part of such a story.

"Yep. That fish pulled at the line like a team of horses. A good-size snapper can be tough to pull in but ain't nothing like a marlin. Rey wasn't about to throw her back after that. Old girl gave him no choice but to stuff her." Larry rubbed his bearded chin between his fingers. "Say, why don't you two take my skiff out for a ride?"

"You sure?"

"I am. I ain't gonna fix all this tackle today. Besides, I can mess with it here on the dock. After all you been through, I'm betting a boat ride's just what you need. Keys are in the starter."

And with that, Larry got up and out of his boat in a second. He patted my shoulder as he walked past me. "I sure am sorry, sweetheart. None of you deserved any of that."

I watched Larry trudge down the docks. He looked back at me and winked as he opened the door to the Crab Shack.

"Who is that?" Jed asked.

"An old friend."

"Awful kind of him to offer his boat."

"Larry's different, but he'd do anything for anybody. He wouldn't have let us argue with him, either. "

"Let's go, then." Jed jumped in the boat.

I hesitated, remembering I hardly knew much of anything about him. "Should I trust you out in the open sea, Jedediah?"

"Well, let me see. I smoke. I'm a foster kid. I have a crooked eye, and I don't walk too straight, either. You know nothing about me." He grinned and held his arms out wide. "Probably not."

I folded my arms across my chest and studied him a moment, then threw one leg over the side of the gray-painted, box-like vessel. "My mama'd have a fit about this, you know. Thirteen and headed into the open bay with a boy barely more than a stranger." I reached for Jed's outstretched hand as the evergreen water threatened to pull me down between the steady safety of the dock and the boat.

"I have no doubt." Jed grabbed my waist with both hands and pulled me aboard like I weighed nothing more than a bag of cotton candy. He drew me close enough to him that I caught the salty smell of clothes left outside to dry and the smell of tobacco.

"Life jacket?" Jed pulled one tight around his chest and held another out to me. "You better wear one. Besides the fact I'm a bunch of trouble, I don't swim all that well. If you fall in, don't count on me to save you."

"You can't swim?"

"I can hold my own in shallow water. But no, I never took lessons. Switched families too often. I guess each family thought the one before them took care of that milestone. Among others."

I put on the life vest and pulled Larry's old raincoat on over it to keep the wind from getting through to my skin. It smelled like old fish and oyster slime, but I was glad to have it.

The engine chortled to a bubbling growl, and I took charge of the steering. If Jed didn't know how to swim very well, I wasn't about to let him drive the boat. At least not in and out of a boat slat. Larry was generous, but he probably wanted his skiff back in one piece.

We putted out from between the docks into the glassy calm of the bay. Almost instantly, liberty ran its fingers through my hair, reaching straight to my soul. I plopped onto a bench next to the motor and watched the rocks and homes we were passing. The late-afternoon sun speckled the water and darted sideways between the thick-trunked palms and beach elder. Stagnant bilge water, bait, and exhaust combined to take me back to that last boat ride with Daddy. The boat pushed the water aside, leaving arrow-shaped ripples in the direction of our journey.

Tired of idling along in the oyster flats and shallow waters, I pointed the boat toward the center of Mobile Bay, where you could go and hardly make out the land. Before we knew it, water surrounded us on every side. Jed turned off the engine, and we floated, the water lapping and licking against the hull. Three or four other vessels dotted the horizon.

"If I could be anything in the world, I'd be a pirate." Jed propped a floatation cushion on the end of his bench and tossed one to me. We leaned back against them, letting the sun warm our faces, chilled from the windy ride.

"They're still out there today, pirates. They're really not nice people, you know."

"Maybe not. But I'd be a nice one."

"How can you be a nice pirate? They steal and live like hobos, never staying anywhere long enough to settle down."

"Then I guess you can say I already am a pirate."

"You steal?" I wondered for the second time if I'd made a mistake taking this boat ride with him.

"Aw, no. I don't steal." He threw his burned-out cigarette butt into the sea.

I felt bad about my assumptions of him stealing all of a sudden and tried to make up for it. "Larry's a pirate, you know. His full name's Larry LaFitte. A direct descendant of Jean LaFitte."

"Jean LaFitte? You're kidding me. He's one of the greatest pirates from these parts."

"Yeah."

"I read about him when I found out I was getting placed with a family in Bay Spring. Used to be nothing around here but groves of beach elder and sea grass and dunes higher than your head, especially down by the coast. A perfect hiding place for pirates, then and now. Some books said LaFitte floated off and lived his last days on an island. But others say he landed here, his ship and crew drifting into Cotton Bayou down by Gulf Shores. Used his ship as firewood so there'd be no trace of him and he could live in peace."

"I feel bad for Larry. He's got a kind of sickness in the head. Daddy explained it to me after the last time we fished with him. Lots of folks who have it live locked away in mental hospitals. But Daddy and my preacher found Larry living under the state pier down in Gulf Shores and took him in. Said he used to be a track star somewhere around these parts. Fought in Vietnam too. Almost died there. His head problems started over there, and he couldn't find help when he came home. But Daddy and Preacher Beckett found him a place to live. Set him up with a boat of his own so he could make a living oysterin'." I pointed to a half dozen oyster boats floating near a shallow spot offshore, their captains working stilt-like rakes along the bottom.

"Daddy always liked stories of folks who got second chances. That's why he liked Larry, I guess. Also why he named his boat *The Jubilee*, after Leviticus 25:10, when God erased the debts and wrongs of everybody's past. God gave 'em another chance. That's what He did for Larry. Gave him a jubilee."

Jed kept his eye on the clouds shimmering white against the deep blue sky. Although it coulda been the wind, his eyes moistened with what I took to be emotion. He leaned back and pulled his hat down over his eyes.

"Folks around town make fun of him, 'cause of how he is, not talking much and still looking like he's homeless. It's like the world sucked the normal out of him and locked him inside some kind of cage in his mind, and now he only comes out when he wants to, and even then, sometimes in pieces."

"He talked to me."

"Yeah, he did. Another reason I figured you'd be all right to hang with, at least for one afternoon." Waves lapped against the sides of the boat, and a barge stacked high with forty-foot containers of all colors loomed on the horizon. "My aunt, Comfort, she's in a place like that right now. Hasn't hardly come out of her house 'cept to sit on the rockers with Solly since a few days after Daddy and Uncle Cole shot each other." I didn't want to tell Jed why she was having a harder time recovering from everything than the rest of us. Turned out, he already knew.

"I've known some girls like her. Girls who've been raped."

"How'd you know Comfort—"

"I read the newspaper." He rolled over onto his elbow and faced me, his eyes meeting mine for the first time since I started telling him about Larry.

"Princella said they paid so no one would put that part in the paper."

"Must've paid them after it went to print. I only saw one report that mentioned it, the day after the shooting."

So the whole town *did* know.

"Anyway, I've known girls who went through similar stuff. Rape. Incest. You name it. You see it all when you're a foster kid."

"I'm sorry."

"Don't be. It's made me realize everybody hurts. And everybody needs a friend. And hurtin' people, they need friends most." He sat up and leaned over the side of the boat to let his fingers glide along the water. "You ever been to a zoo?"

"Sure. There's one over in Gulf Shores with a bunch of exotic animals. Tigers, even."

"Well, think about those tigers, how they pace back and forth, eyes staring past you, caged up but seeing freedom out past the bars all around them. Think they like living in there?"

"Probably not."

He sat back up and leaned toward me. "Especially not if they lived free beforehand. But think about if that's all they've known. They might think they want to get out in the world and explore and run like the other cats, but they might find, once they're out there, the world feels too big and dangerous."

"What's that have to do with Comfort?"

"Those are the people who need a friend. I seen all kinds of people get the hope beat out of 'em. Girls like her, even younger. Babies who have their innocence stolen from them. It's like they're locked up in a cage of fear. You can see in their eyes they want to get out and taste the world again, but they can't, because they're scared. Their prisons feel safe. Sometimes they don't even realize they're all locked up until someone believes in them and sets them free."

"We believe in Comfort. Me, Mama, Ernestine. Especially Solly. They're supposed to get married this summer. Doesn't seem to make a difference, though."

"Don't give up. It will." He fiddled with his fishing rod, put a chub on the end of it, and handed it to me. "Here. Let's see what we can get."

He pulled two co-colas out of the cooler he'd brought. I waited to sense even the slightest tug or nibble on the line. Fishing bored some folks, but waiting, to me, was the best part. Something about throwing in something small and expecting to haul in something bigger. Something about hope.

The water pulled the fishing line farther as we drifted along, and the wind blew the fine string so it hung and curved on the air. Then, more than a twitch but less than a yank, something tugged my line. I waited to be sure, then it tugged again. "Hey! I think I got something!"

As I reeled in some line, the fish pulled back something fierce. I leaned back and reeled, leaned back and reeled.

"I see it! It's a snapper! Here, I'll take it a minute if you want to see." Jed took the rod from my hands, and I leaned over the side next to him. Flashes of bright pink scales flashed through the froth and foam of the dark teal ocean. The line disappeared in the mad mix of it, and the fighting grew wilder the closer Jed pulled him in. Half the great fish's body flipped out of the water. One last yank, and it flew over the side of the boat and flipped and flopped across the deck. We scooted and jumped to avoid its sharp spines and spasms until Jed managed to gently step on its head to use pliers to free the beast from the hook.

"Hoo-eee! What a snapper!" Jed hollered.

The fish gasped for air. Its gills yawned open and shut, and its whole body rose and fell, desperate and pleading for a breath. I crouched down close to it, the fish's eyes glassy with shock. Its body arched and flipped as Jed put one foot across its belly and ratcheted the hook loose. Jed stepped back, and I wrapped my arms around the slimy, wet fish, fighting to keep my balance and stand without letting it slip.

"Anni, what are you doing?"

I pressed my lips against one of its pearly pink gills, then careened the parched fish over the side of the boat. He lay on top of the water, too stunned to move, then turned himself over and swam off in a skitter into the dark safety of the sea.

"What'd you do that for?"

"I don't know. I just had to save it." My chest heaved with shock and fear and glee at saving the life of that fish, the smelly goo of it stuck to Larry's coat.

Annoyance fell from Jed's face, and for the second time that afternoon, his eyes turned moist and pink. "Yeah."

I knew then and for sure I could trust this boy.

Yes, I could trust him indeed.

We sat next to each other on the bench in the middle of that small boat as a barge chugged by, story upon story of containers glaring down and mocking the smallness of us, two kids in a boat saving a fish no one cared about but us.

Le pyebwa jwe ak van, li pèdi fey li.
"When the tree plays with the wind, it loses its leaves."

CHAPTER 15

Anniston

After straightening things up in Larry's boat and thanking him, Jed offered to ride back with me on our bikes.

"Can we stop at your place?"

"Why would you want to do that?" His voice held a sudden coldness.

"Thought it might be nice to see where you live."

"Not today."

We rode side by side toward the country and the orchards, avoiding streets that led to the library and the trailer park behind. The silence between us felt awkward. A big crow flew along the edge of the sky, almost as if flying along with us. Never could figure out why folks don't like blackbirds. They get a bad rap on account of them stealing pecans. Daddy threw fits about them, said they could eat as much as fifteen pounds of pecans a month. Still, they're so pretty when they fly, ebony wings with deep shades of blue like strong shadows pushing the air behind them. Hawks, too, for that matter, the way they circle and float on the air, hanging there despite the pull of the earth, waiting ever so patient until God gives them something to eat.

I was grateful when we finally reached the end of the driveway shared by Comfort's house and Princella and Vaughn's. "Wait here."

Jed held my bike at the end of the forked, red ribbon of dirt leading to Comfort's, while I went to her porch to get the empty basket. Empty except for another poem.

a withered leaf
a pale withered fragment
fractured and afraid

a scream in the dark
smothered by hands
covered in riches
buried in sand

a stump of a tree
beat down and thinned
too late for March
or balmy sea winds

no, little girl
you mustn't say a word

no, little girl
be pretty, not heard

I set the basket on the ground next to my bike. "Let's stop here a minute. I don't want to go home yet."

Jed didn't ask why, and I felt somehow the fact he didn't want to show me his home and the fact I didn't want to go back to mine shared a lot of the same reasons—reasons neither of us had words for yet, and maybe wouldn't ever. We set our bikes on the ground by a fresh-cut stump of one of the larger pecan trees that had been thinned the week before, and I handed him the poem.

His brow furrowed as he read. "Your aunt wrote this?"

"Yeah. She's been leaving poems like this for us—well, for me—every time we bring her a basket of things. She's gotta be getting tired of those walls."

"Maybe. But if she's scared, who can blame her?"

"Once in a while, I see Solly there, knocking at her door, then talking at her through it. It's so sad. I can't help feeling there's something we oughta be able to do for her."

Jed picked a yellow dandelion growing nearby. "Ever done this?" He held the yellow part up near his chin. "See?"

His chin glowed the same color as the dandelion. I giggled, grateful for the change in subject. Then I held one to my chin. "Mine look the same?"

"Yeah." He laughed.

"Have you done this?" I picked another dandelion and snapped the flower off the stem with my thumb. The flower ball flew into the air and pegged Jed on the shoulder. "Mama had a baby, and its head popped off." I recited the poem I'd known since preschool.

"Ha-ha. Very funny. Lemme try."

We picked and popped heads off like crazy, fallin' on the ground, we were laughing so hard. The fresh-mown grass around us smelled like wild onions and syrup and sass, and the yellow flowers popped out all around us.

"Say, what are you doing next Saturday?"

"Same as always. Working here."

As fast as I brought up the cotillion, my heart stopped when I thought about actually asking him the question.

"Why do you ask?"

I hoped maybe I could drop it.

"There's this thing I gotta go to."

"Thing?"

"Yeah. Well, I mean, it's something Princella—my grandma's— in charge of. And I'm supposed to ask a boy to be my date." The sky started spinning. My legs felt like saplings.

"*Supposed* to ask a boy? Or you *want* to ask a boy?" The now familiar tease played in his eyes again.

"Supposed to. I mean, well, I do want to ask you. What I mean is …"

"I'll go."

"You will?"

"Sure I will. I can dance."

"Well, it's a fancy kind of dance. We have to wear gloves, and you'll have to wear a suit and tie."

"I got a suit and tie. Had to go to a funeral for my old foster mom's uncle a while back. Should still fit okay."

"Mama and I can pick you up on the way—"

"I'll come back here after I shower up," he interrupted. "Just name the time."

"Okay. But ... I don't care where or how you live, you know."

He didn't argue with me one way or the other, just picked another dandelion and tickled my chin with it, which started us in on popping heads off at each other all over again.

I reached down to pick up another one and jumped back.

"What is it?" said Jed.

"Look there—I thought it was a dandelion. I only saw the edge of it. Almost picked it up." I pointed to a bright yellow lump on the ground.

Jed picked it up. "It's a canary. Still breathin', too."

"What's a canary doing out here?"

"Someone let it loose." He shook his head. "I see 'em every once in a while. Folks buy themselves a pretty bird but get tired of 'em singing all the time, so they let 'em loose. Think they'll live out here like any other bird. But they don't. Poor things don't know what to do, free to fly after spending their lives in a cage. They're used to someone feeding them all the time. Someone filling their water dish. They don't know nothin' about living on their own. And their color ain't much good for hiding from predators."

He cradled the tiny bird in his rough hands, stroking and smoothing its feathers. The bird, too tired to fight, lay there and closed its eyes.

"What should we do?"

"I'll take it home. Nurse it back. Maybe give it to that pet store on Main Street. They're nice folks in there. Maybe they'll know someone who'll take it once it's well. Someone who cares."

*Bay ak kè a nan kou an bliye; jenn
gason an nan mak la sonje.*
"The giver of the blow forgets; the bearer of the scar remembers."

CHAPTER 16

Comfort

When we danced, the world danced with us, Solly and I. The disco ball, squares of mirror reflecting joy, spun over us. Every glimmer, every note, every beat of the drum a symphony playing within his heart and mine. When he held me, I felt safe. Treasured. Chosen. New.

We danced a lot over the years. School events; church events; even in the quiet of his parents' ranch home when they gave us the living room to ourselves on date nights, when Solly'd put on Foreigner or James Taylor LPs.

Sometimes we sang. He'd bring out his guitar and play the songs himself, sing them to me as he rested his guitar on one knee, and let me rest my head on his other. We had an easiness about us. You could say it was like Sunday morning. Sure. Nothing was hidden between us.

At least nothing that needed remembering.

Folks think I don't show my face around town because of the rape. And part of that's true. Mostly, it's because of the monster the rape let out of the closet, an ebony shadow looming and lurking on the outskirts of my brain. The beast was chained up, contained, controlled by denial, forgetting, wealth, and lies. For years I prayed for God to make Cole stop, and one day, round about my tenth birthday, he did. I waited night after night for him to come back, barely breathing, pretending I was paralyzed by sleep as I strained to hear the creak of my bedroom door in the hours of the night the whole world slept. But Abba, He finally heard me. After that, forgetting it ever happened was easier than admitting it ever did. So I never told Solly. Never wanted to tell him. Never wanted to ruin the beauty of the safe place he'd always been for me.

Now the memories flooded over me, released like a swollen river by Cole's violent, and now public, jealousy over a ring placed with love around the fourth finger of my left hand, a ring smooth and unblemished by the sickness in Cole's head making him think love was sex, and sex was power, and power meant he owned me. Or maybe he thought what he did to me meant he owned himself— even if he bought it with my blood.

Way back before I knew better, I tried to tell someone about what Cole did to me, back when I still wore footie pajamas to bed in the winter and Holly Hobbie nightgowns in the spring. Back then, Cole's games were only beginning to grow in power, promising me adoration, which was all I could understand—adoration ultimately threatening and mocking me with doubts.

"It's all in your mind," my kindergarten teacher said one day when I'd tried to confess what Cole did to me. I'd been finger painting, and the bright red lines of my design, thick and wet, hung on a line to dry next to classmates' pictures of houses and sunshine and flowers.

"You always have been a dreamer," Mama said, though I knew she'd seen. She just kept pouring hot bath water over my suds-covered hair.

"Don't tell," Cole said as he held a toy gun against the side of my head. I couldn't have been more than three or four that time. And who, when they're three years old, can tell the difference between plastic and metal? What child can tell the difference between an older brother who holds her—the one she thinks put the moon and stars and all of her tiny, shiny little world of Bay Spring in motion—and the beast that lives within him? Fleshy, tender lips—the same as yours and mine—cover gnarled teeth. Fancy clothes cover bony fingers. Mouths sweet as sugar one day, hissed and blamed and caused guilt to develop deep into my soul the next if I ventured too close to the door of truth.

And yet truth begged me to come closer, to open up, to tell.

"Stranger danger," the programs on public television warned.

"Good touch, bad touch," the special convocations taught us at school.

And even if someone *had* listened, how could I have found words to describe what I myself wondered was real? My mind, each time he hurt me, became a keyhole-shaped chasm through which I escaped and watched, numb.

Don't leave me, I would wish as Daddy read to me, the sun falling over the boats rocking against their moorings all along the bay.

Keep reading, please.

Don't turn out the light.

But he did turn out the light. Flipped the switch the quarter inch downward that darkness needed to act. And before daybreak, cords of fear came and bound me, plastic gun silencing me.

What words could I ever use to tell Solly? We are soul mates, but even soul mates keep secrets from each other—secrets they're afraid might doom them. Secrets I am sure would doom us. So now I am bound worse than ever, caught in the clutches of those secrets even as they lie dead in the grave. Evil got away with far too much this time, and I am the only one who can keep myself safe now. No one else did.

I watch Anni and her new friend walking in the orchards, laughing, unknowing, dancing like Solly and I once did beneath the arms of the pecan trees. Her friend sits on the stump of a pecan tree cut down to make room for the others around it. The boy is one of the new seasonal helpers. I saw him helping Daddy cut that tree down last week. Daddy showed him how to soak the stump and the base with stump killer, trickling down to the end of the farthest, deepest roots. I helped a lot with the orchards growing up, but thinning the trees … I couldn't do it. I knew the reasons behind the thinning, that the other trees couldn't grow and produce as much otherwise, but seeing the giants I helped raise from saplings chopped off … I couldn't stand it. Daddy always cut them down in the late winter. Before March. Before the new leaves felt the warmth rising up out of the Gulf of Mexico and felt safe enough to finally unfurl.

Anni and her friend laugh beyond my window, chasing each other through the rows. How I wish I could join them. I wish to breathe in air and life. I ache for the childhood I never truly had. I ache to touch the mourning doves crying outside my windows, without a plate of glass, hard and sharp, between us. But Cole is everywhere. If I switch beds or sleep on the couch in the middle of the night, he and the dreams follow me there. If I walk beyond the front porch, even the front door, I feel fear like lightning in all my limbs, striking all courage, all hope, dead.

And so I cannot escape.

And I am nothing.

Oh, I could have been something to Solly. To others, too. I could've been good. I could've been right. But I fell, the knees of my soul forever skinned, before I ever had a chance. Even before Solly pulled my hair because he liked me back in second grade.

… He healeth the broken in heart, and bindeth up their wounds …

I hear the scripture, sudden and clear, and laced with the hearty sureness of Ernestine's accent. I hear it, and though I know Abba saved me once, I wonder if He can—if He will—save me again.

If you make your bed in the depths, I am there.

Even in this, Lord?

Even if you settle on the far side of the sea.

Even this far, Abba?

The dark is not dark to Me, child.

Surely this darkness, this evil this time, hides me from You.

Not even this, My dear one. Not even this.

I argue with Abba, and yet, the sharp edges of isolation cut into places of my heart that need healing. The sting of the rending pulls me, overwhelms my fainthearted fear.

And so, I go.

And I go with you.

For the first time in weeks, I pull on my sneakers, wrap around my wary shoulders a shawl that Ernestine had knit, and I go. Into the angled glare of a sunken sun, kissing the horizon like a lover longing to touch more, I go.

My hand, it cradles you.

My fury, it shields you.

My angels encircle your every step.

And in sunlight, I find solace. Unexpected and smiting the unbridgeable solstice between hurt and healing, peace shows up like a waltzing curl of winter air on stretching beams of light. The Light.

His Light.

Binding up one bruise, and one is good for now, the raw edges of my wound warming, even if only slightly, as I walk with Him in the sunlight.

Pa gen okenn lapriyè ki pa gen Amen.
"There is no prayer which does not have an Amen."

CHAPTER 17

Anniston

"Kote nou te?" Ernestine stirred her steaming pot of jambalaya as I walked into the kitchen. "Where have you been?"

"I was down at the docks. Talking to Larry. *The Jubilee* looks real good."

"Saw you met a new friend," she said.

"You did?"

"*Oui*, child. Can't hide much around these orchards."

"Oh." I studied my fingernails and picked at a dead piece of cuticle on my thumb until it bled. I wrapped my finger tight in the corner of my purple T-shirt.

"*Pa enkyete*. Don't worry, Anni. I'm glad you found a friend."

"You are?"

"Your mama, too. Been worried about you not having someone your own age. Tell me more about him?"

I sat at the kitchen table and watched her sample the soup. "I don't know … He's real nice. He likes rocks. Fossils. He's got hundreds of 'em."

Ernestine smiled at me, the sort of smile that took the weight of worry off, like it flew away on the wings of that blackbird.

"He's nice, but … well, he's kinda mixed-up."

"Mmm-hmm." She stirred the stew a moment. "So's I, Anni. Like this jambalaya. But sometimes mixed-up is the best. Like the holy trinity. *Sen trinite a.*"

She wasn't referring to the Trinity we learned about in church, exactly. She meant the holy trinity of Creole cooking: bell peppers, onion, and celery. I'd chopped up enough of those three with her to know. She grabbed one of each and held them toward me. "The three of these, they inseparable. But by themselves, well, one wouldn't be much good without the other."

"I feel awful mixed-up myself."

I pulled the heads and tails off crawdaddies while Ernestine set some rice to boiling. She wiped her raven-colored, weathered hands on a dishcloth before walking to her room off the side of the kitchen and returning with a worn photo book.

"Sit with me, child."

I pulled up a stool to the kitchen counter, and she turned the album to a page of me, wrinkly and new, fresh home from the hospital in Daddy's arms.

"With him gone, the rest of life don't taste too good."

We turned page after page of me growing bigger, and Daddy's

smile shining down on me. Me playing in the plastic swimming pool, diapers hanging down to my knees. Me pedaling a two-wheeler away from him as he stood behind and cheered. Me stepping onto the school bus and he and Mama waving good-bye.

If anyone knew about good-byes, Ernestine did. Lost her daddy, who was fighting against a dictator for Haiti's freedom, before she was born. Lost her husband in an airplane crash right after they married. Chose to stay here in Bay Spring so she could raise Comfort and Daddy.

"How do you do it, Ernestine? How do you go on?"

"You don't go on as much as you change direction. And which direction you take, that part's up to you. One way leads to forgiveness and peace. The other leads down a road of bitterness. Can't turn back from bitterness. Not very often, anyway."

"You chose the right way, didn't you?"

"*Oui*, child. I think I have. But sometimes I wake up in the morning, and I have to make the right choice again. The shadow of bitterness comes that fast on a heart. And each time I choose, I learn again—*nan tout bagay, Bondye ap travay pou byen pou moun ki renmen l*. God works for good. Romans 8:28."

"But not all bad can turn to good, can it?" *How in the world was Daddy dying good? How could it ever be?*

Ernestine took a minute to reply. "You're right." She put her ebony hand on top of my pale and small one. "Not everything bad can be good. The Bible don't stop at verse twenty-eight. The one after says God uses the bad *fè nou plis tankou Jezi*—to make us more like Jesus. But we have to let Him use it. I still wonder why I lost my father before I knew him. I wonder why I lost my husband before we had a chance to have children. But now I know. You. Comfort. Your daddy. God heard my pain and gave me all of you."

I thought about Jed, how I met him soon after Daddy died. "Today, I asked Jed to the dance."

"Asked who to the dance?"

I jumped at Princella's voice. She'd come into the kitchen without me noticing.

"A new friend from school." Officially, he did go to my school, since the junior and senior high were all in one building. But if I'd said he worked for us, she might've let me have it right then and there.

"What's his last name?"

"Manon, ma'am."

"Hmmm. Haven't heard of them." She lifted the lid off the pot of jambalaya and inhaled the steam rising off the top. "No matter, I suppose. I look forward to meeting this boy."

Later, when we sat down to dinner, strips of bell pepper and onion and chunks of celery fell over mounds of white rice, with crawdaddy meat and shrimp tumbling after. We sopped up the mirepoix with Ernestine's homemade sourdough bread soaked in butter.

The day was a holy trinity.

Joy, pain, and a pinch of something I wasn't so sure was going to add anything good to the mix.

Yon do-kay koule ka moun fou soley
move tan, men li pa tronpe lapli.
"A leaking roof may fool sunny weather, but cannot fool the rain."

CHAPTER 18

Comfort

Qarla's relentless pleading for me to come back and do nails at the Curly Q finally drives me crazy enough to take her up on it. She's grateful for the help with the craziness of the upcoming cotillion. As long as she is there, I feel safe enough. Besides, so focused on telling me about their husbands' law office parties, their charity luncheons, their mothers-in-law, or their not-so-secret affairs, rarely, if ever, do any of my nail clients ask after me. To tell the truth, most avoid eye contact with me. They know, of course, what happened. Some even wait in line for Tiffany, the other nail artist, when my table opens up, afraid to be touched by my hands, contagions of rape.

Not that I care about avoidance. I relish it, really, saving my words for Oralee. Ernestine. Poems for Anni. And sometimes I give my words—but words only—to Solly.

Solly grows frustrated by my hesitation around him, the way I jump at a gentle word breaking the silence, once filled with our laughter and nights full of unending conversation . . . the way I shrink back from the caress I used to welcome—even crave. I can't blame him. He's been more than patient. Though I can buff and shine, clip and paint the fingernails of the ladies of Bay Spring, I cannot bring myself to hold the hand of the man I love. Nor can I allow him to hold mine.

I look at the appointment book to see who my next nail client is. Wynn Culpepper. I remember that last name, which is too strange to forget. But I know it better in Coach Culpepper, head coach of the Bay Spring High School football team.

"Wynn?" I call to the waiting room full of teenage girls and their mothers.

A lady showing more cleavage than hiding it, chewing gum, and reading the latest issue of *Cosmopolitan* must be Mrs. Culpepper, whom the whole town knows is Coach's third wife. She nearly shoves the girl I assume to be Wynn off her place on the pink velvet footstool.

Wynn is a wilted girl who does not look at me, most of her face behind a chiseled chunk of bluish-black hair and hiding the rest of herself in black leather and denim. She might've been trying to look like Joan Jett, but she doesn't fool me. I know all about being alone, and I know that's what Wynn is. Alone.

I put her hands in the bowl of warm soapsuds, not entirely surprised at the strong smell of smoke coming off of them. As I smooth the ends of her nails and avoid making her already-bleeding cuticles sorer, I study her face, still splotchy, either from me calling her name or her mama shoving her or both. When I push the sleeve up on her left arm, I see the cuts, which I realize spell out "STOP IT" in crisscrossed, awkward lines. The scars are raised, indicating she must've picked and cut at them for a long, long time.

Wynn notices what I see and quick pulls her sleeve down over the scars. Our eyes meet, and for a moment I think she might talk to me, say something, say anything. Instead, she turns her head down, focusing on some unseen pain resting in her lap.

"You okay, Wynn?"

Her shoulders rise in an exaggerated, annoyed, sigh. "It's nothing."

"That's not nothing," I press.

She looks up and stares hard at me. "It's none of *your* business."

"No, but I can listen." The constant pain in my stomach pulls into a burning knot, one I'm pretty sure she shares.

She shakes her head in disgust, rolling her eyes before focusing on her lap again. "No thanks."

I let her alone after that. I know her kind, kids who think girls like me will never give them the time of day, whole black-clad gaggles of them moving through high school hallways like amoebas. They smoke in the bathroom across from the lunchroom, the one with burn marks covering the seats. Even the teachers overlook the plumes that are so obviously not Aqua Net floating out the door, like they know smoking's all those kids really have besides each other.

Her mama pays me without leaving a tip, and Wynn leaves without looking at me again. I don't blame her. I don't want to look at myself either.

And yet I wonder what life might be like if we all knew the pain that lay beneath each other's sleeves.

Avan ou ri moun bwete, gade jan ou mache.
"Before you laugh at those who limp, check the way you walk."

CHAPTER 19

Anniston

On Saturday, Princella left for the cotillion hours before we did, so nothing stopped me from sliding down the banister to answer the door when Jed rang it. He smoothed his hair down from the wind messing it up on his way over. Despite all my arguing that Mama'd be happy to pick him up, he'd ridden his bike here.

"Anni? That him?" Mama called from her bedroom.

"Yes, Mama!" I felt my face turn red as I hollered at her over my shoulder. A new nervousness turned my belly as I turned to him. "Sorry about that."

"You sure are beautiful." Jed looked as nervous as I felt.

"*Akeyi*. You must be Jed." Ernestine burst into the hall, tropical dress blowing like butterfly wings behind her.

"Jed, this is Ernestine."

He held out his hand, and when she gave him hers, he held it to his lips and kissed it. "Pleasure to meet you, ma'am. I've heard so much about you."

"Rete isit la tande." She swept herself back to the kitchen as fast as she'd arrived.

I shrugged my shoulders at her sudden disappearance.

He smiled, and my nerves simmered down a bit.

"Why, hello, Jed. So nice to finally meet you," Mama said, coming down the stairs toward us. "Anniston, you may invite him in."

"Oh, yes." I giggled, pulling the door open wider and stepping aside. "Please come in."

Jed stood straight as ever and held his hand out to Mama. "The pleasure is all mine, ma'am." He kissed her hand, too. Mama might've blushed harder than me.

Ernestine ran back in to the front hall holding a pair of brand-new white men's gloves and a small box in her hands. "Jed's boutonniere."

"Want me to help you pin it on?" Mama asked me.

"I think I can do it."

"Don't poke me, Anni." Jed winked.

I pinned the pink flower on his navy-blue suit jacket, then smoothed down both sides of his lapels before I realized I was actually touching him and pulled back quick.

Jed fiddled with a box of his own. He opened the lid and pulled out the prettiest corsage I'd ever seen—three white magnolia flowers with baby's breath tied up with a blue ribbon that matched the one around the waist of my dress.

"Hettie said to get you one of these to fit your wrist so we don't mess your dress up with a pin," he said, slipping the corsage's elastic band over my fingers and settling it on my left wrist.

I hate to say it, but everything went downhill from there.

Mama dropped us off at the entrance to the Bay Spring Resort Hotel. I wished for my thick gym socks in the worst way as I wiggled my freezing, prickly-feeling toes in the ends of my stiff and shiny new shoes. Shoulda worn my sweater like Mama suggested since yet another spring cold snap seemed here to stay.

No parents except selected chaperones were allowed. Someone's father, dressed in a tuxedo, bowed toward me and handed me a pink rose. Jed never attended formal cotillion classes, so I'd filled him in on the most important things, like what to wear, how we'd have to link arms and hold hands.

The dancing didn't worry me, either. Thanks to Princella's decades of involvement in the Bay Spring Cotillion, I'd been taking ballroom dancing since kindergarten and knew the dances by heart, like the fox trot, waltz, and polka. I even knew how to do the tango, so I assured Jed I could lead and show him steps, and no one would know the better.

"Don't worry. I do know some moves," Jed said when we discussed the details last evening by the creek. "A crooked hip don't keep me from dancing."

Red carpet runners and signs pointed the way through the lobby to the ballroom, which we would've found anyway, following a long line of kids from school leading into its great, dark mouth. We could already feel the *thud thud* of the band's drums and vibrating of the bass guitar. We barely recognized some classmates, they were so shined up and polished.

Most of the girls wore peach, white, pink, powder blue, or other pastel-colored dresses and tights. Tights or pantyhose were mandatory. All the girls wore white gloves and black patent-leather shoes. And all the girls carried a crisp, cream-colored dance card. Some fidgeted with them, and others showed off their growing list of signatures to their friends. Sally Roberts held hers out like a fan.

"Would you look at that?" I said to Jed, elbowing him in the side and nodding toward Sally.

"What about her?"

"See how she's waving her dance card around so everyone can see it's chock-full to overflowing with requests?"

"I won't be signing it."

We both laughed as we walked inside the ballroom.

"Would you like some punch, m'lady?"

"Why, I'd love some, sir."

Jed walked over to the punch table, upon which a giant swan ice sculpture sat and eyeballed the crowd. I found a seat on the other side of the ballroom, far away from where Princella, Faye Gadsden, and the adult chaperones gathered and chatted. Folks considered Faye Gadsden, cochair of the Bay Spring Auxiliary, one of the most cultured women in town, next to Princella. Her husband, Miles, served as the town judge, which I knew from all the stories in the *Bay Spring Banner Sentinel* about him sentencing folks to jail. Luckily, Princella hadn't seen me come in yet, so I wouldn't have to introduce her to Jed and have him be introduced to her friends.

The live band had their name spelled out on the bass drum: Muddy and the Flaps. I saved a seat near the stage, one of many in a long row of chairs circling the dance floor. Boys and girls who were members of the Bay Spring Junior Cotillion but didn't bring dates sat on separate sides of the floor. The boys sat all proper, feet flat on the floor and white-gloved hands on each knee. The girls crossed their feet at the ankles, folded their hands, and rested them on empty dance cards on their laps. Some girls wore pink or white corsages on their dresses. Many wore them on their wrists. But no one wore magnolias like I did.

A few of the girls new to cotillion wore red roses, which I knew from Mrs. Gadsden was a huge, what she called, faux pas. "Red is for true love, and it's simply not possible for a single one of you at your age to know what true love is. If someone offers you a red corsage at your age, you are to refuse it graciously and not wear one at all." She talked to us like explaining such obvious things bothered her more than swatting flies off a table at a church picnic.

Some kids stared at Jed as he made his way back to me with our punch. He stopped and said a few words to the band members, who paused between songs to prepare for the introductions and kick off the big dance numbers. The three men wore light-blue, bell-bottom tuxedos and Buddy Holly glasses like Solly's, and the lady singer wore a matching blue, lacey cocktail dress. All four gathered around Jed, smiling and patting him on the back and shaking his hand.

"Do you know them?"

He sat down next to me. "Yeah. They played up in Tuscaloosa all the time at street dances. My old foster dad there played guitar with them on occasion. They're pretty darn good."

"If you call the waltz and the fox trot good."

"It is when *they* play it. Their classical stuff is almost better than their rock and roll. Heard 'em at a couple of weddings more formal than this, and even the old people joined in the dancing."

"Oh, great."

"What?"

"Here come Mrs. Gadsden and Princella."

Princella wore an all-red dress covered with sequins on top and flowing chiffon on the bottom. Mrs. Gadsden wore a lace-covered, powder-blue dress, also floor-length. Both of them wore dyed-to-match shoes and white, over-the-elbow gloves. Standing next to each other, they looked like a glob of Aquafresh toothpaste.

Princella scanned the room. When she saw me, she turned her gaze to Jed, scanned him up and down, her eyes stopping first at his hair, which grew over his ears, and then at his shoes, which were sneakers on account of his bad hip. She scrutinized him up and down again, then turned her eyes, brewing like a dark bay storm, on me. I focused on the dance card in my lap, folding it up like a tiny fan.

Mrs. Gadsden tapped the microphone, sending thuds of noise echoing across the ballroom. I jumped, and everyone stopped talking and moving around. "Welcome to the Fifty-Third Annual Daughters of the Confederacy Cotillion and Bay Spring Auxiliary Auction. A lot of hard work and hours of preparation have gone into this spectacular evening, and we can't wait for everyone to have a splendid, splendid time." She paused like she expected folks to clap, and a few chaperones in the back did. "First, I'd like to introduce Princella Harlan, president of the Bay Spring Ladies Auxiliary and grand hostess of tonight's gala event." Mrs. Gadsden paused for a moment, apology in her eyes as she glanced at Princella. "Despite recent family tragedies, she worked tirelessly and without pause to bring you this year's event. If you aren't already aware, Mrs. Harlan graduated summa cum laude from Alabama Southern with a degree in elementary education. She married Mr. Vaughn Harlan and devoted her time to her beautiful home and children. Now, in addition to her service to this auxiliary, she donates her time and gifts to the Alabama Southern Football Booster Club, acts as a chapter advisor to the Kappa Alpha Omicron sorority, and participates in various duties with the Alabama Pecan Growers Association."

Mrs. Gadsden handed the microphone to Princella. I'd never seen her nervous before, but sweat glistened on her forehead and upper lip. "Thank you, Faye. It's an honor to be here, as it is every year. And now, I'd like to introduce to you Mrs. Faye Gadsden, wife of Judge Miles Gadsden, two of the most devoted members of Bay Spring society." She faltered, then fished around in her beaded handbag and pulled out a note card. She adjusted the microphone, her hair, and her dress, and cleared her throat. She covered the microphone with her hand and whispered something to Mrs. Gadsden, who laughed nervously and patted her on the shoulder.

A screech of feedback cracked through the air, and Princella's face turned about as red as her dress. I wondered if she'd have been near as flustered if Mrs. Gadsden hadn't brought up Daddy and Cole.

She cleared her throat. "Since 1972 Mrs. Gadsden has single-handedly brought an impeccable level of etiquette and high-level ballroom dancing to this cotillion program, thanks to her award-winning background. Why, last fall, Mr. and Mrs. Gadsden were crowned three-time Southeast Regional Champions of the Ballroom Dancing Association of America, in both the Smooth and Rhythm categories. She is an advocate for children's issues on local and state levels and sings soprano in her church choir. She wishes for me to read this message to everyone." Princella paused to clear her throat—again. "'I was raised in a home where manners are very important. This came naturally to me, and I thoroughly enjoy passing them along to the next generation of society.'"

Princella stepped aside and handed the microphone back to Mrs. Gadsden.

"Thank you, Princella. And now we're almost ready to begin. Let me take a brief moment to remind everyone that although we trust you are an exceptional group of young adults, you are expected to maintain rules of the dance, including rotating partners according to dance cards. And now, on with the dance!"

The lights dimmed, and the disco ball above the wood dance floor dropped lower and spun slowly. Pieces of light fell across the room like snowflakes, and Muddy and the Flaps played "Moon River"—a pretty good waltz to start off with. The drum brush swished like the dancers on the floor.

One-two-three, one-two-three ...

Warm shivers I'd never felt the likes of before moved up and down near the bottom of my belly as I held on to Jed and he held on to me.

One-two-three, one-two-three ...

We laughed and poked a little fun at some of the other couples and generally made the most of it. Luckily, no one else signed my dance card, so we stuck together every time the song changed.

After about a half a dozen songs, I had to use the bathroom. Princella caught me on the way out of the ballroom.

"Who's your friend?"

"His name's Jed, ma'am. He's new to town."

"Where'd he come from?"

"Tuscaloosa."

"You do realize he's completely wrong for a place like this." She leaned in close to my ear, and I tried to back away. Her breath smelled like strong cough medicine. "I would've expected something more for you, Anniston. Someone who at least looks like they're from good breeding stock. Someone who at least looks normal."

I didn't know what to say.

"At least he minds his manners."

"Yes, ma'am … well … I have to go to the bathroom." I turned and skirted away from her before she could say anything else.

Good breeding stock? Someone who at least looks normal?

Her words stung and squeezed into a hard knot inside of me. I hoped I could avoid her the rest of the evening. As I walked out of the bathroom, relief opened up my lungs enough to breathe when I saw her leaving the lobby to go outside—probably for one of the "fresh air" breaks she often took at church or other public events. She'd be out there a while.

When I returned to the ballroom, Jed was talking to the band members again, who were preparing to play another song. He'd taken off his navy-blue blazer and was rolling up his shirtsleeves as I made my way toward him on the dance floor.

The lead singer winked at him. "This goes out to our friend Jed, who's new in town and wants to show y'all how it's done." The lead singer hollered into the microphone. "A one … a two … a one … two … three … four!"

The guitarist plunked out a string of notes, and Jed danced like nothing I'd ever seen before, making his arms do a wave back and forth, slow at first, then catching up to the beat of "Sweet Home Alabama." He moved across the floor in what looked like Michael Jackson's new style of break dancing, and sure enough, before long, Jed turned in circles and moved in all sorts of fancy ways with his arms and on his back, spinning on the floor. Soon, other kids got up and circled around him, and we swayed and grooved like a hot crowd at a street festival.

I glanced around at the chaperones, who didn't act like they minded one bit. Either that or they were so busy talking about grown-up stuff they weren't paying any attention. Princella was outside, and Mrs. Gadsden busied herself straightening up the punch table. The next song pounded out rock and roll harder than the last one. More boys flung their jackets across the room. A few girls kicked off their shoes, so they could spin and slide on the hardwood floor.

The guitarist moved up to the mic for the next song, a new ballad by Air Supply, "All Out of Love." As soon as the music slowed, Melinda Sue O'Malley and Tommy Sharp pressed their bodies together closer than two oysters in a halfshell. They broke every rule of touching in cotillion, including the one about boys keeping their hands off girls' behinds.

Good God in heaven, were we ever gonna get it.

And sure enough we did.

A shimmer of red streaked across the side of the ballroom. In an instant, Princella yanked the microphone from Muddy. The guitars and keyboards wheezed a long, sad sigh as their musical vibrations trailed off into the silent, heavy air. Princella's smooth beehive hairdo stuck up all over her head, windblown, fuzzy, and fried. For what seemed like forever, she clung to the microphone and stared at all of us, her eyes like the spotlights used at store grand openings, shooting into the mess of us and announcing the gravity of our behavior. The chaperones, some of whom danced right along with us, fixed their eyes on their shoes or the ceiling and moved in close.

Finally she spoke. Growled, really. Maybe even howled.

"Exactly. What." She lifted her head higher and sniffed. "Is going on here?"

No one dared answer.

Even Mrs. Gadsden looked a little astonished by Princella's sudden interruption.

A few girls found their shoes and gloves.

A few boys found their jackets.

They pulled them back on as if shielding themselves from the trouble about to explode.

Princella didn't look flustered anymore. Far from it, in fact. "Anniston Harlan!"

My spine burned like someone threw boiling water down the back of my dress, and everything in the room between me and her turned black. I couldn't hear or see a thing except her curled-up lip and eyes cutting deep and hard into mine.

"Come up here *this instant*, and bring your *retarded friend* with you."

The words came out of her mouth and twisted my belly like I might throw up. The burning down my spine moved up my shoulders and down my arms and the blackness swirled around me.

"I said, '*Come here*,' Anniston!"

Jed grabbed my hand and the two of us walked together toward Princella. I held his hand like I'd never let go. I wasn't sure I ever could.

"What in God's name have you done here, the two of you?" she hissed, when we got up close to her. I caught another big whiff of that medicine smell. Only then I knew it wasn't medicine. She'd been into the drink out in her car.

"Do you realize you not only ruined this dance for yourselves, but for every single one of the cotillion members here tonight? A formal apology will be expected. From *both of you*."

"Yes, ma'am," I said.

"Yes, ma'am," said Jed.

Mrs. Gadsden made her way to where we stood, as Princella dissected Jed and me with her steely eyes. "Princella, I think that's enough."

"And you!" Princella ignored Mrs. Gadsden and turned to Jed. "Who do you think you are coming in here as a guest and turning this place into a veritable night club, encouraging the band to play that horrid music! How dare you, with your bent-up legs and—"

"Princella …" Mrs. Gadsden moved alongside Princella, put a hand on her shoulder and tried to stop her, but I knew Princella was like a train, flying too far and fast down a track to slow down, no matter whose body stretched across the rails.

"—and your stupid eyes. How can you see to walk straight, let alone dance with my granddaughter? You should be ashamed to be a guest of a Harlan, the mess of a child you are. I've cleaned up enough messes in my family than to have to put up with the sight and likes of you. Now get out of here, and don't you ever show your face around my family—or this circle of people—again!"

Though Jed had tears in his eyes, he stood up straighter and did not reply.

"He will not leave without me." The words, thin and shaky, surprised me as they fell out of my mouth. Fear like pins and needles ran up and down my legs.

Princella's hand grabbed my upper arm and squeezed so hard her fingers pressed down to my bones. "Then both of you leave! Get out of my sight!"

My right eye lost all vision and the side of my face hurt like a baseball bat hit it after Princella pushed me away with one hand and slapped my face with the other. The force knocked me to the ground. I wiped the wetness of my face, thinking it was tears, but my white glove smeared with blood. The cut on my cheek stung like fire.

Without looking at anyone, I ran. I ran as fast as I could out of the ballroom. Out of the hotel. Into the night. I ran. And ran. And I didn't look back.

Apre dans tanbou, la a se lou.
"After the dance, the drum is heavy."

CHAPTER 20

Anniston

Tears poured down my face. I didn't wait for Jed and only slowed down when I heard him calling after me.

"Anni! Wait up!"

I couldn't talk, because sobs took over my breathing.

"Anni. C'mon. Hold up!" Jed limped up next to me, but he didn't say anything more. He listened to me cry while we scuffed toward town. Though Jed walked right next to me, I felt so alone. I couldn't figure out where I fit in anymore. I used to be sure, when Daddy was here and our family was whole. I knew I oughta feel sure of my place with Mama and Ernestine, and part of me was sure of Jed. But now everything mixed together—the shooting, what Cole did, Princella … Where was the holy trinity in all of this? Where was that verse twenty-nine Ernestine talked about?

I considered taking my questions directly to God about all that, but words for prayer felt stuck. Reaching for God felt like reaching for a safe place in those dreams where I'm running from something evil but I keep falling down. The evil presses closer, and my legs weaken. Felt like the harder I tried to reach for God, the farther away He got, and the more my heart fell to pieces.

As we trudged along, the heat of my hurt kept some of the cold away. We were in for a late frost. The skies spat bits of near-frozen rain at us. Through my tears, I saw the wilted magnolias on my wrist and cried harder. The cracks in the sidewalk jumped up at us at uneven intervals, making it impossible to avoid stepping on them. I always played the step-on-the-crack-and-you'll-break-your-mother's-back game. No matter what. And since I couldn't avoid stepping on the cracks that night, I imagined Princella's back breaking every time my foot fell against another jagged divide.

Without me realizing it, we'd walked all the way to the front of the Bay Spring Public Library. The front light shone down on the steps but did nothing to bring color to the deep blue and gray of the night. Streetlamps cast light on the world and created angled shadows as if we were on a stage, as if nothing in the last hour really happened at all.

Jed set me down on the steps and put his jacket around me. "Wait here," he said, then ducked around the corner. I figured he was headed toward the trailer park. For what, I wasn't sure. But anywhere other than that cotillion was okay with me. I pulled his jacket tighter around me and watched my breath as it froze, then disappeared.

Same breath that froze and disappeared the night Daddy died. I leaned my head back and searched for Orion the Hunter, the Big Dipper, or any familiar constellation, but the clouds were too thick. No stars shone. I wondered if the world would ever be warm again.

A rumbling came closer, and an old, yellow-and-white pickup truck with dim headlights came around the corner from where Jed disappeared. Sitting at the driver's wheel was the same woman from the beauty shop who Jed had thrown money at. She stopped the truck at the curb in front of where I sat. Jed hopped out of the passenger side. "C'mon. We'll take you on home."

"That your mama?" I whispered in his ear, grateful for his arm he offered and entwined around mine.

"Foster mom. Yep." He gave me a boost up into the high truck cab, then hopped in next to me. "Hettie, this is Anniston. Anniston, my foster mama, Hettie Devine."

"Ma'am." I offered my gloved hand, then pulled it back, ashamed of the blood staining it.

"Humpf."

Being as that was the one and only sound she made, I couldn't tell if she felt annoyed with me or with being out in general, but at least I had a warm ride home. Her face was smooth like someone who might be Mama's age, but her strawberry-blonde hair, done up in a too-tight permanent wave, and smudged streaks of makeup under her eyes made her look much older. Heat flowed through the truck's vents and warmed us. Our breath steamed up all the windows as she insisted on fixing me up. She leaned in close, and I could smell cigarettes on her as she dabbed peroxide onto the cut on my face.

"I called your mama and told her I'm bringing you home," Jed said, putting his arm over my shoulders. "She's awful concerned."

Mrs. Devine taped a piece of gauze over my cheek, pressing the tape down a little too hard.

If Daddy were here ... I wish he was here.

Jed and I didn't say anything all the way to my driveway. It bothered me that he didn't want me to see where he lived, but not as much as my cheek, which really smarted. On top of that, my heart split wide open thinking back to what Princella said into the microphone about him. Shame made it hard to even look at him. I needed to let him know I was sorry for the whole mess. I couldn't stand the thought of losing him on top of losing Daddy. But after all she'd said, how could he possibly want to still be my friend? I put my hand on top of his and let it stay there, hoping what remained of our friendship would melt away the chill in our fingers.

Jed gave Mrs. Devine directions, and I let her drive me as far as the driveway.

"Sure you don't want Hettie to drive you up to your house?"

Mrs. Devine glared at Jed, as if to say she'd already done more than her share of good for him for the day.

"I'm sure. I'll be fine. I need to walk a bit. Thanks for loaning me your jacket, Jed. I'll be warm enough."

"Well ... Okay." Jed stood beside the door of the truck as I climbed out. His forehead wrinkled up, indicating he wondered whether I should be left to walk alone. But part of him knew and understood.

"Thank you, Mrs. Devine." I tried to smile at Jed, but tears came instead. "Thank you, Jed." I stood with the truck door open a minute, letting the frosty air free up the tightness in my chest. "See you soon?"

"See you soon, Anni. See you soon." He leaned down and kissed me gently on the temple opposite from where Princella hit me. When he backed away, sorrow played in his eyes, a sorrow more for me than for him.

The wheels of the truck crunched off down the road, and I turned toward our driveway, black and endless under the cloud-covered sky. Walking past Comfort's house, everything Princella said back at the dance hurt so bad I couldn't go home and face Mama and Ernestine yet. I veered toward the creek, but instead of going there, I walked past it to the graveyard. The place didn't scare me at night. Peace blanketed the earth there, a silent, holy place where time stopped and sleep came to weary people.

Lights from Comfort's house shone into the graveyard, making the tombstones cast long, tilted shadows. Stories and wonderings filled my mind as I wandered between the stones. I passed the Cossey family, all eight of them killed on November 4, 1924, when their car stalled on a railroad track before a freighter came around the corner out on Bone Hill Road. The youngest child had only been nine months old and the oldest child, a boy named Patrick, one day away from turning thirteen like I am now. Rumors say if you're out on Bone Hill Road at the time of day when they died, you can still hear the wailing of the young ones on the wind. But I don't believe that. Folks turn crazy when they talk about ghosts and such, making up any sort of story to make a tragedy creepier. I passed several more white stones belonging to Civil War soldiers, several Harlans among them. Then I came to a large, grassy section, in the middle of which sat the two largest, newest, gray granite stones in the cemetery, awkward and out of place compared to the older, simpler stones around them.

COLE HARLAN

MARCH 19, 1941–NOVEMBER 23, 1979

BELOVED SON

THERE HATH PASS'D AWAY A

GLORY FROM THE EARTH

Centered between "Beloved son" and "There hath pass'd" was a photo of my uncle, already yellowing beneath the hard, clear covering. He looked nice enough, smiling and wearing an Alabama Southern football jersey. He had dark hair like Princella's and Daddy's, and green eyes like Comfort's. Nothing about the photo let on to what happened on November 23 or that he was responsible for any of it. The only evidence was Daddy's grave a few feet away with the same date of death. Vaughn got one of those double gravestones for him, the kind where they'd bury Mama next to him someday and carve her name and death date in alongside.

REYMOND HARLAN

JANUARY 23, 1943–NOVEMBER 23, 1979

BELOVED HUSBAND, FATHER,

SON, AND BROTHER

No nice quote or scripture added. No photo. Just the letters of Daddy's name sunk into the mottled slab of stone.

Just dead.

I knew good and well that hating someone was a sin, but I couldn't help but hate Cole for taking Daddy from me. Princella worshipped the ground Cole walked on, and it hurt something fierce she cared more for a dead person than for the living, breathing ones around her like me, and especially her own daughter, Comfort, who she paid no attention to despite her being hurt so badly.

"Why?" I said out loud, looking Cole's picture in the eyes.

"Why?" I screamed at Cole's grave, throwing first one, then a whole bunch of half-rotten sticks fallen from the great oak at the place I figured Cole's head lay. I threw sticks. Then I threw clumps of grass. Then I threw dirt and rocks and whatever else I could find. I dug and clawed at the ground for anything my hands could fit around to throw at his easy-smiling face. I didn't have a white dress to keep clean and hold me back anymore, since a mess of blood, dirt, and grass stains covered it.

At some point, I stopped throwing and curled up in the half-wet grass, my back pressed up against Daddy's gravestone. I stared at the creek and tree limbs swaying in the drizzle-laden black night, groaning against the weight of the wind, dappled by the light from Comfort's porch.

Komansman chante se soufle.
"The first steps of singing are breath."

CHAPTER 21

Comfort

I am asleep, but the crying wakes me. At first, I think it must be the wind whistling through the crack in my bedroom window. But when I rise to close it, I know. I've done enough crying myself lately to know the difference between a sob of grief and a sigh of the wind. As I move toward the window, I hear the crying, louder.

Not unlike my own, the cries come in and from the depths of night, muffled but for gasps of air between sobs. I walk to the front door and pull it open far enough to peer into the fog rising around and swirling through the arms of the pecan trees and the great oaks sheltering the graves beyond.

Leaving the house in daytime is one thing.

Leaving in the middle of the night is another.

I feel like the disciple Peter, knowing I am called, hearing Jesus tell me that opening the door will bring freedom and not pain ... that pressing through the mist will bring relief and not more shame.

I pace, fighting against my fear and the want—the need—to help.

"You're dead, and you can't stop me," I say, hoping Cole can hear me in his grave. "You can't defend yourself now. How does that feel? I might just tell the whole world what a sick and pathetic man you were, and you can't stop me. You thought I was meek and quiet and compliant. But you were wrong. My secret, the one you told me never to tell, the one locked in a place you could not reach no matter how deep you thrust your knives into my soul, is that I was strong. I was smart enough to make myself dead, more dead than you are now, whenever you hurt me. So you may have taken my body, but you did not take my soul. Even this last time."

I open the front door and pull Ernestine's quilt around me.

The darkness is not dark to Me, child. Night shines like the day. Darkness is as light to Me.

I hear You, Abba.

Still, my chest quivers with fear, and my rain boots, rubber hard from so many days of cold and disuse, form to my feet as I plod toward the cries of the hurting girl across the graveyard. Of course I know it is Anni before I reach her, crouched there against her father's gravestone, pressing herself close to the granite as if straining to hear his heartbeat once more.

"Anni," I say.

Comfort, the Spirit whispers.

"It's okay, baby." I help her stand and pull her to me.

I hold you like you hold her, says my Abba.

I wipe her tears with a threadbare spot of the quilt and feel the warmth of liquid affliction against my fingers.

I hum as we walk together toward Oralee and Ernestine, shadows standing in the backlit doorway of the looming, pillared house, and I hear Abba singing over us both:

I've cleansed you with My tears of blood
and the sweet, salty water of My tears.
You are beautiful.
You.
The real you,
whole and unscathed.
You made it through the fire.
You really can come out.
The light is bright, but it can heal
if you step into it.

The light outside the safety of my little house is bright, and I squint, even at this late hour, as if bandages, wrapped around my eyes for too long, have been removed. I strain to hear the song of Abba, and like a Raggedy Ann, I can see the heart on my chest that says I am real, but I cannot feel that it is so, even with Anni's shaking body tucked in beside mine as we walk.

Maybe I don't have to feel real yet.

Maybe, for now, opening the door is enough.

Se aprè batay nou konte blese.
"It is after the battle that you count the injured."

CHAPTER 22

Anniston

As the quilt wrapped gently around my shoulders, I couldn't say I was surprised. I'd heard the footsteps before they reached me and knew.

Comfort pulled the quilt snug and put her arms around me. "Let's go home, baby."

Her voice, a whisper, sounded like a long-lost melody. The smell of lavender in her long blonde hair washed over my pain and smoothed over bumpy places in my heart like the roll of the sea over a hacked-up beach. We walked, silent, past her front porch where the asters lay wilted from the frosty rain. I put my arm around her waist and the bones of her back and ribs stuck out like my dog's, Molly's, when we first found her as a stray.

Comfort's eyes fixed on mine, and I could see hers water up. Sadness swept over me again about the whole night, the whole of unspoken hurt and untold wanderings, the whole of the pain hidden by this pecan-covered piece of land.

Mama and Ernestine stood on the front porch as we made our way up the drive. When we got there, they near knocked me off my feet, both of them hugging me like they hadn't seen me in weeks. And maybe the me who came home that night hadn't been seen in a while.

Maybe not ever.

Mama hugged Comfort next, and when they parted, tears streamed down their faces.

Mama got down on her knees this time. She held my face in her hands like looking into a glass wishing ball, then shook her head with sorry. "She'll be in the grave, too, if she ever lays a hand on you again."

Someone set a glass of warm milk and three of Ernestine's oatmeal-praline cookies on my bedside table before I climbed into bed. I pulled a loose string from the fraying corner of the Joan Walsh Anglund sheets. Images of happy boys and girls playing and dancing covered the pillowcases and bedspread. Molly curled up against my stomach and let out a long sigh.

"I know, girl. I know." I put my arm around Molly and turned to face the window and moon and stars beyond. I kept the window cracked open, even on chilly nights, so I could hear the crickets and smell the weight of the hills and closeness of the ocean. Night music floated in and soaked my heart, swirling from the nightmares I faced each night even before I slept … the ones I kept to myself, too afraid to share with anyone, even Ernestine.

The hole in the center of Daddy's chest fills my mind, blood flowing all around despite his great hands clasped there, pressing against the life flooding out of him. And me, pressed against the closet door, wondering still why my good and kind daddy lay stuck in a cold, black hole in the ground on account of standing up for his sister.

Princella's raised voice in the rooms below blamed Daddy for everything. Vaughn argued back at her. Vaughn and Ernestine always said Princella has her reasons for all her hate, and I was sure she did. Like a pecan farmer knows in his bones when his crops are destined for a storm, I always knew something was off-kilter about my family, even before the shootings. Life around here was like a hiccupping movie reel at school, one of those the teacher tries every which way to fiddle with, turning the projector knob back and forth to try to bring focus, glimpses of clarity skipping by, crooked frames never quite settling in.

I folded the pillow under my head and pulled the frayed quilt up higher as fear overwhelmed my heart, moaning like the wind slipping through my window. Making sense of my life felt like a ferry crossing Mobile Bay, bleating its whistle as it moves farther and farther away from the distant shore. I listened for the sound of those ferries, I pulled my knees up close to my heart, and played my nightly game with the now-visible moon, daring it to stare back at me and see who could go the longest without blinking.

Each night I played that game, and the moon always won.

Pale kare kare. Pa eseye twonpe.
"Speak plainly. Do not try to deceive."

CHAPTER 23

Anniston

"Hey there, Anni." Solly came to help Vaughn prune the trees. Splotches of light leaned through the breakfast room windows, and Molly chased the reflections as they bounced along the walls in random places.

I tried to pull my too-short hair over my swollen eye. "Hi, Solly."

"Mornin', Solly." Mama's greeting vibrated in my ear and throbbing head.

Solly leaned down to my level as he made his way toward the coffeepot. "Whoa there, darlin'. What happened to you? You didn't pick a fight with one of those squirrels in your traps, did ya?"

I tried to smile, but my cheek smarted tight as a balloon about to pop. "I'll be okay."

Solly's dimples faded into a worried frown.

"You might want to keep your voice down." Mama handed a mug of steaming coffee to Solly. "Princella's still asleep. Vaughn will be down in a minute."

He rubbed his stubbled chin for a moment, eyes questioning Mama as she packed a cooler full of drinks and snacks. "Y'all have big plans today?"

"Yeah, where're we goin', Mama?"

"We're takin' a little road trip," said Mama.

"New Orleans," said Ernestine.

"What's the occasion?" Solly asked.

I was as eager as him to know the answer to that.

"Truth," said Mama. "It's time for a little truth around here."

The highway running north and south along Mobile Bay teased drivers with views of the ocean and homes with gardens straight out of the *Southern Living* magazines stacked on Princella's coffee tables. Wisteria spilled over the tops of stone walls and picket fences, begging passersby to stop and visit. Peach and pecan stands and run-down gas stations peppered the land along our drive, along with homes and shacks and chicken coops. I couldn't tell which buildings were for people and which ones were for animals. Made me wonder what it would be like to live behind such weathered walls. Once in a while, a shaggy, panting dog and a human watched from their sagging front porch as we passed.

"If I Can't Have You" by the Bee Gees played, and I sipped on a Yoo-hoo.

"Are we going to the Garden District, Mama?" I wasn't sure what she meant by truth, but I hoped it included beignets. I could almost taste the powdered sugar melting on the tops of them already.

"Right near there. We're going to have lunch with some old friends." She and Ernestine grinned at each other like some big secret set between them. Most times, trips to New Orleans were full of good food and shopping. I'd brought a book to read to pass the driving time, but I didn't feel like reading today. From my spot in the backseat, I stared out the window and listened to the "American Top 40" show on the radio. Ernestine worked on quilting squares.

Mama drove. She didn't say much until we got to somewhere between the Biloxi and Gulfport, Mississippi, exits. "I'm so sorry, Anni. Sorry about last night. Sorry about how Princella treats you. Sorry for your worries over Comfort." She let out a long sigh. "Mostly I'm sorry about Daddy. This … this wasn't how our life was supposed to be."

"Mama …"

"No, wait, you need to hear this. I didn't know things would get this bad. The family's always been a mess, but killing? And now, Princella raising her hand against even you? She comes from a long line of hurt—one she swore you and nobody else would ever find out about. One that's trickling down to you, and we've got to stop it from coming down any farther, no matter how determined she is to forget about her own past. Some things shouldn't be forgotten, no matter how much someone thinks they ought to be."

Mama turned the AC up a notch. "I'm so sorry you have to hear such things at your age. But you're a strong, brave girl, so I know you're big enough to hear it. I wish a heart as good as yours didn't have to learn humans are capable of doing such evil to each other. Especially people in your own family ... Especially people in your own family."

Mama concentrated on the road in front of us, white lines falling under the car in an awkward rhythm, each pulling me closer to learning about the things she spoke of. I couldn't tell if she spoke for my benefit or for her own. I think she tried to work truth out of the mess for herself, too.

One thing for sure, she was right. Some things you shouldn't forget.

As the car passed over the road, I remembered better times. Happy times. Times I'd spent with Daddy.

"Ready for this, Anni?" Daddy held my head against his chest in the exact place his heart beat. "Lemme get a good look at ya." He put his hands on my shoulders and tilted me away from his body. "My sweet baby girl, getting to be such a young lady." He smelled like soap and laundry detergent. And his smile—oh, Daddy's smile melted me.

A junior is as far as I ever made it in Girl Scouts, tiring of all the rules, requirements, and obligations. But square dance night was one we all looked forward to, even me.

Daddy tucked a daisy from one the table centerpieces behind my ear and offered me his arm, floating me to the center of the Thomases's barn.

"Partners to your places, like the horses to their traces!" said the square dance caller into the microphone. The band, made up of a banjo, a couple of guitars, and a drum set, warmed up their instruments. "Let's all boil some cabbages down now, 'hear?"

It was one of my favorite square dances, and the caller gave us instructions, especially for the first-timers. But me and Daddy, it was our third year in a row, and we remembered the steps easy.

"Bow to your partner. Bow to your corner. Allemande left!"

We swirled and swooshed by my fellow troop members and their daddies, grinning till it hurt.

"Pass on through and do a pull-by, then promenade all the way home!"

Boil them cabbage down, down.
Turn them hoecakes 'round, 'round.
The only song that I can sing is
boil them cabbage down.

Possum in a 'simmon tree,
raccoon on the ground.
Raccoon says, 'You son-of-a-gun,
'shake some 'simmons down.'

"Allenmande left, then allemande right. Four ladies chain, and we'll do it all again!"

Daddy barely took his eyes off me, no matter where we were in the circle. Times like those, I was glad I had no brothers or sisters. No one to share the way he made me feel like such a treasure.

Butterfly, he has wings of gold.
Firefly, wings of flame.
Bedbug, he got no wings at all,
but he gets there just the same.

Boil them cabbage down, down.
Turn them hoecakes 'round, 'round.
The only song that I can sing is
boil them cabbage down.

"Turn your corner, like swingin' on a gate. Right through. Left through. Don't be late!" The caller loved trying to mess us up, in which case, we'd about fall on the ground, we laughed so hard. Worked up a sweat, too, all the turning and swinging, switching and swirling.

Ladies do, and the gents, you know,
and it's right by right by wrong you go.
And you can't go to heaven while you carry on so.
And it's home, little gal, and do-si-do,
And it may be the last time, I don't know,
And oh, by gosh, and oh, by Joe.

"Weave the ring!" the caller hollered, the last call of the dance. And somehow, when we finished all the round and round and back and forth, we ended up standing before each other, face-to-face, laughing until we couldn't laugh no more.

The whine and crackle of the radio as Ernestine fiddled between Peaches & Herb, the Bee Gees, Styx, and Billy Joel brought me back to the conversation she and Mama were having. Ernestine gave up and shut off the radio altogether.

"That's the nature of secrets," Mama said. "The more they're stuffed away, the angrier they get, scratching and clawing to get out in the open, tearing us up inside as we fight to keep 'em tucked away. But the heart knows—the heart that's not holding the secret in knows, especially when it's a good heart like yours, Anni. The secrets of others get their slime all over the innocent. I can't sit back and let secrets keep clawing at you. It's time we broke the cycle of sins and lies in this family wide open."

And you can't go to heaven while you carry on so.

The line from the old square dance echoed in my head as Ernestine handed me a baggie filled with crumbled pralines.

"Sometimes evil is acquired. Sometimes it's inherited. Sometimes it rubs off like the scent of perfume left on unwashed clothes, sweet at first, but then the stench seeps through. I've been around the Harlans long enough now, I saw the evil growing like a cancer. Now it's spread to places it should've never been allowed to spread."

Sadness like a wave turned my stomach. Now that Mama and Ernestine talked about it, I knew the evil about which they spoke. I felt it in my dreams, the ones where I was chased. I knew I never had a direct reason to be scared of anything, so maybe, like Mama said, I felt sin all around me, even though I couldn't see it.

And you can't go to heaven while you carry on so.

Mama continued. "Vaughn came from a long line of pecan farmers. More important, he came from a long line of gentlemen. He had the best of everything—education, a future as heir to the plantation. When he was young, he could have married any young lady in town, and everyone respected him. So when he brought Princella home from college, why, everyone knew she was completely wrong for him—not because she was poor, but because she had a dark and bitter heart."

"What was so wrong with her? Did something happen to her to make her that way?"

Only movie characters were as bad as her. Cinderella's stepmother. The queen in *Sleeping Beauty*. Images of those cartoons flashed through my mind.

Mama continued. "Yes and no. One of the biggest things was how Cole was born. See, Princella was the girlfriend of one of Vaughn's teammates, who dumped her after he got her pregnant. Vaughn admired her all along from a distance, but she still loved the baby's father. Regardless, Vaughn felt sorry for her and took it upon himself to care for her, marry her, give her a good name, and help her raise that child—Cole. Of course, back then, and with nowhere else to turn, Princella took him up on it. The whole Harlan family grieved Vaughn's decision. Still, he held fast to his gentleman ways, caring for Princella and treating her like a queen.

"As Cole grew, Princella near worshipped him, to the point of neglecting your daddy and Comfort after they were born."

"That's how you came to live here, right, Ernestine?" I interrupted.

"That's right, child." She winked.

"She lavished Cole with gifts, hoping that might ease his tantrums and disrespect. While his personality on the outside made him the most popular young man in Bay Spring, he was a liar and downright mean at home. With Vaughn's help, Princella groomed him from grade school to be a starting quarterback, a role he fell into naturally. Cole knew that. He took to dating as many girls as he could without worrying about how many hearts he broke, as well as having long nights out and coming home late and drunk.

"In the meantime, Comfort and Rey grew closer and closer and fell farther and farther away from Cole. Rey took to studying and music mostly, and Comfort took to friends and her books. She preferred to stay out of the limelight, but her beauty and Princella's constant social pressures pushed her into the cheerleading and all those pageants.

"Cole went on to college, where he kept womanizing and drinking. Vaughn clung to his gentlemanly ways and tried to keep Princella happy. He pulled Cole out of jail for underage drinking many times and used his buddy Miles Gadsden to smooth over complaints of harassment from different girls.

"When Cole came home from college, he often acted inappropriate with Comfort, making crude comments and patting her on the behind and other things. Vaughn and Princella pretended not to notice, even when Rey and I tried to talk to them plain about it. The more Cole's behavior carried on, the more upset Comfort became. She tried to steer clear of him, but when Cole got an idea in his head … The engagement made him snap."

I shook my head, still struggling to believe that a person could be so awful. "He had everything. Why didn't he just leave her alone?"

"I don't know. We'll probably never know. But sometimes, when a person has everything, they still want things they can't or shouldn't have for the pure power and greed of it. That's what starts wars. And that's what makes a man rape."

I watched the second hand of my Hello Kitty watch make tiny jumps around the numbers.

And I felt the sore spot on my cheek throb.

Rad sal lave nan fanmi.
"Dirty clothes are [to be] washed in the family."

CHAPTER 24

Anniston

Crossing Lake Pontchartrain into the concrete bustle of New Orleans gave me excited butterflies every time. We weaved our way through the city until we got to St. Charles Avenue, where Mama pulled off the interstate. Elaborate, colorful homes stood alongside bland, neglected buildings. Those with scrolling, ornate metalwork seemed to scold the sad, older structures for being so worn-out and tired. We parked on an unfamiliar side street nowhere near any of the places Mama usually took me in New Orleans. I couldn't see the lake or the river or any buildings like the ones near Daddy's college, Tulane.

"We're here." We headed toward the entrance of an old church with a four-story brick building attached to the back of it. Between the sidewalk and the back building, a chain-link fence surrounded a playground full of boys and girls of all shapes and colors. Some raced Big Wheels on the blacktop. Others squealed, their color-tipped braids flying as a merry-go-round spun them like a blender. In a grassy section, younger kids—some wearing only diapers—splashed on a water table full of balls and boats.

When we got to the front of the church, I read the sign out loud: "St. Augustine's Freedom Home for Women and Children. Established 1932. Why we stopping here?"

"When I went to nursing school in town, my apartment was near here," Mama said. "My roommates and I came and volunteered here as often as we could, a couple times a month, at least. I met your daddy here too. Thought you might like to see it."

The wood doors were full of carvings and stained glass, like they belonged on a castle. A blast of cold air-conditioning greeted us as we stepped into the musty-smelling foyer with worn, crimson carpet. A black sign with white letters stuck on it read, "Welcome, all who are weary and need rest." On one side of the foyer, a makeshift office was set up with tables, file cabinets, a phone, and a couple of typewriters. The black lady behind the desk nearly climbed across the top of it to get to Mama.

"Oralee! Look at you, not a day older than when you was here in college!" Jeans and an orange, polyester shirt with a long, pointed collar stretched across her thick body, and her graying hair was braided in cornrows with orange beads.

Mama hugged her tight, her eyes wet wih tears. "Aamina, it's been way too long."

"Oralee, I'm so very sorry about Rey. So very sorry."

The two of them stood rocking and holding each other for a while, until Mama stepped back and wiped her eyes. "Aamina, meet Anniston."

"Well, it's about time. And so grown up. I'm sure you don't remember we met when you were learning to crawl. Your mama brought you here to show you off. She's sent me a few pictures over the years, but you a young lady now."

"Pleasure to meet you, ma'am."

She grabbed my hand and yanked me into her thick arms for a hug. She smelled like night cream, green beans, and snickerdoodles.

"And you must be Ernestine. You been a godsend to these girls, from what I understand. Welcome!"

Ernestine extended her hand, but Aamina hugged her, too. "What's with all the handshakes? Let Aamina hold on to ya!"

"A pleasure to meet you, Aamina."

"You must be hungry after your drive. Come on into the back— we're about ready for lunch service."

We followed her through the middle of the church sanctuary, which smelled like the old, lemon-oiled wood of the pews, and out the back. A hallway sloped down steep and opened up into the newer part of the building. A sign hung on the wall, pointing right to the dining hall and left for the clinic. We turned right toward the dining hall, a gym that doubled as a cafeteria. Women of all ages smiled and talked, some holding babies or the hands of wriggling toddlers. Others stood by themselves, shoulders drooping, wearing threadbare clothes that were either too man-ish, too tight, too short, or all of the above.

Aamina led us to a serving line like at my school cafeteria, with the same plastic trays that had separate compartments for milk, vegetables, and the main course. I felt starved, and the cheeseburgers, sliced pears, green beans, French fries, and carton of ice cream looked scrumptious. When we were through the line, we found a spot away from the crowded tables where we could visit easier. Aamina said hello to everyone she passed, and every one of them seemed happy to see her.

"We've got an afternoon of fun planned for you—helping with the preschool, observing intake, and serving dinner to our friends."

"Thank you so much. I hope it wasn't so short of notice that we're a bother."

"Oralee, you never a bother. And our friends love when new folks come serve."

"Are there babies that need rockin'?" asked Ernestine.

"We got a whole room full of 'em for you, Ernestine." Aamina's laugh was like happy notes on a xylophone.

"Where do they come from?" I asked.

"Who, child?"

"The women and children. Do they live here?"

Aamina raised an eyebrow at Mama. "Your mama didn't tell you about what we do here?"

"No, ma'am."

She winked at Mama. "Well, okay then. We best start at the beginning. Back in the 1930s, during the Great Depression, shelters overflowed with folks needing a place to live. Mothers and children, especially, had no place to turn if their husbands left—and a lot of them did back then. Couldn't feed their families, so they up and left, figuring at least they could take care of themselves by finding work in the city. Jobs were scarce though. Enough men grabbing them

up, weren't none left for women. A Catholic priest named Father
Michael O'Shaughasee saw the need and asked the archdiocese to
help start St. Augustine's Freedom Home in a mansion that once
stood on this site. So many lined up the first day they turned folks
away, which broke Father Michael's heart. Eventually, the church
raised enough money to build this new building in 1957, so now
up to one hundred women and children can stay. The church pays
teachers to help run a preschool and day care while mothers find jobs
and get back to work as much as possible. Eventually, most of the
women leave us able to support and care for themselves.

"I used to live here myself, until I got healthy enough to get
a job and live on my own. Now I work here full-time. Wouldn't
leave for the world. These women here, most of 'em been through
things you can't imagine. They've come here seeking shelter from
families or boyfriends or spouses who near beat 'em to a pulp. Come
here bloody rag dolls before they think to go to a hospital, they're
so scared. That's why we got that free clinic you saw on the way in.
Nurses and doctors volunteer to patch 'em up until they feel safe
enough to get to a hospital or outside doctor. Some of 'em come here
pregnant—by choice or, more often, by rape or incest—and they
stay here. We see they get proper pregnancy care, and often, they and
their babies come back to stay after delivery. They're welcome to stay
as long as they need, as long as they're working on more schooling or
jobs or a way to eventually be independent again—some for the first
time in their lives."

"That's so sad."

"Indeed. These ain't subjects most folks talk about. Everyday
folks are too busy to see the hurt around 'em, or if they could see,

they too busy to care. Often, helping hurting people makes a hurting person feel too much of their own pain, and they never come back to volunteer again."

Mama finished a bite of burger. "It's amazing how much a smile and warm touch can fill a person up and give them hope to live."

"See that friend over there?" Aamina nodded toward a table where a pale woman with long blonde braids hoisted a chubby baby boy high in the air, the two of them laughing and carrying on like no one else was in the room. Made me laugh, too, they laughed so hard and big. "Her name is Mary. Mary'd been selling herself to men since she was ten and her mama died of a drug overdose and her daddy—well, she never did know him. She came to us when she was nineteen and scared to death of her pimp and thinner than a splinter off a porch rail."

"What's a pimp?"

Aamina looked at Mama to make sure she should continue.

"Go on, Aamina."

"A pimp's the name they give a man who enslaves girls and women and sells them to others for sex, making them turn over part or most of the money they make in exchange for a place to live, food, and clothes. A girl can't leave her pimp without being beaten. Mary was lucky. She ran away without getting caught. Others can't or are killed by the pimp or his thugs for trying.

"So we gave Mary a bed and helped her change her name. She's in beauty school now.

"Baby's name is Ben. His daddy has a real good job in construction, but Mary and Ben are staying here until she and the daddy are sure about the wisdom of a marriage and the ability to build a life together."

"Why do people do that to each other?"

"Desperation, drugs, they're born into it, groomed for it ... hunger and exhaustion makes 'em not care no more."

"She looks so happy, like none of it happened to her."

"That's what the Lord can do with a life. Like the story in Daniel, when the king put Shadrach, Meshach, and Abednego in the furnace of fire. God stayed with them the whole time—He was the fourth man who appeared in there with them. And when they came out? None of 'em even smelled like smoke. The only thing that burned was the ropes around they wrists. That's what the Lord can do with a person who's walked through fire. Free 'em from chains that keep 'em bound up tight and from clouds of despair and smoke and flame. If that person lets God help." Aamina kept her eyes on Mary and Ben and smiled.

The afternoon passed quickly, and we made lots of new friends. I played on the playground and helped in some of the younger children's classrooms. Ernestine rocked all the babies she could, and Mama helped Aamina with staffing the front office.

After serving dinner, we sat in the front office for intake, which Aamina said's the best part of the day. Said she loves seeing folks take the first step toward healing and making better lives for themselves. Said a lot of outsiders think seeking help is for weaklings and that the past should be left in the past and not dealt with.

"But not dealing with the past," she said, "is like having a skunk in the middle of your living room. You don't notice it after a while, but everyone around you smells it, and it rubs off on folks who visit, and no amount of tomato juice baths will ever wash the stink away. You can only bury the past when you acknowledge it and don't allow it to sidle up against your leg no more. Even then, digging the hole to bury the thing is hard work. It's the hard work of healing most folks never want to do."

The intake room was inside an old side entrance to the sanctuary. Pale-pink wallpaper with giant, ivory magnolias covered the walls. Aamina said brides used it to prepare for their weddings. At 6:30, the current St. Augustine residents checked in for the evening. Then at 7:15, check-in opened up to newcomers.

The first woman who came in didn't look any older than the upper classmen at my school. She wore a faded, tie-dye shirt, running shorts, and blue-and-white flip-flops. A red bandana held her long blonde hair off her face. A little girl about three or four years old slept on her shoulder. She wore a yellow sundress—nearly the same color as her curly hair—that tied at her shoulders. They were both way too skinny, and I noticed matching bruises on and around each of their thighs.

"I'm Aamina. Welcome to St. Augustine's." She held out her hand and the young lady shook it limply.

"I'm Sunny, and this here's June."

"Sunny, pleasure to meet you. Hey, June. Hey, baby." Aamina rubbed June's bony shoulder. "Goodness' sake. She's burning up."

"Yeah, she's been sick. I ran outta her medicine, and now she's sicker than last week. Can you help?"

"Well, the clinic's only open a few hours each day. This is for folks who need a place to stay."

"Need that, too." Sunny lowered her eyes and rocked June from side to side.

"Okay, if that's the case, have a seat. We'll need to ask you a few questions—basic information we take on everyone. Otherwise, everything you say is kept confidential, and we tell no one you're here unless you tell us you're accepting their calls."

"Not much to tell you. June and me—her daddy beats us. And we had enough."

June snuggled closer into Sunny, and I saw three bruises the shapes of fingers on her limp upper arm.

"One more thing. You have to be at least eighteen for us to take you in."

"Turned eighteen yesterday. Got here as quick as I could."

Aamina pursed her lips like she had to think about the awfulness of that. Finally, she spoke. "Okay. Let's start with June. My friend Oralee came to help tonight, and it happens she's a nurse. So we'll get June checked over and see what she needs. Then we'll check you over too. Won't take but a half hour or so. Then we'll get you something warm to eat and settle you into your beds. Mothers and their children stay together."

Mama put a hand on Sunny's back and led her and June to a bench across the room where another intake worker waited to help with paperwork. In the meantime, I saw Ernestine greeting a tall girl with long, black hair parted down the middle that fell in soft waves around her face and down the middle of her back. Pretty enough for a Miss Alabama contestant, the girl kept her arms crossed in front of her tight, like she fought to hold something in. I recognized the Greek letters on her T-shirt from pictures of Mama and her sorority friends. At first, I thought the girl came to volunteer. Then her smile turned into a frown and tears flowed down her face like the creek behind Comfort's house. She nodded to whatever Ernestine said to her, and it drove me crazy not hearing their conversation.

Aamina must've read my mind. "It's always the ones you least expect. I'll put money down on her being pregnant and from one of the universities. Come down here so's none of their friends'll know they're in trouble."

"Why can't they tell their friends?"

"If they were true friends, they could. But a lot of folks is friends on a surface thinner than a thawing lake. One wrong move or misperception and it's over."

"But if she's having a baby, isn't that exciting?"

"Not if you're unmarried and in a sorority it ain't."

Ernestine brought the girl to where we sat. "This is Jenny."

"Hi, Jenny. What can we do for you, darlin'?" Aamina said this like showing up at intake at St. Augustine's was the most normal thing in the world.

"It's okay. You can tell 'er." Ernestine put an arm around the willowy girl.

"A ... a few weeks ago, I was at a party and ... things were crazy ... outta hand ..." Jenny searched Ernestine's eyes for help.

"Go on, child. We're all here to help."

Jenny inhaled like a person about to dive under water. "A few of the boys, I don't know how ... I got locked in a room with 'em, and I couldn't get out ... no one heard me ... the music and shouting was so loud ..." She stared up at the ceiling, her eyes fluttering, trying to fight back tears. "Now I'm pregnant ... I can't go back ... I can't go home ... I don't know ..."

"Sweet Jesus." Aamina flew out of her chair and wrapped a trembling Jenny in her hefty arms. The girl's shoulders shook with sobs. "You come to the right place, baby. You come to the right place."

Only three other women came in that night. In the meantime, I helped Sunny and Jenny sort through the donations room for a couple of outfits, new underwear, and pajamas. Then we fixed 'em up with toothbrushes, hairbrushes, and other toiletries. Each one of them got a brand-new Bible, too, a study Bible with Jesus's words in red. I took off two of the friendship bracelets Ernestine and I made and stuck them in next to Psalm 34, which I told them was my favorite scripture, next to Isaiah 61, on account of how it talks about angels setting up tents around us, protecting us, and pulling us outta trouble, and how God stays close to the brokenhearted. "I hope you don't mind my sharing this. I thought you might like it."

I don't know which they liked better, the verse or the bracelet, but it felt nice to leave a bit of me tucked into those pages for them.

The ice cream part of the Dilly Bar dripped down the stick over my hand.

"Better hurry up and eat that. Told ya to get something in a bowl." Ernestine grinned at me from the front seat and ate a spoonful of her Peanut Buster Parfait.

"Thanks for taking me there, Mama," I said between bites.

"So you liked it?"

"Yeah. I like learning about things you did when you were younger."

"And I like showing you. But that's not the big reason I took you there today."

"It's not?"

"I needed you to see where Princella grew up."

Well, good thing I was sitting down, because you coulda knocked me over with a feather right then and there. "Princella? Grew up there?"

"Yep. She did. She and her brother."

"She has a brother?"

"Yes, but they don't ever speak. I'm not sure I remember what his name is or where he lives. They had a falling out over something trivial like a piece of their mama's jewelry, and she wrote him off forever."

"That's crazy."

"That's Princella. Anyway, Princella's mama brought them to St. Augustine's when they were barely in grade school. Much like June's daddy, their daddy hurt them in awful ways. St. Augustine's took them in. When Princella was fifteen, her mama died of diphtheria and the folks at St. Augustine took her and her brother in as their own."

"Then why does she hate poor people so much if she was one herself and so many people helped her?"

"Good question." Mama turned off the interstate onto the Bay State Highway. We cranked down our windows to breathe in the dark relief of the salty air. "I'm not so sure she hates them, as much as she hates the parts of herself she sees in them."

"Mmm-hmm." Ernestine rested her head against the back of the seat.

"Princella worked hard in school and got a full scholarship to Alabama Southern. Room, board, everything paid for. A group of St. Augustine donors sponsor one child every four years for college, and that year, they chose Princella."

"That's cool—"

"Woulda been, but Princella took the money and ran. Oh, she went to ASU for a while, and boy did she ever let loose. Got involved in the social high life, never told a soul about her upbringing. Fell for that football player—Cole's biological father—who dumped her as soon as he found out she was pregnant."

"But what about college and how she was in a sorority and all? How'd she do all that being pregnant?"

"She didn't ever finish. She lies about it all the time. Made up some big story about a New Orleans wedding, too. No one in Vaughn's family—including Vaughn—ever said otherwise. So folks around town all believe it."

"So if Princella didn't tell anybody about St. Augustine's and kept it such a big secret, how did you find out?"

"When your daddy and I dated, Princella caused me a lot of trouble. I never measured up. The people at St. Augustine's were some of my best friends. So I talked to Aamina and the others about her. As soon as I said Princella's name, Aamina knew. I brought in a photograph to confirm, but Aamina knew she was the same Princella. They'd been bunkmates more than once during the years they lived here together. It nearly broke Aamina's heart to hear how Princella turned out. Said maybe me and Rey could redeem some of the good St. Augustine's poured into her." Mama shook her head and sighed.

"You don't think you have redeemed anything, Oralee?" Ernestine asked.

"No ... I don't know. I don't know if any of Princella can be redeemed."

"*Oui*, but look in your rearview mirror."

In the mirror I could see the lines around Mama's eyes crinkle into a smile. "You're right, Ernestine," she said. "You're always right."

BAY SPRING BANNER SENTINEL,
MONDAY, MARCH 17, 1980
By Shirley O'Day, Social Reporter

Saturday night marked the Fifty-Third Anniversary of the Daughters of the Confederacy Cotillion and Bay Spring Auxiliary Auction. It grieves me to report the event was a disaster of highest proportion that violated not only social but Southern rules of etiquette as well.

Several ladies invited guests who had never set foot in a junior etiquette or cotillion class, which was quite evident to all. Which goes to show, Southern belles and gentlemen are born and not made, and rules are bred, not taught.

Mrs. Faye Gadsden and Mrs. Princella Harlan wish to extend their sincere regrets and apologies to everyone in attendance Saturday night and assure the town that such a ruckus will not occur again in the future. They also recommend no one allow the band Muddy and the Flaps to return for any Bay Spring event.

Finally, as author of this column, I feel it is my civic duty to remind everyone there are rules in the South, and they are not made to be broken. When everyone follows them, life is sweet and refreshing as iced tea. If not, things get rotten as a red tide.

Due to the embarrassment of this evening, I won't be announcing the names of the eighth-grade debutantes nor the queen of the cotillion in this week's column as has been the usual tradition. Instead, I will honor them individually next week.

MAY 1980

Lafimen pa janm leve san dife.
"Smoke never rises without fire."

CHAPTER 25

Comfort

Spring runs into the start of summer without me hardly noticing, except for the seven tornadoes that touch down within five days of each other this first week of May. They nearly demolish the towns of Southside, Lineville, Louisville, Clayton, Theodore, Gulf Shores, and Hubbard's Landing, barely missing our orchards.

As if Alabama hadn't suffer enough after Hurricane Frederic.

Makes me wonder what kind of a summer we're in for, storms coming at us faster than we can recover. People say the connection between weather and people is a myth, that the bone-aching worry that comes ahead of time when the sky is bright and clear is coincidence when the storm rolls in. But I wonder anyway. I have an achy feeling that won't go away.

A bruised reed I will not break.

I wish I could believe You, Abba.

A smoldering wick I will not snuff out.

All I am is ashes.

I will bring justice.

How I wish You would.

I will take hold of your hand. I will keep you and make you to be a light to others who walk your path.

How? Help me see how.

I know and see what has taken place. I will make you new.

Let me go down to the sea again, to hear the call of Your ocean of grace. To bend my weary body to You. To sing like I did when I was younger. To shout from the dunes Your goodness. Let me live to see the day I can do all these things. I can't take another storm.

You can't take another storm. You're right. But I can.

Even when I leave my home, I feel the arrows pointing at me, waiting to take another shot. Tornadoes on the horizon waiting to flatten me.

These things are part of a battle, child. A battle bigger than you.

Then please fight for me.

My child, I've already won.

Pousyè pu leve san van.
"Dust does not lift without wind."

CHAPTER 26

Anniston

School dragged on when it got close to summer. Dragged on even worse ever since I faced people with my black eye after the cotillion back in March. I pressed myself as close to the walls as I could, passing clumps of students and avoiding everyone's eyes on the way to my locker. Jed would be there, waiting, so he could walk me to my first-period English class, something he'd been doing since the dance.

So much happened to him he didn't ask for—a crooked eye and a catawampus hip, never knowing his real parents, more foster parents than he could count. If any of it bothered him, he never let on. Didn't even make him angry. I think I felt madder than him about how the kids at school treated him, the way they looked the other direction when he tried to say hello or quick turned down a hall if they saw him coming or stared at their lunch trays when he searched for a table. Sure, he'd been the new kid this year, and new kids always had it rough, especially in a small town like Bay Spring, and a limp and a crooked eye didn't help.

Lucky for both of us, no one ever sat at the table by the teachers' aides, so we'd claimed it as our own. I considered what a relief it'd been not to sit with the other girls in my class at lunch anymore. All they talked about was boys and hair and clothes, how their mamas took them all the way to the fancy New Orleans boutiques to find their cotillion dresses. Nikki Hatch talked about getting to second base with Grady Bingham. Melinda Sue O'Malley said Tommy Sharp tried to get to third. And Cara Lynn Harris complained how Eddie Prince wouldn't even hold her hand. But as proud as they were of their so-called boyfriends, all those girls turned beet red and couldn't say a word to save their lives through their jittering teeth whenever the boys came around. How that was any fun at all was beyond me.

Me and Jed weren't like that.

And we certainly weren't afraid of each other.

At first, none of the girls who tolerated me sitting with them over the years noticed or cared that I didn't sit with them anymore. I wasn't exactly a topic of discussion. But of course, eventually, Sally Roberts had something to say about it. Her and her big mouth.

A few weeks after the dance, I was stepping away from the cafeteria cashier and nearly choked on a big whiff of her Love's Baby Soft. She headed to her usual table, and I headed toward Jed, who was saving me a seat across the lunchroom.

"Where you goin', Anniston?"

"Over here. I'll see ya later."

"Is he your boyfriend now? How embarrassing," Sally said, scrunching up her nose.

"He's my friend, and he's not embarrassing," I'd said, continuing to walk toward Jed, whose smile turned to a frown because he heard every word Sally said.

"Fine, then. Sit with your weirdo friend. But don't expect to sit at our table anymore." Sally walked off in a huff, shaking her little skirt-covered hiney like she was the coolest thing since jelly shoes.

"Sorry about that." I plopped down in the chair next to Jed. "She's a real jerk."

"She's afraid. And I'm used to people being afraid of me." He bit into his cheeseburger like hardly anything happened.

"Well, they shouldn't be."

Ever since then, it'd been me and Jed, and Jed and me.

"Happy birthday, Anni." Jed was waiting at my locker, and he handed me the prettiest purple bouquet of lemon beebalm tied up with twine I'd ever seen. And though I knew he'd found them along a roadside, he found them for me, just the same.

"How'd you know?"

"Mrs. Nowlan's bulletin board." He grinned, and I melted.

"Thank you."

"You're welcome." He pulled my locker door closer to hide us, leaned over, and kissed me on my cheek.

This morning, Jed and I had class together. The school held an annual poetry day each May, when every freshman English class paired up with an eighth-grade English class, supposedly to help the eighth graders transition to high school next year. We figured it was an excuse for half of the teachers to sit in the lounge and smoke, since there wasn't really a transition to speak of. We stayed in the same building with the same teachers and same kids we'd known since grade school. Jed's class combined with mine, and I sat next to him as Mrs. Nowlan began.

"William Carlos Williams said a poem 'must be real, not realism, but reality itself.' What do you think this means?"

"It speaks about pain," I blurted.

Jed looked up quick from the notebook page he was filling with graffiti sketches of 3-D arrows and stars, peace symbols, and all kinds of robots and superheroes punching their way into space as they flew around bubble letters that spelled out *freedom*. I looked closer and saw one with my name in the middle—Anni— surrounded by roses and songbirds. Heat like electricity shot straight through to my toes.

"Interesting response, Anniston. What do you mean?"

"What good is poetry … any words, really … unless they open us up to what's going on inside a person?"

"Indeed. But how does this apply to 'The Red Wheelbarrow'? Sixteen words. Just sixteen. And yet these sixteen words by William Carlos Williams represent, for many, poetic genius."

"Everything is so bright—the red wheelbarrow, the glaze of the rain, the white chickens," Cara Lynn said, a little too loud. She was always trying to be the teacher's pet.

"Yes. He uses few words to create striking images. Good. Other thoughts?" Mrs. Nowlan scanned the room.

"Maybe the red means blood running out of a broken heart. The rain tries to harden it but washes it clean, so clean that even white chickens aren't afraid of it anymore." Jed leaned back in his seat, shoved his pencil over his ear, and crossed his arms behind his head.

Mrs. Nowlan didn't quite know what to say to that. My face flushed hot. I wondered if Princella's pain would wash away from her and our family, and if maybe there was a chance we could be clean and free like those chickens someday.

"Interesting perspective, Mr. Manon. Anyone else?"

"Maybe it is what it is. A wheelbarrow and chickens, like the man wrote. Why does everything have to be read into?" Grady chomped on his gum a little too loud, then winked at Nikki across the room. Nikki turned about the same shade as I imagined that red wheelbarrow.

"Thank you, Grady. Let's move on."

We spent the rest of the class talking about meter and rhyme and didn't get into the meaning of much else. But Mrs. Nowlan did give us time to write our own versions of "The Red Wheelbarrow" using the same stress and pattern as Williams. I wrote mine for Comfort:

so much depends

upon

a patch of

asters

pushing through

kudzu

beneath the oak's

shadow

"Where did that brilliance come from, Manon?" Grady punched him in the arm like he chewed his gum—a little too hard—once the bell'd rung, and we'd all shouldered our way into the hall.

"Lay off, Grady." Jed kept close to my right side.

"No, really, Manon. You're some kind of geeeee-nius."

"Whatever."

Grady yanked on Jed's shoulder, causing him to drop his books. "Don't walk away from me when I'm talking to you."

Jed sighed. "What'dya want, Grady? Wanna pick on me because it'll make you feel bigger? Better? Stronger? Because it'll impress Nikki over there?"

Nikki pulled her locker door open and peered out from behind it.

"Jed, leave it be." I'd seen Grady pick fights before, and they never ended pretty.

"You're not welcome here, Manon. You're trash. Foster trash. And we don't like trash filling our halls like dirty rats. You need to go back to your trailer and find a new place to live. That's all."

"Why don't you shut up, Grady?" My voice sounded like I was a squeaky, scared little mouse.

"And you, trash lover." He stuck a finger in my shoulder. "You make it worse. Bringing him to the dance and ruining it for all of us. Good thing someone in your family set you straight."

Before I could say anything, Jed's fist came flying at his face.

Grady was on the floor with his hands over his nose, full of blood.

Mrs. Nowlan ran out of the room. "What's going on here? Oh, my goodness, someone get Mr. Morrison—get anyone—quick!"

Lè w'ap neye, ou kenbe branch ou jwenn.
"When you are drowning, you hang on to the branch you reach."

CHAPTER 27

Anniston

It was a well-known fact that Grady Bingham regularly beat up new kids, so Mr. Morrison suspended Grady. Since it was Jed's first offense, Mr. Morrison sent him home, along with me, so we could "blow off steam." Mama drove us since Mrs. Devine was the only attendant that day at the Tom Thumb gas station where she worked.

"He was only sticking up for me, Mama," I said as we piled into her car.

"I know, honey. I'm not mad."

"You're not?"

"The way I see it, more folks need to be stood up for around here. Look at it this way, you get half the day off for your birthday." She grinned at us from the rearview mirror.

"Then would you care if we hung out a little while?" I asked. Jed mentioned studying at the library for the rest of his now-long afternoon.

"What'd you two have in mind?"

"You could drop us at the library, ma'am."

"Well, Mr. Morrison might not approve. But sure. I'll have Ernestine pick you up in a couple hours. We've got cake and your favorite dinner for you to get home to tonight. Sound good?"

"Thanks, Mama."

"Thank you, Mrs. Harlan, ma'am."

We waited on the library steps until Mama drove away, but Jed grabbed my arm when I started for the doors.

"Wait. There's something I want to show you."

"But I told Mama—"

"Won't take long. We'll come back here and study in plenty of time for Ernestine. C'mon." He bounded down the steps and rounded the corner, and good night if he wasn't taking me to the trailer park.

The trailer park wasn't big. Only a dozen or so trailers, most of 'em set up on concrete blocks. Some folks kept theirs up real nice with flower beds and oyster-shell paths trimmed neat and gingham curtains fluttering in the breeze. The number forty-eight was stuck to the front door of what I knew to be Jed's trailer from the same butterscotch-yellow-and-white truck parked there that Mrs. Devine took me home in after the cotillion. Rust stains ran down the faded white door from the screws holding the numbers in place. Jed's foster parents didn't keep their trailer up as nice and wasn't a flower bed in sight, but maybe gardening wasn't their gifting.

"Are they home?"

"Nah. Wouldn't bring you here if they were. Hettie's workin', and John's down in New Orleans gambling. They saved up all my money for him to go."

"What are we doing here, then?" I wasn't so sure Mama'd approve of me being alone in a house with a boy. Even Jed.

"Getting my smokes, for one thing." The outside door creaked and rattled like it might fall off when he opened it, and the inside one didn't sound much better. Smelled sour inside, like food left out too long and smoke and dirty socks all mixed up together. Hardly any light shone through the dingy curtains, which were shut tight and didn't look like they were opened much, if ever. I rubbed my arms, feeling all of a sudden wary of the place.

"I'll stay out here." I sat on the vinyl couch, covered in a horrid flower pattern, attached to the wall by the kitchen.

"Suit yourself. I'll be right back." He disappeared into a room at the end of the trailer, which must've been his bedroom, 'cause he came back with a fishbowl. White fish, almost see-through, flittered around the water, pausing to nibble at each other or the pebbles at the bottom. "Wanted to show you these as long as you're here."

"What are they?"

"Blind cave fish. Found 'em up north in Key Cave. They got blind cave crayfish and endangered gray bats up there too. They don't need eyes, so they don't have eyes. Or maybe God made 'em that way from the start."

"Why are they clear like that?"

"Don't need the sort of skin and scales that protect 'em from light. Critters like them are called stygobites. They can't live outside of caves, which is why I keep 'em in the back of my closet where it's dark all the time."

"What are we called, then?"

"Humans." He laughed and gently poked my nose with his finger. "There are some animals, like spiders and salamanders, that can live in and out of caves both. They're called stygophiles."

"How'd you learn all this stuff?"

"On my own. At the library. Same as with my rocks."

From the direction of his room, a bird started chirping, then singing, really singing. Prettiest bird song I ever heard. "Is that the canary? The one we found that day?"

"Yep. Feeling better, ain't he?" Jed took the fish back to his room and brought the canary out in a small cage. Newspapers were spread across the bottom. Little swings and rings and ropes swayed across the middle for the bird to play on.

"How'd you know it's a he?"

"Wasn't sure at first. Then, after he ate enough and got to feeling better, he sang. Only boy canaries sing."

He put the bird back in his room and came back, a pack of cigarettes tucked in the rolled-up sleeve of his T-shirt. He ushered me out the door and winked at me as he lit one up. "Now let's go to the library."

I found a couple of novels to read, and by the time I came back to our table, Jed was back with a stack of his own on animals, geology, and such.

"It's not fair, the way you have to live, no mama or daddy and giving all your money to those folks."

"It's not all bad. They don't even notice my animals." He kicked his feet up on the table and dug into one of his books.

It occurred to me then that maybe he wasn't so unlucky. He'd learned how to be happy where he was, like a salamander, half in this world and half in a world of his own. Maybe someday I could learn to do the same.

The windows were open wide when Ernestine and I got home. As I grabbed a co-cola from the fridge, I heard singing outside the doors that led from the kitchen to the rose garden and the edges of the hills beyond, which were full of pecan trees tinged with the green of early summer leaves. Quiet, so she wouldn't see me, I listened to Princella as she pruned back her roses.

> I want some red roses for a blue lady.
> Mister Florist, take my order please.
> We had a silly quarrel the other day.
> I hope these pretty flowers chase her blues away.
> Wrap up some red roses for a blue lady,
> send them to the sweetest gal in town,
> and if they do the trick, I'll hurry back to pick
> your best white orchid for her wedding gown.

Weddings.

Comfort and Solly should've been planning theirs, but no one mentioned whether or not it was happening since Daddy died.

Did that cross Princella's mind as she sang?

I watched her a little while longer. She handled each branch like an infant, tender and almost breakable between her gloved fingers. Maybe she worked slow and careful to avoid the thorns. She wiped her face with her arm, then she sniffed, which is when I noticed a couple of tears splat onto the patio.

Could she really be crying?

I left the kitchen so she wouldn't see me spying on her.

"Anniston? Can I see you a moment?"

Vaughn's voice echoed through the front hall, and I jumped a half a mile, not knowing he was in his study as I walked by. "Yes, sir?"

"You're home early."

"A little."

"Your mama told me what happened."

"He's a good friend—"

"I'm not talking about Jed. I know he is. Come sit by me a minute, will you?" He motioned to me to come to the leather couch, where he sat holding a framed, black-and-white photograph. The scent of pipe tobacco and old books made the room feel strong and safe.

He handed me the frame. "Recognize these people at all?"

At first, I thought the Alabama Southern football player was Cole and the woman on his arm was familiar, but I couldn't place her for sure. And the photo looked too old and gray to be that recent.

"That's me and your grandmother."

I looked closer at the unlined, clean-shaven, boyish face of Vaughn. Looked a lot like Daddy, actually. Then I looked closer at Princella. Decked out in her Alabama Southern cheerleader uniform, she was smiling from ear to ear, like she really had something to smile about. I never saw her as happy as she was in that picture.

"She was the sweetheart of the team. I was crazy about her. We all were. She was the life of the party. Charming. Gorgeous. But she fell for the guy who snapped this photo. Cole's biological father."

Cole's father. The one who dumped her when he found out she was carrying Cole. No wonder she was smiling. She was smiling at the man she loved behind the camera. I suddenly felt very sorry for Vaughn. He must hurt, too, knowing she didn't smile at him that way. Knowing she lost the part of the only man she truly loved when Cole died. Raising Cole and losing both him and Daddy.

"I love her still, you know."

I didn't know how he could.

"Anniston, what she did to you is wrong. The way she raised her children, that was wrong too. But deep inside, she's got a good heart. See, sometimes the parts of a person most broken are the hardest parts for them to forgive in themselves and in others. Their hate of themselves comes out as a hate of everyone around them, even the ones they should love most. They'll never change until they look their hurt in the face and take it on."

I thought for a moment, sifting through what he said. I thought about Daddy and Comfort, being raised like outcasts in their own home. I thought about the Freedom Riders on the flaming bus. I thought about Jed punching Grady because he hurt me. How poetry and words should be real and red and true. And I thought about Princella out there crying in the middle of her rose garden.

"How's she supposed to look hurt in the face if no one hands her a mirror?" I gave the frame back to him and took my schoolbooks and my big white dog up to Comfort's old room.

"Happy birthday, Anni!" Mama set the caramel cake in front of me, candles lit, waiting for me to make a wish. But wishes wouldn't come to mind.

Finally, when the candles dripped wax onto the icing, I squeezed my eyes shut, still saw nothing to wish for, and blew them out anyway. I suppose I coulda wished for my daddy back. Or for a way to move away from Princella. But this was my place in the world, and no wishing would get me out of it.

Princella sat across the table, and pushed a long, thin box toward me. "I know we haven't been on the best terms, Anniston. But I do wish you well."

I glanced at Mama, who acknowledged I should go ahead and open it. Under the paper was a black velvet box, the first velvet box I'd ever received. I felt almost embarrassed by what I knew to be a generous gift even before opening the lid, especially after all that had happened between us. When I did open the lid, I was shocked.

"Every girl needs a strand of real pearls. And you're more than old enough to have your own."

"Thank you, Princella, ma'am." When our eyes met, I saw a tenderness I was unaccustomed to, maybe even love. Or maybe an apology wrapped in money. Either way, I couldn't help but be grateful.

"You're welcome."

"*Kè kontan anivèsè nesans*, child." Ernestine, sitting next to me, patted my hand and set a small box in front of me.

I pulled the brown paper off, to reveal a stack of colored blocks.

"Pull up the top one. Try it."

I did, and the whole stack of blocks swung down, all of them held together by colored ribbons. I turned the top block over, and the same thing happened. Each time I turned it, the blocks flipped and fell into a new line, like an unending puzzle.

"Have you seen one, child?"

"No, I can't say that I have. What is it? It's super cool."

"They call it 'Jacob's Ladder.'" It's just a toy. Something small. But I thought maybe it'd be something that helps bring you hope."

"It will, Ernestine. I know it will."

"I have something for you too, darlin'." Vaughn, who'd stepped out for a moment, came back carrying a weathered guitar case. "Not much to look at, but maybe somethin' you can use."

"Oh, Vaughn." Mama put her fingers over her mouth and teared up.

"This here acoustic guitar was your Daddy's. His first one. I got the strings replaced for you, and tuned 'er up, so if you'd like to start playing, why then it's all fixed for you."

"Thank you, sir. This really means a lot."

Mama piled the gifts on big time after that: summer clothes galore, books, and my own set of nail paint and makeup.

And when the evening was over, as I was lying in Comfort's old bed, next to Daddy's old room, I thought of a wish.

I wished this was how it always was at our house.

Lespwa fè viv.
"*Hope makes one live.*"

CHAPTER 28

Comfort

Daddy brought me along for grafting every spring I could remember—like Rey brought Anni—to search for the best branches from trees producing the best tasting, strongest pecans. While the sky shines aquamarine, I help Daddy and Solly, Anni, Jed, and the other workers harvest the scions. I imagine the raw cut ends of the spring scions feel like I do, stinging from unwanted vulnerability. It's progress, I suppose.

Out in the orchards, surrounded by the familiar work that creates stronger, better trees, I feel. Here in the rows with my loppers and my grafting knife, I take, instead of being taken from. Shame and pain subside as I sever branch after branch after branch. Maybe I'm letting out vengeance. Maybe my fear is turning into rage as I force the arms of the pruners together, slicing through another green, inviolable branch. I wrap the raw end of the scion with damp paper towels and plastic wrap so the ends don't dry before they're grafted and the pruning isn't in vain.

When we've gathered all we need, we take the scions, Daddy and I, to the rows of rootstock, where Solly, Jed, and Anni have already begun the second part of the process, called the "four-flap" or "banana graft." Solly takes a sharp knife and makes an X across the raw end of a lopped-off branch, about the same thickness as the scions.

Seagulls from the bay cry overhead, prairie warblers from the brush, Louisiana water thrush from down near the creek, and the awkward imitations of mockingbirds echo, all of them unaware or uncaring as we move among the rows. Rootstock grows like crazy this time of year, having soaked in the nutrients of the rainy season and the rays of the spring sun. The bark slips off easily, giving itself over to the annual opus of our hands.

Anni and Jed come behind Solly and peel four sides of bark back until about four inches of the chartreuse insides of the branch are exposed and cut back. Then we put a rubber band around the four flaps until the scion is ready to tuck inside.

With another sharp knife, Daddy whittles the bottom few inches of four sides of the scion, leaving slivers of bark along each corner. He tucks the new, bare, chartreuse stem inside the arms of the root-stock branch and wraps it with green tie tape and Parafilm. There, it rests for the summer and begins growing only after wintering and coupling with the arms of its surrogate.

The others move farther down the row of rootstock, and Solly and I work together. I turn to grab another scion from the aluminum bucket on the stocky wooden ladder.

Solly nuzzles the back of my neck with his lips.

I jerk and recoil.

The bucket dumps and clatters to the ground.

"Comfort, it's me. It's just me." I see the tears collecting in his eyes as he holds his arms out wide like the flaps of the grafts waiting to embrace the tender scion shoots.

I step toward him, my arms heavy with wraiths of emotion, but I do not reach for him. Instead, I unwrap the fragile end of the scion, whittle four sides of bark away, and place it in his gloved, outstretched hand.

Chen an ki yelps pa mòde.
"The dog that yelps does not bite."

CHAPTER 29

Anniston

Daddy always said pecan trees don't like wet feet, which explains why the ones on the tops of rolling hills grow taller and wider than others. Trees struggle in the low places, roots soaked and withering in water from all the spring rain setting stagnant in the silt and clay. Low or high, the orchards welcomed Jed and me as sure as the hot summer that greeted us at the end of the school year. I'd taken a summer job working the counter at the Curly Q on Saturdays when they needed extra help, and when I wasn't there, I helped Jed in the orchards, which is how we made up for not seeing each other in school.

Mowing and trimming around the acres of trees was our primary job, and Jed loved driving the mowers. Aside from that, we helped fertilize trees—especially the younger ones—sprayed for bugs, and emptied and reset squirrel traps.

Depending on the time of year, Vaughn ordered zinc and lime to provide extra nourishment for the trees. Mostly he relied on nature to give the trees what they needed. Decades ago, the Harlans covered the ground of the orchards with what Daddy called "helpful and nutritious weeds" like crimson clover, which made the rows look like they were dressed in a red carpet. They planted arrowleaf, too, tiny bunches of yellow flowers that look awfully pretty when a boy like Jed hands them to you on a summer morning when the dew is still thick and glistening white on the hillsides.

He handed a bunch to me, tied with a string of burlap, on the same morning I brought him a slice of peach-pecan pie to celebrate what I knew to be the occasion of his birthday. Mrs. Nowlan put all the summer birthdays on her bulletin board the last week of school so they wouldn't be forgotten.

"What are these for?" I took the bunch from his hand and considered how pretty weeds could be depending on the intent of the person giving them.

"You."

"Wait, I have something too." I handed him the paper bag. "Best not wait to see what's in there."

"Mmmmmm. And what's this for?" He stuck a finger's worth of pie in his mouth and grinned. Crumbs from the crunchy, brown sugar topping stuck to his chin.

"It's your birthday, ain't it?"

His smile faded, and a knot filled my belly. Had I done too much? It was only a piece of pie. And I hadn't even made it. Ernestine did.

"I s'pose it is. Thank you." He rolled the bag back up and pulled out a pack of cigarettes. When he lit one, the smoke twirled in the air above his head. "What do you say we head outta here for a while? I got a good piece of mowing done. Been out here since before seven."

"Sure, then. You shouldn't have to work too hard on your birthday anyway."

He led me to the creek, near where I'd met him that first day, and we roamed the muddy places looking for fossils. The knot tightened inside me since he pretty much quit talking since I brought up his birthday. I couldn't stand it any longer.

"I'm sorry."

"For what?" He stopped where he was, ankle deep in the middle of the creek.

"For bringing you pie."

He tossed his spent cigarette in the weeds, bent down, and poked around in the water some more. "Aw, Anni, it wasn't the pie."

"Then what?"

"I'm sixteen today."

"Sixteen! Well, are you having a party? Are the Devines having one for ya?"

"Shoot, no. Old man John wouldn't let Hettie have a party for herself, let alone me. Drunk as a skunk most of the time and asleep with 'Do Not Disturb' across his forehead the rest."

"I sure am sorry about that. Everybody should have a party when they're sixteen."

He threw a fist-size rock into the creek so hard it scared me and every living creature within one hundred yards. "Aw, the heck with it."

He took off running down the creek, mumbling words I figured I'd rather not hear. He ran so fast I couldn't keep up. And before I knew it, the world was silent. Only thing moving was the old swing Comfort used to swing me on when I was little. Now the rope hung limp, frayed, and lonely.

Surely he'd come back.

The silence, except for the trickling of the creek around my feet, reminded me of Shelley Cartright, who drowned in Mobile Bay a couple of years ago. A third grader at the time, Shelley and her family'd been swimming and searching for sand dollars off Dauphin Island, and while no one watched, an undertow swept her out to sea. By the time they realized it, Shelley floated facedown in the water, dead. The trauma of it near wrecked her mama and daddy, who blamed themselves. Now when I see Mrs. Cartright at the Piggly Wiggly, she carries a sadness about her and looks at me and other children like she can't bear to see us living when her own girl is cold and still and buried under the dirt.

We'd attended Shelley's funeral, because they were members of our church. The crying was like garbled moans of warbler flocks settling in our orchards each spring. Like those broods of birds, all black and huddled in tight groups, the mourners shivered and hunkered toward each other, trying to keep in whatever heat or hope was left in them. There weren't enough tissues to soak up the tears. The whole church smelled like lilies, and to this day I can't stand that sweet, honey-thick smell. Those darn lilies smelled up the whole church at my grandma's funeral, too, on Mama's side, back in Anniston, Alabama, a few years back. Too much lily made me woozy, like eating too much chocolate at Easter.

There was no way Jed could drown in this silly old creek, but the thought stuck and scared me, with his crooked walk. What if he slipped and broke something? I decided then to head down the creek toward town in case he needed help.

"Jed? Jeee-eee-d?"

A seagull called, lonely and wild and far, far away.

My lungs tightened in the silent, unmoving air.

"Disgusting!" I jumped back as a fat black mud snake slithered into the creek right in front of me. The scent of moss and mold and green stuff floated on the edges of the creek and coated my throat all thick and wet.

"Anni! You'll never believe what I found." As fast as Jed disappeared, he was back—as soaking wet and happy as Molly after a day of swimming in the pond—splashing down the middle of the creek toward me. His legs flailed from side to side as he ran, pushing through the muck of the mud and water.

I fell flat on my hiney, Jed scared me so bad, as worked up about that snake and the possibility of him lying hurt somewhere as I was.

"What is it?" I said, using a sapling to pull myself up, and annoyed with the cold globs of mud soaking through to my backside.

"Look what I found." He huffed and puffed from his running. "It's a super-rare brooksella. I mean, brooksella themselves aren't really rare. They're from the Cambrian age, and they're all over Alabama. But this one—there's two of 'em, stuck together. It's a *double* brooksella. I've never seen one like this. Not ever. You keep it, Anni. It's a great one to start your collection."

"You sure?"

"Positive."

Most of the fossils he showed me looked like plain old rocks, and I looked them over real close to see the fossil embedded in the bumps and crannies. But he wasn't kidding—this was something to behold. Etched across the top, like an ancient message, were two raised stars, each the size of a silver dollar, arms joined and clinging to each other and spread out like they were smiling and happy to meet us.

My fascination disappeared when I saw widening spots of red on his drenched, white T-shirt. "Jed, you're bleeding!"

He looked at me like a puppy begging not to be punished.

"What are those?"

"I—I, uh—I ran into some high weeds and brush down the creek."

I stepped closer to him, and he stepped back. "You sure about that?"

He turned from me for the second time that morning, saying nothing.

"Jed, you can tell me."

"You don't want to know."

"Yes, I do. I'm your friend!"

"No. You don't need to know about such things."

"Are you kidding me? My uncle shot my daddy to death in front of my own eyes. And my aunt is on the verge of withering away to nothing because that same uncle raped her. What do you think I can't handle?"

He pulled his shirt over his head, the muscles in his back and shoulders tensed and wiry.

Then he turned around.

Bloody red spots, all the same size, and a bunch of others scabbed or healed over, covered his chest. "This is why there won't be no party for me. Never has been. Never will be."

"Are those—are they from cigarettes?"

"What else? In the middle of the night when John thinks I'm sleeping ..." A single, fat tear, full of so much pain I thought it might explode, splashed into the creek. Tears always fell fatter for someone hurt like that. "He gets his jollies off of surprising me, off the screaming or something. If I don't bring back enough money from my job, he burns me. If he finds out I keep some for myself, he burns me some more. Handle *that*." He walked back toward the orchards.

"Jed, stop. You can't stay there. You can't go back. We've got to tell someone. I'll tell Solly. Or Mama. They can help. Maybe you can come and live with us."

"Anni." He turned back toward me and set his hand on my shoulder. The knot inside me ignited into something hot and sweet. "Look, you're real nice and all, but maybe we shouldn't be friends. Shouldn't have ever been friends. Back at the dance, your grandmother was right. I ain't good enough for you."

"She's wrong! That's not true!"

"It is." He climbed up on the mower.

"But—wait, I made you this." I pulled the string out of my pocket and handed it to him. "It's a friendship bracelet. For your birthday. I made one like it for me. See?" I held my wrist up toward him. "Blue for the bay, green for the orchards, and yellow for the sun."

The hard line of his jaw relaxed some as he took the bracelet from me. But it hardened up again real quick. "Go home, Anni. Go back to work at the salon. And don't think about me anymore."

I bawled, right then and there, as he drove away from me on that mower. I couldn't help it. And I didn't care if he saw. The tears came and came, harder than at Daddy's funeral. Maybe because of Daddy's funeral. Maybe the losing felt near the same.

"Wait!" I cried. "Wait!" I hollered again.

But the mower kept moving farther and farther away, cutting everything down to the silty, red dirt.

And I sank to my knees into the crimson clover.

Le lapli a ap rive, wawaron nan chante.
"When the rain is coming, the bullfrog sings."

CHAPTER 30

Anniston

Over a week passed with no sight of Jed. Not even when I walked Molly through the orchards. I tried to fill the empty places burning up inside me with extra work at the Curly Q, and on this particular afternoon, I was surprised, after bending down to tie my shoes, to see Mandy Appleton across the counter from me. Not that it was strange to see her at the Curly Q. But I hadn't even heard the gold jingle bells ring when she came in the salon.

"Hi, Mandy. Do you have an appointment?"

"Yes. Hi. Sandra should be expecting me." Mandy had no clue what my name was, let alone that my grandmother wanted me to be exactly like her.

Sandra, finishing up on a highlight, hollered from halfway down the row of chairs. "Hey, Mandy! A few more minutes, and I'll be ready to do you up right, girl!"

Mandy smiled, then studied her nails and popped her gum several times on the way to taking a seat in the high-back, overstuffed, pink-velvet chair in the waiting area. She bypassed the June issue of *Seventeen* for the May issue, which featured Diane Lane and a story on summer romances. Figured.

"Are you ready for the pageant, Mandy?" Tiffany Allen, the second nail artist, asked as Comfort glanced up from working on Gerty Matthews's eighty-three-year-old nails.

Mandy peered over the top of the magazine. "With Sandra's help I will be."

"How could the judges not pick you again this year? You've got everything Bay Spring could ask for in a county fair queen. Looks. Smarts."

"My acceptance letter arrived from Mississippi State this week. I'll be studying English literature."

Whoop-dee-do. You and every other debutante.

I focused on rearranging the nail polish in the glass case from lightest to darkest and polished the glass for the fourth time that morning. What happened between me and Jed burned inside, and sitting still made it worse.

The golden bells jingled, and in walked Lorraine Doyle, one of Cole's old girlfriends who he'd probably dated the longest of anyone.

"Can I help you, ma'am?"

"I need my nails done. They're way past due."

"Comfort's about to finish up with Mrs. Matthews. Ain't that right?"

"Be about ten minutes," Comfort said.

Lorraine cleared her throat. "How long for Tiffany?"

I shivered, though half the air-conditioning had left the salon when Lorraine walked in. "Um, well, Tiffany just got started."

"I'll wait." She spun around on her heel and sat next to Mandy on a pink, leopard-print painted ladder-back chair. She chose the June *Vogue* with Kim Alexis on the front. She tried to be sneaky about it, hiding behind that magazine, but I watched as she stared at Comfort.

Gerty Matthews hobbled over to the counter, leaning on her cane as if it kept her alive. "Thank you, honey." She patted ten extra dollars into the palm of my hand. "See that Comfort gets this tip, hear?"

"Sure thing, Mrs. Matthews, ma'am." I wondered why I couldn't have had more of a storybook granny like Mrs. Matthews. I bet she made actual Toll House chocolate chip cookies and talked kindly to her grandbabies, sitting with them for hours working puzzles and loving them no matter what their hair looked like.

Lorraine still stared—even sneered now—at Comfort.

"Take a picture. It lasts longer." I covered my mouth with my hand as soon as I said it, not believing myself. But I couldn't help it. All the sad and mad and unfairness of Jed, added to the way this lady treated Comfort for what she thought she knew happened way back last Thanksgiving, mixed all up and came spilling out.

"What did you say, young lady?" Lorraine directed her sneer at me.

"If you don't mind, ma'am, please quit staring at Comfort."

"What business is it of yours who I look at? And how dare you talk to an elder that way."

Qarla walked to the front of the store as Comfort bowed her head with shame. "What's going on up here, ladies? Anniston, do you need some help?"

"Anniston?" Lorraine snickered. "Oh, I see. Anniston *Harlan*, right?"

"Yes, ma'am." I pressed myself as far as I could into the back of the swiveling counter chair.

"Is there a problem, Ms. Doyle? Comfort can do your nails now, if you're not wanting to wait."

I wished Qarla wouldn't have asked.

"I won't have that whore touching my hands."

"Excuse me?" Qarla took a step forward.

"You heard me." Lorraine set the magazine on her lap.

"And I'll not have that kind of talk in my shop."

"Are you asking me to leave?"

"You heard me."

"You, lady, just lost yourself a client."

Lorraine flew out of the salon, taking the magazine with her.

"Have a good day, Ms. Doyle!" Qarla called after her.

Mandy set her magazine down by this time, too, and I was surprised to see she looked as stunned and sorry for Comfort as anyone.

"I'm sorry, darlin'." Qarla went around the nail table and put her arms around Comfort, who raised her eyes toward me. They overflowed with tears.

"I've got to go. I'm sorry."

"Stay, honey. Qarla's got your back."

"Me, too," said Tiffany.

"Me, too," said Sandra, who'd come up to the front to call Mandy back to the chair.

Mandy got up and walked over to Comfort's table, and I braced myself for what she might say. "Miss Comfort?"

"Yes?" Comfort said through a wad of tissues.

"May I say—well—this might not be the right time to tell you this, but—well—I've always thought you were the most beautiful woman in Bay Spring. I mean, the whole reason I do pageants and all that is because I've always wanted to be the next Bay Spring sweetheart, like you."

Comfort packed her purse, stood, and put a hand on Mandy's arm. "You don't want to be me, darlin'. Trust me. I'm the last person you'd ever want to be."

Qarla and I began to clean up for the afternoon after Comfort left.

"Shoot. Comfort left her Bible," Qarla said. "Never comes here without it these days."

"I can drop it off when Mama takes me home."

Clouds hung low as I walked toward Comfort's house late that evening. Bullfrogs sang in a crescendo, like the plucking of guitar strings. First one lingering hum, then another one, then another, until a whole chorus of the brainless amphibians sang in harmony.

Too bad humans don't listen to each other so close.

Must be the frogs' survival depended on listening to each other.

Solly's truck sat parked in front of Comfort's house, and I cut through her side yard past the open living room window. Lace curtains curled back and forth.

"—listen to me. You've got to stop doing this to yourself." Solly's voice, usually calm and soft, was insistent, almost raised.

"And what exactly am I doing that needs to stop? That I *can* stop? Can you tell me that?"

Solly paced past the window, and I quick hunched down and walked catawampus toward the house and crouched under the window so I could hear. I knew eavesdropping was wrong, but I couldn't help myself.

"Comfort, you can be well. You deserve to be well. These past few weeks, I've seen you start to live again, and I'm so grateful, but there's still a part of you that's unreachable. As long as that part of you stays hidden and locked up, he still hurts you even from his grave. I've respected your need for solitude for months now, but since I've seen you can be better, I can't stand to see the hand of fear still holding you by the throat, threatening to suck you back in. I lost you once, and I'm not about to lose you again. We can still have a life together—"

"Stop right there. Don't—don't say that."

"Why not? Tell me, why not? Give me one good reason. I'm not him, Comfort. I'm not Cole. I'd never, ever hurt you."

"I know you're not, Solly, and that's why I can't be with you."

I heard her cross the floor toward the window I was crouched under, and I tried to tuck myself in closer to the foundation of the house so she wouldn't see me.

"You're not making any sense, Comfort. You're none of those things! You're beautiful. You're—"

"Stop, Solly, stop. I'm not—"

I heard him walk closer to Comfort.

"Stop. Don't touch me, Solly …" Comfort's voice cracked. No amount of harmony in the world could've covered the sharps and flats of her tone.

"Shhhh, darlin'. It's okay. It's okay." Solly spoke to her like a daddy singing a lullaby—like Daddy sang to me—and I felt tears puddle on my eyelids. "Comfort, look at me. Hon, look at me … He might've wrecked you for a while, but he didn't destroy you, the you God made in His image. Maybe the mirror you're facing is cracked, and you can't see the truth of you past the messed-up, skewed, and crooked shards of glass. But you're still there, Comfort. You are. He mighta stolen an awful lot, but he didn't kill you."

I'd heard more than I could stand. Tears trickled down my face as I got up, tiptoed to the front porch, and set Comfort's Bible on one of her rocking chairs. As I did, a tattered bookmark fell out with a picture of a horse running across a pasture on it and the poem, "If you love something, set it free. If it comes back to you, it's yours. If it doesn't, it was never meant to be."

I tiptoed off the porch and crouched low until I reached the driveway. As I walked, the clicking songs of the crickets whispered all around me and a moth, white and gleaming in the moonlight, darted back and forth in front of me.

I remembered what Ernestine always said: *"Yon papiyon blan pote bon nouvèl."*—A white butterfly brings good news.

Lord, I need some good news. We all do.

But it seemed the days of good news were gone forever.

Yon chat boule nèt juèt pou boule nan dife.
"A burnt cat dreads the fire."

CHAPTER 31

Comfort

scattered and chafed
by wind
blown days
forgotten
swaying softly gently
by ominous
pain

*

thunderhead horizons
a striped scarf holding

in chaos
summoning
confusion desperate
separations
of
hope
Who can
after all distinguish
the storm from the raging sea

It's the evening after Solly and I fight, and I set my pen in the scratched-up Ball jar with half a dozen others and watch the sky grow leaden outside my window.

Bruise-colored storms roil on the horizon, and I can't get it out of my head that Mandy Appleton thinks she wants to be like me. Before anything happened with Lorraine Doyle, I watched Mandy devour page after page of tanned, twiggy bodies and stories about getting and keeping boyfriends in the magazine, as if she could not and would not compare to anyone on those pages. Funny thing is, if she really knew those girls, she probably wouldn't want to be like them, either.

Folks—and not only folks around these parts—have in their minds the dirt-encrusted, tin-roof-covered, handout-seeking crop pickers when they think about who does things like Cole did to me. Worse, they think folks like me who get that sort of abuse either did something to deserve it—or they treat 'em like they did.

Homecoming queens have it easy, folks think. *The darlin' of the football team has a free ride to everything good and beautiful and popular and perfect.*

If Mandy only knew.

Lorraine had a right to treat me the way she did. I probably did do something to deserve night after night under the weight of my big brother's breathy steals of innocence. Maybe I wore the wrong sort of sundresses as a toddler. Maybe if I'd had brown or red hair instead of blonde. Maybe if I hadn't been in tumbling. Or gymnastics. Or cheerleading. Or dancing. Maybe if I'd have been nothing.

Maybe if I'd never been born.

That last thought crosses my mind, and I soak it in like a truffle, the sweet shell of truth melting into a paroxysmal ecstasy of yes.

This is what I've been searching for. Death will set me free.

I try to push the thought away. Taking my own life, that would be as wrong as Cole taking Rey's, wouldn't it?

But then, maybe it would be a gift. A gift to my mother, certainly. A gift to Solly—sweet, stubborn Solly, who refuses to leave me for someone new. A gift to this whole rotten town. Leaving the aftermath of this life would be like Hurricane Frederic fleeing the coast last fall. Sure, it was hard on everyone at first. But now, survivors are starting over. Broken homes are being rebuilt. Communities have a chance to make things new.

I search my medicine cabinets for leftover prescriptions. Sleeping pills. Pain relievers. Anything I can mix to keep from facing another day. Anything to keep another sunrise—yellow, then pink, then blazing red—from searing my soul.

Death twists the last trickles of hope out of me, like Ernestine wringing the sudsy water out of a sponge. Near dancing inside with the chance to end this pain, I pour bottle after bottle of pills into one big, plastic bag. A box of razor blades catches my eye, and for a moment, I consider using them instead. Might be easier with a razor, pain floating along with the blood right outta me. Death holds me in its strong, icy arms, and I feel weightless at last. Abba tries to break in, asking to have His dance with me back, but the broad shoulders and chiseled jawbones of doom woo me. Twirl me. Make me feel like a princess—

"Comfort?"

Go away. The eyes of my new lover hold me, and I am glad to let him.

"Comfort, are you home?"

The phantasmal suitor evaporates as the knocking keeps on at my front door. I stuff the bag of pills, empty bottles, and the box of razors into my pillowcase and shove it all under my bed.

Another day, Abba. Let Death take me home, please, another day, soon.

Le yo vle touye yon chen, yo di li nan fou.
"When they want to kill a dog, they say it's crazy."

CHAPTER 32

Anniston

"Hope this pizza tastes good to her. She needs something to cheer her up after that nonsense at the salon yesterday," Mama said.

Ernestine wiped the sweat off her brow. Over eighty degrees still, even at almost eight o'clock.

"Pizza. *Barbara Mandrell and the Mandrell Sisters* and *The Love Boat*. Saturday night like old times." I needed something to cheer me up too.

Rap-rap-rap.

No response.

"I told her we were coming. And her car's here." Ernestine fished for Comfort's house key in her giant pockets and inserted it in the lock. "Comfort? It's us. You in there, child?"

Rap-rap-rap.

Through the transom, a shadow shifted and light moved. Ernestine turned the knob and cracked the door open a few inches.

"Sorry about that. Come on in." Comfort's face was all red and splotchy, like she'd been crying.

"Mushroom, green pepper, and onion. Your favorite," I said, making my way toward her kitchen with the pizza. The front hall was bright, and a chipped white table, topped with an old lamp shaded with white lace, greeted us. A painting of magnolias bursting out of a basket hung above the fireplace in the front room. Ivory paint covered the walls of every room. Yet despite the brightness, the place smelled empty. Not bad, just musty and unmoving, like a store full of antiques no one had visited or mulled over for a long, long while.

Small, white hexagon tiles covered the kitchen floor, blanketed with red-and-white-checkered rugs. Comfort pulled four pale-blue glass jars out of the cupboard, plunked some ice in them, and poured sweet tea until the ice rose and danced near the top of the glass. As we sipped on our sweet tea, quiet settled among us like the morning fog that hangs between night and a new day. Comfort's hair, like the sun shining on straw, flowed over her shoulders, and a band of freckles covered her cheeks. Her green eyes, though deep and welcoming like a lake in summer, skirted around us like a cat unused to strangers.

"Thank you." Comfort took a deep breath and focused on a spot on the floor. "For what you're trying to do here. Thank you."

We settled in for pizza and *Barbara Mandrell*, laughing at the comedy sketches—and the rest of our nutty little town.

"Let's watch the stars. Want to?" Ernestine suggested before *The Love Boat* aired. "Those old rockers don't get enough use. And it's such a nice evening."

"Well …" Comfort hesitated. "Okay. Yes, that would be nice."

"Y'all head on out there. I'll cook up a pot of popcorn and bring it right out. Got some bacon grease in here, child?"

"In the door of the fridge there. Thanks, Ernestine."

Comfort grabbed the crocheted shawl from the armchair, and each of us curled up in one of the big wooden rockers rough from peeling periwinkle paint, the same color as the window boxes.

Night turned the whole world velvet. Stars shone brighter. Moonlight bathed our sunburned skin. We rocked and pointed out the few constellations we could remember: Cassiopeia and her upside-down (at least this time of the year) husband, Cepheus; the Big Dipper; the Little Dipper; and Draco. The moon, like a sliver of fingernail, smiled at our efforts to squint out these and the planets like Saturn and Jupiter. I knew one of the big spots on the moon was called the Sea of Tranquility, which is near where the Apollo 11 astronauts landed on the moon. I wondered if our family craziness disappeared if someone were to look down on us from way up there. I imagined myself walking on the silvery surface, and the greatness of space hugging my weary spirit. For the first time since Daddy died, I felt some order around me.

A deep-rumbling car with one burned-out headlight slowed on the road that ran in front of Comfort's house.

"Comfort! Hey, Comfort! That you?" an unfamiliar, deep voice hollered from the driver's-side window. The car stopped and idled. In the distance, another pair of lights headed toward us.

"Who's there?" Mama hollered back.

"Wasn't talking to you, lady. I said is that Comfort Harlan?" The driver, who appeared to be close to Daddy's age, pulled the car onto the grass and hopped out of the vehicle. Another man was slumped over, sleeping, in the backseat.

"Jimmy," Comfort said, taking a step back from the man who came toward us out of the shadows. The edges of his white tank top blew in the wind, and he held a can of beer in one hand.

"It is you, darlin'. Been a long, long time. Didn't even see you at the funeral. Mighta been nice if you'd shown your face at my best friend's—your own brother's—funeral."

"What do you want?" Comfort backed toward the door.

"Look here, you leave now, understand?" Mama walked toward the man, but he paid her no attention.

A truck pulled to a stop behind Jimmy's car, and Solly climbed out of the cab.

Hurry, Solly. Please hurry.

"I think you know what I want ..."

"That's enough—get outta here, Jimmy!" Mama yelled, but it didn't stop him. He came up onto the porch

"Same thing you give all the boys. Same thing you gave your brother all the time. Slut." Jimmy held on to the *l* of that awful word with his tongue, slurring it, so it took an extra long time coming out. Then he balled up a wad of spit in his mouth, sending it flying onto Comfort's cheek.

She crumpled to the floor of the porch like he'd punched her as Solly came flying and pounded a fist into Jimmy's nose.

Jimmy somersaulted backward into the yard. "Damn you, you son of a—"

"Shut up! You shut your mouth! Don't you ever come around Comfort again! And if you do, I swear I'll kill you!" Solly screamed.

"What the—man, settle down. I was just trying to have some fun." Jimmy wiped his face with his arm. "My face!" he said, his hands and shirt covered in blood.

"You were just getting the hell outta here is what you were doin'! Now git before I sink my boot so far into your rib cage it'll take half a dozen surgeons to get it out!"

Jimmy scrambled to his feet and ran back to the car, the black night swallowing his car up as fast as it appeared. Solly threw the beer can after him as Comfort buried her face in her skirt. She rocked back and forth, and it took me a minute to figure out if she was humming or mumbling. Then I recognized the song from Sunday school and from what she hummed the night Daddy died:

We are climbing Jacob's ladder
We are climbing Jacob's ladder
We are climbing Jacob's ladder
Children of the Lord.

Solly scooped her up and carried her into the house. Comfort didn't move or blink. She only stared up at the black velvet night and the stars that shone more dimly and farther away than ever.

"*Seyè, gen pitye!* What on earth happened to you, child?" Ernestine held the door open as Solly carried Comfort into the house to bed. She hadn't heard a thing over the sound of all the popping corn. She searched our faces for an answer to her question, but none of us could explain.

Soon enough, Solly was strumming softly on his guitar and talking gently to Comfort from behind the closed door of her bedroom.

"We should leave them be," said Mama.

"*Oui.* Let's go home, child." Ernestine put her arm around me, and we walked back to the big house. Once we got there, Mama and Ernestine tried to drown out the awfulness of what happened with a new episode of *Fantasy Island*.

Afterward, since I wasn't tired, I plopped down on one of the lounge chairs on the back patio, in the middle of Princella's rose garden, and set about picking the chipped polish off my toenails. Red wheelbarrows, glistening rain, white chickens, and gleaming constellations mixed up in my head, making me seasick, teeter-tottering between the constant struggle to right our wrongs and getting thwacked to the ground again by Princella, the likes of Lorraine Doyle, and loogies from the likes of Jimmy.

The creak of the screen door startled me as Ernestine came out. She pulled a chair up beside me, stuck her nose in the air, closed her eyes, and swayed to some internal song or rhythm. "*Ou vle pale osijè de sa?* Want to talk about it, child?"

"He called her a slut." The weight of what Jimmy'd done and the way those ladies at the supermarket spoke tumbled off my chest, and the words splatted like a wet towel at Ernestine's feet, waiting for her to pick them up and do something with them.

Ernestine shook her head with the shame of it.

"Was she?" I couldn't help blurting the words out before I could think. I knew what *whore* meant. I knew what Daddy and Qarla told me. But what if Comfort did have sex with boys all over town? What if—with the other secrets in the family—no one talked about this other side of the story and no one wanted to admit it? I jittered all over, fearing how Ernestine would respond to my question. Usually I felt free to ask her anything, but I wasn't sure I wanted to know the truth.

She sucked in a breath, and instead of a reprimand, she asked, "What do you think?"

"I don't know."

"You think you don't, but you do, child. *Koute kè ou.* Listen to your heart. You know."

"How? I can't hear anything through this mess." The sting of anger on my tongue tasted like French fries, too hot and salty, but I couldn't keep myself from eating more. "Feels like I'm wandering around a graveyard of people who aren't alive, and every time I think I've done something good or we're on our way to being normal like other families, something like tonight happens. The whole world's spinning around all normal, 'cept us. So maybe she was a slut. Maybe she did ask for it. Maybe that's why we're such a mess, and I can't make a friend to save my life, and neither can she. All I hear is silence, Ernestine. Silence and my mind screaming with questions. That's all I hear."

"*Vin isit la ak chita.*"

"What?" The more serious she was, the more she spoke in her Haitian tongue, and the more it drove me crazy.

"Sit down in front of me, and let me braid your hair."

"I don't want—"

"Sit."

I knew not to argue with her, so I huffed on over and sat with my back to her. She ran her knobby fingers through my hair and divided it into pieces, followed by the back-and-forth, back-and-forth of the braiding.

"Comfort hummed a song tonight. You know that song?"

"'Jacob's Ladder,'" I said. "You used to sing it to me, and we sang it in Sunday school."

"Mmm-hmm. And do you know what it means?"

"Jacob dreamed about angels going up and down a ladder reaching to heaven. Always reminded me of those escalators at the department stores."

"Mmm-hmm. And do you know what that means?"

"No." Good thing she couldn't see me roll my eyes about the fact I knew I was about to hear her give a sermon. "Ouch!" She'd pulled a strand of my hair too hard.

"Jacob had one of the most messed-up families in the Bible. They was messed up, torn up, and strung out. His mama, Rebekah, was a schemer, and his brother, Esau, was a bitter, jealous man. But Jacob's father, Isaac, blessed him. That made everyone hate him even more, and left him with no choice. He set out to a new land, which in those days was a big deal. They thought their gods wouldn't go with them if they left their hometowns. But Jacob's God—who is the One God and our God—wanted Jacob to know *Bondye pa kite pèp li a*. He never leaves His people. And He goes right along with them into uncharted territory."

"What's that have to do with anything?"

Ernestine wrapped the end of a braid in a rubber band and started in on another row of hair. "Jacob was alone out in the desert. He didn't have a pillow—just an old stone to rest his head on at night. When he fell asleep in that cold and lonely desert, God came to him in a dream and showed him the angels going back and forth, to and from the earth."

"I still don't get it." I picked at my toenails again.

"Not much to get about it, child. Simply means God comes to us when we're most alone and got nothing, not a place to lay our heads. Means His angels are always tending to us, taking our pain up to heaven and bringing down peace for our hearts." She finished another braid. "Look at me."

Her eyes filled with tears. "Comfort is not and wasn't ever any of those things that man or anyone else says. She's alone in a desert, and she can only find cold, hard places to rest. I told you 'bout Jacob so you'd use it to learn to search for your own ladders, places in the clouds where the sky opens up and you can feel the angels pulling pain outta your soul and replacing it with a song. Watch for ladders around Comfort. Look for ladders around your whole family. They're there. They're everywhere. If we learn to look. Even in a mess of a situation like this, child, them ladders are everywhere."

"But, Ernestine—"

"Hush." She turned my head away from her and began braiding again. "Comfort's got a battle going on bigger than any of us can help mend, and she's got to want to get better. She's got to learn to let the Lord and His angels take her pain. But first, she's gotta learn to look for the ladders."

We didn't say a word, either of us, after that. She kept braiding until my whole head was in cornrows.

I counted the stars again.

And prayed.

That night, when I fell asleep, I dreamed about the graveyard where Daddy lay, shadows of the stones long and wavy, like people reaching toward salvation on those religious TV shows. The trees rattled and whistled an eerie version of "Jacob's Ladder." On and on through the rows of stones I walked, looking for ladders, looking for someone.

I found one ladder and tried to climb it, but the rungs broke, every one of them, no matter how high I tried to climb. Legs heavy and my hips stiff, I could barely keep myself standing to take steps. I fell into a big patch of tarry mud, sinking deeper and deeper. The more I kicked back to the surface, the weaker I got. Every time I grasped at the sides for a hard piece of earth, it crumbled, and I sank farther, muck seeping through my clothes and over my chest and up to my neck.

I tried to scream, but nothing came out, and a bony hand covered my mouth, silencing me and pushing me farther into the ground. When I searched for the owner of the hand, I saw Cole's face from the tombstone laughing and laughing like a madman, like a maniac, hair slicked back with sweat and grave stench, howling so loud the whole world could surely hear it.

Then the other sleeping bodies in the graveyard rose up and laughed too, until the laughter became a haunted song like an organ playing only the black, sharp keys.

Dolo toujou couri lariviere.
"*Water always runs to the river.*"

CHAPTER 33

Anniston

After Jimmy came by, Comfort quit coming out so much again, except on the occasions she went to work. Solly's car was often parked at her house, but not near as often as before. He mostly helped in the orchards when he came.

Summer barged in for good, like a boiling pot of okra, fierce and steamy, leaving us feeling slimy and overcooked. One day in early August, Ernestine and I sat under a big oak in the backyard, trying everything we knew to keep cool while pecan pies for the Moonlight and Magnolias Music Festival baked inside. This batch would go in the freezer, along with several other batches made ahead of time, until we thawed 'em out a couple of days before the festival.

"You did a mighty fine job on those pies today, Anni. *Bon travay.*"

"Thanks." The hammock I lay on swayed, and out of the corner of my eye, I saw Princella and Vaughn's car rolling down the driveway toward us. They'd been out shopping and who-knows-what that morning.

"Is your mama back from work?" said Princella, looking me over as she exited the car.

"She's inside resting, ma'am."

Without hesitating, she walked up to the house, obviously in a huff. Vaughn followed her, nodding to me and Ernestine as he passed.

I leaned over to Ernestine and whispered, "What do you reckon's wrong now?"

"Lord only knows. *Sèlman Bondye konnen.*"

My ears tickled trying so hard to hear the conversation inside. "Want some lemonade?" I asked Ernestine.

"Best not go in there, child."

"I know, but I'm thirsty." I headed toward the house and heard voices in the kitchen rising as I got closer.

"—doesn't matter where I go—the Curly Q, post office, Vaughn hears about it at the barber shop."

"That's not my concern," said Mama.

"It oughta be. The Harlans are one of the oldest families in Bay Spring. And I spent years restoring my own personal dignity around here. We cannot allow what happened to Comfort get out, let alone be the topic of conversation at every social and private gathering. No one can *ever* know about it."

"How can you say that? People been talking about it nearly a year now. The whole town already knows. It was in the paper. For heaven's sake, everyone knows it wasn't toy trucks him and Rey were fighting about."

Unnoticed, I watched them argue from outside the screen door. Ernestine was right. I didn't need to bother with getting myself lemonade.

"Cole and Rey were cleaning guns to shoot wild turkey like they did every day after Thanksgiving. An unfortunate mental illness came over Comfort. That's all the town knows, and I'm here to make sure that's all they ever know. Vaughn, back me up here."

"It's the way it needs to be." His shoulders slumped, and he would not meet Mama's eyes.

"The town knows everything, Princella. They always have. Surely you know that. Pretending something different happened doesn't help anybody. Especially Anni."

"In that case, you're free to find your own place to live. Free to give up Rey's rights to the plantation."

Mama slammed her hand on the counter. "Princella, I hope you rot—"

Solly interrupted Mama before she could finish cursing. He burst through the front door and screamed, "Oralee! You here, Oralee? I need help!"

Fear emptied me of heat and filled me up with cold panic at the level of alarm in his voice. I pulled the screen door open as he ran into the kitchen, a dark red swath of blood staining his torn-up, sweat-soaked shirt. His chest heaved like a colt after a race.

"What is it, Solly?"

"It's Comfort. Come quick! She's in a bad way, and I need help. Vaughn—call an ambulance, now!"

Se nan chemiz blanch yo wè tach.
"It is on the white shirt that one can see the stain."

CHAPTER 34

Anniston

Vaughn dialed for the ambulance, and Mama and Solly took off running back to Comfort's. I stuck my head out the back door. "Ernestine! C'mon, we gotta go! It's Comfort!"

"Lord Jesus, help us," she said, then switched to Creole. *"Seyè, a ede nou. Seyè, a ede nou. Seyè, a ede nou. Seyè, a ede nou,"* she said over and over and over again.

All the arguing forgotten, Mama and I, Vaughn, Princella, and Ernestine, hobbling as fast as she could behind us, hurried down the driveway to Comfort's house.

"Mama, help her!" I screamed, my heart thudding in my ears when I saw Comfort lying there beneath the pergola covered in weeping vines of wisteria. She lay there, curled up like a baby, in a white T-shirt, blood and torn-up patches of grass everywhere. Her eyes gazed at nothing, and her skin reminded me of thin, white sheets hanging in the breeze. Even her lips were white. Each of her wrists was wrapped in torn pieces of what must've been Solly's shirt, now soaked in blood that still trickled from them. Spots of blood on her nightgown grew larger while we watched.

"Leave me to die, Solly. Tell 'em to leave me to die." Her eyes stared blank at the clouds floating past while Solly gathered up the small ball of her in his arms, and Mama felt Comfort's neck for her pulse.

Pins and needles ran up and down my arms.

Felt like the world was spinning and darkening, even in the middle of the day.

The blood on the carpet, running straight outta Daddy's heart—that's all I could see.

His life and love for me nothing more than a river of blood reaching toward me hiding in the closet.

Would anyone notice if I passed out?

Ambulance sirens came closer, the scream of them a welcome slice into the thickness of our panic.

My knees melted, and I wouldn't have been able to move 'em if I had to, just like in my dreams.

Too much blood.

She was dying, like Daddy. I knew it. I felt her life leaving her, like I'd felt it leaving Daddy.

I felt life leaving me, too.

Solly held Comfort like the night Jimmy came by, like she weighed less than a leaf, and carried her to the ambulance as it pulled into the drive. The whole time, Princella screamed and moaned like the awful howling winds of those tornadoes a few weeks back.

"I'm coming along," Mama said to the paramedics. "She's lost a lot of blood already. Pulse is 130s and thready, and her arms and legs are like ice. Good luck finding a vein, guys." Mama climbed in the ambulance, and the doors shut on them, the swirling red of the lights blinding me like the blood coming out of Comfort's wrists.

"C'mon." Solly motioned to me and Ernestine, and we climbed in his truck to follow the ambulance to the hospital.

"What about Princella and Vau—"

"Never mind them. They can get there themselves. Let's go." Solly peeled out of the driveway, red dust swirling in a fit, blurring the sight of Princella on her knees, and Vaughn standing above her trying to help her to her feet. I turned back around and concentrated on the flashing lights of the ambulance in front of us, so I wouldn't be sick.

By the time we parked, Mama stood at the doors marked "Ambulances Only," waiting for us. Same doors we came to less than a year ago. Same doors that mighta been a way to save my daddy if he hadn't died right then and there. "They're waiting on results to see exactly how much blood she's lost. They may need to give her a transfusion or two before they take her to surgery to repair her wrists. Gave her some lorazepam and morphine to calm her down and keep her comfortable." Mama turned to Solly. "It's probably best if only you see her for now. She called out for you when we were in the ambulance. I think it'd be good if you saw her."

"Thanks, Oralee." Solly squeezed Mama's shoulder as he walked past her through the double doors of the emergency department.

I fell into Mama's arms and let her hold me. "Shh, baby girl. Sh-sh-sh. It's gonna be all right. Gonna be okay." She moved to and fro as she held me, rocking me like I remembered her rocking me when I was small.

"Can we pray, Mama? You, me, and Ernestine? Can we pray for Comfort?"

"Aw, sure, darlin'. Let's go sit over there where it's quiet." She directed us inside to the waiting room and a semicircle couch covered in fake blue leather. A TV hung from the wall with the sound turned down, some news anchor talking, but none of us could hear a word he said, and we didn't care to. We held hands and prayed in silence, the three of us in a circle, automatic doors of the emergency room opening and closing, opening and closing. I could hear a child crying and the beeps of monitors and equipment through the double doors leading to the treatment rooms.

"Lord, please help Comfort. Please," I whispered, and squeezed Mama's and Ernestine's hands.

Zanno kase nan sak, grenn li pa pèdi.
"[When] the necklace [is] broken in a bag, its pieces are not lost."

CHAPTER 35

Comfort

The light I swim toward fades.

Air thins within me, and I thirst for more. Desperate, I search for the surface. I must breathe. I need air, more than anything I've ever needed.

The music of death slows, and my manic lover slips through my arms.

Or do I slip from his?

The water pulls me in directions I never intended, pulling me down farther. I flail for life, even as it ebbs from me. My limbs burn for air, lungs near-bursting from the ache for oxygen. My mouth, my throat, form the shape to scream help, but whatever life is left within me is not enough to move sound through water.

Then I feel pain, and I know.

I am still here.

Abba, why didn't You let death take me? If one day in Your house is better than a thousand elsewhere, why didn't You let me come to You?

I press a plastic button with my thumb and feel an icy burn of medication move up through the veins in my arm toward my heart. I feel for my wrists, covered in gauze and tape, stiff and hard over the blue veins I cut. I strain to not open my eyes, clinging to leftover wafts of death lingering behind my eyelids and unwilling to realize the nightmare awaiting me in the day.

"Comfort."

The sound of Solly's voice gives me no choice but to face life. He is here. He came.

"You shouldn't have come." My words struggle and tumble past the cottony thickness of my tongue.

"Yeah, well, I came anyway."

I open my eyes and fight to bring the duplicates of him together. I turn my head away from him, so he won't see the tear roll down my cheek. He scoots his chair closer to the bed, and I feel the warmth of his fingers as they lace between mine.

"They said you're gonna make it."

I stifle a sob, not sure if it comes from relief or from the grief of wishing they'd have let me die there under the wisteria. I push the button again and let the fog of medication woo me to sleep—weightless, demonless sleep.

For now, I do not mind how long Solly sits beside me.

For now, I let his life enfold me and bring me back.

Le syèl la tonbe, mouch yo pral kenbe.
"When the sky falls, the flies will be caught."

CHAPTER 36

Anniston

The moon was lifting the thick, wet blanket of daytime off the earth by the time Comfort's surgery finished and the nurses settled her into her room. We walked into the star-canopied night—me, Mama, and Ernestine—grateful for the cool, weightless air. Solly took us home, so he could pick up some things to take back to Comfort. He'd be staying with her at the hospital, since she required watching every minute on account of trying to kill herself. The nurses called it "suicide watch." If Solly didn't go back, one of the nurses would've done it instead. Better someone she knows, we figured, since the next couple of days would be hardest for Comfort. Mama explained she'd wake up frustrated and ashamed her plan didn't work, but in the end, most folks who try are glad to have another chance at living.

When Solly pulled up to the house, we found Princella slumped against the steps at the base of the pillared front porch. Her gray updo hung in sad and droopy chunks around her face. She didn't notice us, even when we got up close to her. She cradled a large, mostly empty bottle of wine like a baby, and the hems of her beige, Ultrasuede pantsuit were stained red from the driveway. Mama gently shook her on the shoulder.

"Princella." She didn't move. Mama shook her harder. "Princella, wake up."

Princella moaned and tried to focus her eyes on Mama. The whites of her eyes were red and watery.

"Princella, get up. Let's get you up to bed," Mama said.

"You sure you don't need me to stay? I can call the nurses at the hospital …" Solly worried.

"No, Solly, you get on back to Comfort. We can handle this. Anni can help."

"'Kay. I'll check on y'all tomorrow then."

"Thanks, Solly."

Ernestine went to fetch Vaughn, and me and Mama held Princella by the waist, one of us on either side of her, and shuffled toward the front door. The wind blew through the pecan trees, the shells clacking as if applauding us for our efforts.

Princella interrupted my thoughts with a wet, wine-laden gasp and hiccuped in my direction.

I couldn't help gagging. "Is she gonna be sick, Mama?"

"It's a possibility." Almost as soon as she said it, Princella crumpled over and gagged. Me and Mama let go of her and jumped back in the nick of time as Princella heaved and choked out what seemed like gallons of puke.

Mama's face scrunched at the acidy smell. When we were sure Princella was finished, we helped her to her feet and stumbled toward the door again.

Vaughn came out to see about all the commotion, cigar smoldering between his fingers. He took a draw on it and blew a cloud of smoke into the clear night air. Then he chucked the rest of it into the grass. "Not again, Princella."

Princella laughed a tired, angry cackle. "Isn't it a shame?"

"That's one word for it. Look at you."

"I think I look pretty good, all things considered." Her words jumbled and slurred together. Vaughn took my place holding Princella up, and he and Mama half pulled her the rest of the way up the stone steps stretching across the porch.

"Wait here, Anni," said Mama. They nearly dragged Princella up the curved staircase, and I heard the soft thud of her landing on the bed. I waited for them in the den, where the floor-to-ceiling bookshelves overflowed with football trophies, photos of Cole, and signed photos of Alabama Southern coaches and players who played pro ball. One corner featured a couple of photos of the whole family, one of Comfort in her cheerleading uniform, and another of her and Daddy in what appeared to be homecoming court. Mama and Vaughn startled me when they came back downstairs.

"I'm sorry you had to see that, Anni. Thank you for your help," said Vaughn.

Mama, looking furious, stood behind him.

"She gonna be okay?"

"She'll be fine," said Mama. "Let's go over to Comfort's and see what we can do."

I kicked at stones on the driveway as we walked. My bones ached all over, even when Mama and Ernestine used the happy smell of lemon Pine-Sol to scrub away Comfort's wavy trail of blood that led from the bathroom sink, where the razor blade lay, through the house and out the front door. On Comfort's dressing table, I found a yellow-edged note card, words a soft jumble of blue, felt-tip ink.

> *Come Master come*
> *Find me*
> *here*
> *Let me finally*
> *Find*
> *rest in You*

Bondye di, "Èske pati ou a, epi mwen pral fè m".
"God says, 'Do your part, and I'll do mine.'"

CHAPTER 37

Comfort

I am assigned a nurse or an aide or some other stranger in a hospital uniform to watch over me every hour of the day. After a few days of not reopening my wrist wounds, I am trusted enough to be given a moment of privacy in the bathroom. Layer by layer, I peel away gauze until the lacy bandage no longer hides the slit edges of skin. Rusty blood oozes past stitches straining to hold me together.

I avoided watching all the other dressing changes. I watched the nurses' faces, pale masks tight with the pressure of holding in disgust. Disappointment. Impatience with someone like me, about whom they imagine all sorts of lurid, ghastly pretexts.

Besides, I know well what the scars of slit wrists look like. I know the precise angles, the length, the off-color streaks of skin from my work as a nail artist. They wear long-sleeved shirts, even in the height of summer. They are careful to keep any skin above their palms covered. Others are not so careful. Either that, or they are not so ashamed. So when I turn their hands over to rub in lotion or dry their cuticles, I see.

The last chunks of gauze fall soundless to the floor, revealing angry puckers of sutured skin. Incisions, macabre smiles, stretch from my wrist halfway down my forearm. I hoped lengthwise would've made things go faster. Not that it matters, since I'm still here.

I lose track of how long I stand there, unprepared for unclad mirrors before me.

Me.

Gaping at the barrenness of my reflection, I crumple to the floor and sob, sliding down the antiseptic vanity, pressing my face against the tiny, cold, octagon-shaped white floor tiles. A nurse forces herself into the bathroom and calls for a couple of panicked coworkers to come help take me back to bed.

Why did Solly save me?

So you can live.

The voice smarts.

Live, Comfort. Choose to live.

The voice bores into secret places privy only to pain.

See My torn and bloody wrists.

I see, and my soul hemorrhages at the verity of the vision before me. If I can put a finger, a finger, against my Abba's wounds—but no. Wounds cannot heal wounds.

Can they?

I reach toward Abba again, unable to stop myself. In shame, I reach, without the intention of coming close. Not really. Without believing any power, high or low, can infuse my soul. How could it?

Who touched Me?

I did not.

You did.

No, Abba, I only reached.

Reaching is faith, and faith is the intercourse of the eternal.

What good is that to me?

You took a risk.

I ran from life.

You reached for Me.

So have dozens of others.

My only concern is you.

People. My mother. The town. They will say it cannot be. I cannot heal.

Trust Me.

Can You—even You—create a clean heart from this filth?

Yes, and I can renew your spirit.

My fingers trace the wound invisible beneath bandages again.

Have mercy on me, Abba?

Be still as My love falls upon you, blotting out your shame.

But the dross of my pain, it covers everything.

I cleanse with the fire of justice and sanctify with the sweet smell of hyssop.

I am crushed.

I restore.

They stole everything.
I reclaim.
All I have is broken.
Broken mends best.

Chaj ou pa ka pòte, ou mete-l atè dousman.
"The load you cannot carry, you put it down carefully."

CHAPTER 38

Anniston

The days came and went, and during this time, I figured out what people meant when they said "slow as molasses." I spent most days working at the Curly Q, still looking for but never seeing Jed working in the orchards on my days off. Mama and Solly visited Comfort, and when the time grew closer for her to come home, Ernestine and I visited her too. Solly stood outside the double doors to the nurses' station waiting for us. Mama pushed a buzzer, and someone at the nurses' station let us in.

"She's better today. Cheeks pinkin' up this morning."

"How's she feel about visitors?"

"I told her you were coming, and she smiled and said, 'Good,' so I think it's fine for you to visit. But she's still tired. So not too long."

"I got her this in the gift shop." I showed Solly the pen and journal.

"She'll like that, darlin'. Come with me."

The smell of bleach and hospital cleaners burned my eyes. The first thing I saw when I walked into the room were the thick, white bandages covering Comfort's wrists. I must've stared at them without realizing.

"Doesn't hurt. Not anymore." Comfort smiled at me slightly. Her lips were still pale, too pale, like the pink inside of a seashell. "Y'all can sit down."

Ernastine and I sat on the air register under the window. Mama sat in a chair in front of me, and Solly sat in a chair right next to Comfort's bed. She grabbed his hand. He held hers like a fragile piece of china in both his, rough and suntanned.

I handed her the pen and journal. "Here you go. I got this for you. Well, Mama helped."

"Thank you, Anni."

"You're welcome." I wanted to ask her a million questions, but fear grew fat in my throat.

Thankfully, Mama spoke up. "The doctors say you're going to be fine, Comfort. That's such good news. You gave us quite a scare."

Comfort tugged at the corner of her bedsheet. "I know. I'm sorry it came to this. I am." Tears puddled in the bottoms of her eyes.

"We're the ones who are sorry, Comfort. We shoulda been doing more to help you—more to help you get help."

"Wasn't nothing you coulda done. I've been so tired. Tired of living with a fog of sadness I can't climb out of. Tired of the stares of folks in town, Jimmy, mamas grabbing their children's hands and pulling them close when I pass them in the grocery, everyone in town acting like I have something contagious." She pulled another handful of tissues out of the box and sopped up her nose and eyes.

"But, Comfort, none of that's true." Mama's voice cracked. "And even if folks have perceptions, you don't have to own 'em. It's time to start fighting, taking back the life that belongs to you. This whole family wronged you by being so afraid. We allowed Princella to stuff you into a pit."

"A miry pit," said Ernestine.

"It's not your fault, Oralee. After everything happened, I got so tired of surviving. I wasn't, really. People think death happens when someone's heart stops beating, but I know a soul can leave a person while they're still breathing, and you can walk around soulless and empty."

Mama wiped her eyes. "I'm tired, too, Comfort. I'm tired, too."

"Ladders, children. Look for the ladders." Ernestine stared out the window at nothing in particular, then got up and sat next to Comfort on the bed. She held Comfort's other hand. *"Bote pou sann dife,"* she said. "From Isaiah 61. You feel like the life you been living ended when Cole hurt you—and parts of it probably did—but the Lord has ways of making endings turn into beginnings. You have to help Him out, though. Like the paralyzed man who came to see Jesus for healing, the Lord healed him. He sure did. But then Jesus said to him—"

"'Pick up your mat.'" Solly finished the sentence for her.

"*'Ranmase nat ou.'* Carry that burden and give it to Jesus and then go—go down the new road He has for you and look for the ladders along the way. *Nechèl.*"

"I don't know if I can."

"We know," said Ernestine. "Your friends and family. Reach down in your sweet heart to the places Jesus holds in His nail-scarred hands—places can't no one touch but Him. Those places are safe. Those places are whole. Take power of the Holy Spirit from those places, and you will see He will form you into something new and strong."

A nurse stepped around us, took Comfort's blood pressure, and gave her a couple of pills.

"What are they giving you?" Mama leaned toward the bed to get a good look.

"Dr. Howard—do you know him?—he started me on something called tricyclic antidepressants."

"I do know Dr. Howard. Greg. He consults on a lot of the patients who come through the ED and on the floors. He's exceptional. And he's constantly reading the latest journals for the latest treatments."

"He told me about group therapy, too. A whole group of people who've been hurt like me meet every week. He thinks it would help me to know I'm not alone in what I've been through. Do you really think there are others like me—enough of them to form a whole group like that?"

"I know there are. After they've been hurt, some come to the ED for help. Other times, in the middle of the night when I'm talking to a patient, they'll tell me how their father or grandfather, an uncle or family friend, did unimaginable things to them." Mama choked up again. "No, Comfort, you are so not alone."

"Mama, she's always made fun of her friends who go to therapy, like it's a disease or something to laugh at. Says family problems should stay in the family. I never thought about talking to anyone about it." Comfort fiddled with the ends of the ties on the thick, new bathrobe we brought her.

Ernestine stroked the hand Solly wasn't holding. "Gettin' help is anything but weak, child. Gettin' help is for the strong. Hiding and pretending something never happened is the worst thing of all."

Comfort sat up straighter in bed and pushed a stray piece of hair off her forehead. "Dr. Howard said my trauma is a lot like what war vets go through, that trauma mixes up the way all the chemicals and nerves work in the brain. There's a brand-new name for it. I can't remember—"

"Post-traumatic stress disorder?" Mama asked.

"That's it. Some depression, too."

I thought about Larry and the way he'd been since he came back from Vietnam.

"Explains why you're so jumpy," said Solly.

"Yeah. Dr. Howard says without medicine taking the edge off my fear, healing's even harder. But maybe with medicine and help … maybe I can?"

"Sounds like Dr. Howard gave you a good dose of hope, child."

Comfort sat back. "Yes. Yes, I think he did."

On the way out of the hospital, we passed Princella and Vaughn coming in. Princella held a vase full of roses from her garden.

Ernestine leaned close to Mama and whispered in her ear. "Don't you say nothin', Oralee."

Mama huffed in protest, but when we got close, she politely said hello.

"Oralee. Anniston. Ernestine." Princella nodded at us, and Vaughn threw a chewed-up cigar in the bushes. Princella's hair was done up fancy like she came fresh from the Curly Q.

"Thank God Solly's in there with her," Mama said after we got far enough away from them.

"Amen."

Men Anpil fè chay la pi lejè.
"Many hands make the load lighter."

CHAPTER 39

Anniston

That next Monday, I woke up extra early. I'm not sure if something woke me, or if worrying about the approaching end of summer churned me awake. Molly followed me out to the front porch, where I rocked and waited for the newspaper to come. Steam rose from Solly's Styrofoam Tom Thumb cup of coffee as he sauntered up to our house. The edge of the sky turned from gold to the pale blue of angel wings as he sat in the rocker next to me, and our chairs creaked in similar rhythm.

"Summer's ending soon," I said as a sliver of sun slipped into view.

Solly studied his coffee, then turned the corner of his eye toward me. "Yeah. I can't believe it's the end of August."

"Comfort's coming home soon."

He sighed and focused on stirring his coffee. "Yep."

"What are you gonna do now?"

"You sure don't ease into a subject, do ya, little lady?"

"I s'pose not. I'm sorry." I curled my ankles around the legs of the rocker and slumped down, realizing I was prying.

"Aw, it's okay. A tough thing to talk about."

I tried to keep quiet and wait for him to do the talking. I picked at the fuzzies on my nightshirt while I waited for him to go on.

"Always did have an eye for Comfort. But it wasn't until I was about your age that I fell hard for her. She helped at the Crab Shack snack counter, and I brought my allowance to buy snacks from her while my daddy worked on his shrimp boat down at the docks. Once we got to know each other better, she'd go on break when I came, and we'd have a cola together. Her and I, we stayed together through high school, and then we went to the local technical college together too. Her for beauty school. Me for landscaping. Been through a lot, me and her."

Sadness fell over his face as he gazed across the meadow toward Comfort's house. His eyes were so blue, Comfort must've nearly drowned in them. "When I got my manager job at the Proper Petal, I asked Vaughn for Comfort's hand. Never thought that would make Cole—that it would mean the end—"

"None of us thought any of this would mean all it has." I put my finger up to the scar on my cheek.

"I'm so sorry, Anni."

"Ain't nothin' now. Hurts more on the inside."

"Yeah. Yeah, I bet it does. And I know what you mean."

"So did you and Comfort split up? She's been lettin' you visit her." The knot in my belly tightened, wondering if I pushed for too much information again. But he answered quick.

"Yes and no." He punched a pattern in the lip of his foam coffee cup.

"Are you still engaged?"

The jaw muscles on the sides of his face hardened as he frowned. "No. Not officially. But I'd marry her still, today." A tear as big as a fly plunked into his coffee, and he set his cup down to rub his eyes. "She sent her ring back to me."

"What?"

"She sent her engagement ring back to me. Right before she cut herself. Postman delivered it the day after she went in the hospital. She put a note in there telling me to move on, that I needed to find someone else whole and unbroken. Someone who wasn't so dirty. That's the word she used, *dirty*." He put his face in his hands, and the rocking chair squeaked beneath him.

That was it, then? It was over? Me and Jed were over. Solly and Comfort were over. Would it stop being the end of things? Or was that all life was, a bunch of endings?

"Mama said she's coming home next week."

He sat back in his rocker and dried his eyes. "Yeah."

Surely there was something we could do to move or at least change the direction of the storm hanging forever over our heads. And if I couldn't change Jed's decision about us, maybe I could do something to help change the course of things for Comfort and Solly. "Maybe y'all aren't having a wedding. But maybe we can do something to celebrate, just the same."

"I don't know, Anni. I just don't know." He used a lot of effort to push himself up out of the chair and then plodded toward the orchards.

Se kouto sèlman ki konnen sa ki nan kè yanm.
"Only the knife knows what is in the yam's heart."

CHAPTER 40

Comfort

"I was supposed to get married." I hardly believe I speak, since I promised myself beforehand I wouldn't say a word. I might be required to attend the support group for abuse and rape survivors before the hospital will release me, but I don't have to like it. Maintaining a regular schedule of meals, one-on-one counseling, and journaling—those parts get easier every day. But the support-group counseling—I dreaded that from the first time they mentioned it.

By this time, the hospital lets me wear my own clothes. I pull my oversize cardigan around me tighter and sink into my chair, cheeks pinking with the heat that comes with revealing more of myself than I intended.

"Oh, honey chil'." The woman next to me, a black woman about Oralee's age and three times as big around, shakes her head with sympathy. The Tab T-shirt she wears strains to cover her enormous bosom. I can't help wonder what happened to her as she holds out a box of tissues toward me. "I'm Maelle."

"Comfort," I say, reaching for the tissues, grateful to sop up the trail of tears that have hardly stopped since I first looked at my scars. They say that happens—once the scab of pain's picked off, the weeping comes for a long, long while.

I wonder about everyone there, same as they must wonder about me. They didn't call it a rape-survivor group for nothing. Thirty minutes into my first meeting, and my preconceptions about what it would be like are blown away. The metal folding chairs I was sure underprivileged, uneducated, pitiful women would sit in instead fill with faces I recognize. Faces I know. The cashier, Sammy, who works the Piggly Wiggly registers in the early mornings, for instance. She sits across from me, still wearing her work clothes.

"I wanted to say somethin' to you all those times you came in the store. But you weren't ready. And if there's one thing I learned, you gotta be ready to talk," she says as soon as I sit down.

I wonder if this is a group Wynn Culpepper, the girl from the salon, might need someday, same as Cindy Peabody, salutatorian of the high school when I was a freshman. Cindy, sitting next to Sammy, leans down and occupies her toddler, a little boy in denim overalls named Charlie, playing at her feet and chewing on a wooden train engine. "I'm here 'cause I had a nervous breakdown a month after Charlie was born. Didn't remember anything about my life before the age of ten, but it all came flooding back. My stepdaddy molested me for eight years back then. Mama kicked him out last year after I got up the courage to tell her."

Not everyone is as forthcoming about their trauma, including me. All I can tell them is I was supposed to marry Solly.

"Do you love him?" The woman on the other side leans closer to me. I recognize her as a long-time client of Qarla's. She had a recent affair with the mayor, if I remember the gossip correctly. Lives alone in a gigantic house on the bay—gated driveway and everything. Her jet-black hair is done up like Jackie Kennedy's, oversize sunglasses perched on top, and she wears a white tennis skirt, a bright-pink polo shirt with the collar standing up, and a green sweater around her shoulders, its sleeves tied in a loose knot.

"Vicki, our new guest might not be ready to answer questions yet." The group leader, Connie, comes to my rescue. She's an older woman, graying blonde hair pinned in a loose bun, spectacles dangling from her neck. I admire her flax-colored, embroidered kaftan, topped off with a floor-length cardigan draping beneath her and puddling onto the floor.

"All I mean is if she loves him, she shouldn't give up on that," Vicki says to Connie. Then she turns back to me. "Honey, you can get better. Healin's possible. So if it's true love, don't give that up."

I consider her encouragement. I do love Solly. I don't want to give him up. I didn't know how I'd live without him before all this mess. And if I did feel like answering Vicki, I'd tell her I can't imagine living without him, still.

"Sorry I'm late, guys—" the dark-haired beauty bursting into the room stops short when she sees me.

Mandy Appleton.

I drop my eyes, unable to look at this girl who said she wanted to be like me. How could I have known how alike we already were?

She takes a seat on the other side of Maelle. I see her trying to meet my eyes and smile, but I keep my head down.

The group breaks up after an hour of introductions and folks sharing progress, setbacks, and tears. As I head back to my hospital room and the others head toward the lobby, I feel like a seagull lighting off the end of a dock. Because while it might be a while before I share more, I have learned two very important things today: that everyone around me, and especially the most unlikely ones, carries her own heavy burden.

And that I am not alone.

Wè jodi-a, men sonje denmen.
"See (live) today, but think about tomorrow."

CHAPTER 41

Anniston

Took some convincing to talk Mama and Ernestine into having a homecoming for Comfort, but once they agreed, we took to planning the best, Southern-fried celebration ever. We didn't want to overwhelm her, so we kept it to our family and Solly, who, although hesitant, agreed.

First, we cleaned her little cottage from top to bottom. Ernestine washed and pressed the bedding and curtains. Mama and I scrubbed the kitchen and bathroom with lemon-scented cleaner and followed up by rubbing down the furniture with lemon oil. We cut the prettiest flowers from the garden—verbena, magnolias, carnations, and baby's breath, jasmine and lavender. Then we stuffed them into vases and jars, buckets and pots all around the house. The ceiling fans whirred, and a bay breeze floated through the windows, opened as wide as we could get them. Vaughn came by to fix a few inside light fixtures and fill the gas porch lanterns outside too.

Out on the patio, Mama taught me how to make string lamps by dipping crochet string in glue and wrapping it around a balloon, which we popped after the string dried. We were covered in glue by the time we were done. Ernestine used her paints to give the string balls some color when the light shone through them after we attached them to the string of white Christmas lights. Candles flickered everywhere, on the table and floating in a glass punch bowl full of water. Luminaries in brown paper bags lined both sides of the garden paths.

Mama brought over her antique collection of rose china. None of the patterns matched, but when put together, they turned the table into a harmony of color like a garden itself. Solly picked the menu and brought the food. He said he might've liked to be a chef if he hadn't heard the Lord calling him to landscaping. On an old chalkboard borrowed from the Proper Petal, he wrote the menu and placed it on an easel in Comfort's front entryway, so she'd see it first thing:

SLAW DOGS
RED POTATO SALAD WITH CREOLE MUSTARD
BISCUITS AND HONEY
PAN-FRIED SWEET CORN
PEACH-PECAN PIE
HOMEMADE ICE CREAM
FRESH-SQUEEZED LEMONADE

And of course, we would play music. Solly brought his guitar. Ernestine brought out her squeezebox, and she let me use her *frottoir*. I brought Daddy's fixed-up guitar, so I could join in with the few chords I'd learned since my birthday. And Mama brought a tambourine and a couple of old bongo drums, so whoever had an extra hand used those to keep the beat.

By the time we organized everything, I don't know if we were more scared or excited for Comfort to come home. Solly went to pick her up, and waiting for them to come home felt like waiting for Christmas morning. The only guests who didn't come were Princella and Vaughn. Princella had a headache, and though Vaughn said he wanted to stay—which part of me thought he genuinely did—he stayed home to take care of her.

It was just as well. Comfort was pale, her face drawn, and circles shadowed her eyes as she climbed out of Solly's truck cab. Solly's hand rested on the small of her back as she held up her long, patchwork skirt to climb the whitewashed, front porch steps. With each one, Comfort's cheeks pinked up and puddles of tears began to rim her bottom eyelids. Still, her voice sounded small, timid. "Hi, everybody."

"Welcome home!" Mama said first, then we all got up and gathered around her. Even Molly ran around her in circles, jumping and sniffing and kissing Comfort's hands with her black, wet nose.

"*Jezi, di ou mèsi.* Thank you, Jesus. Mmm-hmm." Ernestine held her hands together as if in a prayer of thanksgiving.

Comfort opened the front door and took notice of everything we'd done on her way to the kitchen. "Y'all have surely outdone yourselves." She kept shaking her head, as if trying to loose herself from these good things she felt she didn't deserve. But we figured if we kept treating her like she deserved good things, eventually she'd believe it for herself.

Once in the kitchen, Solly offered to pray. "Dear Jesus, we praise You for this time together. We thank You for friendships that outlast and out-love hard times. We ask You to bless and protect this time together and that You'd give us courage to put our fears and pain at Your feet, to know the goodness of Your truth, and that You would guide us beside still waters and give us peace. In Your precious name we pray, amen."

Everyone cleaned their plates during dinner, and then Mama and I made the homemade ice cream. Night sounds came out as daylight sank under the horizon. Ernestine lit more candles, and the whole patio nearly floated like a fairyland of magic—lights and our hearts dancing on streets of freedom.

Mama scooped rock salt as I dumped cups of ice into the sides of the ice-cream maker, and we took turns cranking the handle. I remember when I was younger thinking the salt would spoil the ice cream, until I learned in science class it doesn't go into the ice cream—it makes the ice colder so the mixture freezes faster. My teacher called the salt a *catalyst*. Made me think about other catalysts around us—things you might not think are good but that end up making things better, like manure in a garden, bees on flowers, hard wind making the wood of a tree stiffer and straighter as it grows.

"Let's check it." Mama stopped cranking, and we took the lid off the chamber that held the ice-cream mixture. We each dipped a spoon into the cold, frothy mixture, which was thick like cake batter.

"Mmmmmm! Perfect." Tasted like summer and love. I thought about Jed and wished he was here too. But Solly brought bowls of peach-pecan pie out before I could think about him too much. Mama scooped ice cream on top, which melted like butter onto the warm, pecan-covered fruit and crust.

Comfort sat on a lounge chair with a quilt wrapped around her shoulders. Said she felt cold a lot since the day she went to the hospital. Solly brought her a bowl of ice cream and pie, then sat down beside her with his guitar. Solly played "Blackbird" by the Beatles first. His fingers strummed and moved along the strings like ripples on a lazy creek, his voice like water on a parched throat. His smile focused on Comfort and hers on him, like they were the only two on that patio.

Ernestine reached alongside her chair and pulled her squeezebox onto her lap, grasped each end, and pulled back and forth in an easy in and out wheeze. "Let's *jwenn eksite*!"

I rubbed the *frottoir* in time to the tapping of Solly's hand against his guitar.

Every sound mixed to a beat as happy as a calf kicking its feet in the air after it's released from a stall. We sang all sorts of songs: "Lord of the Dance," "This Little Light of Mine," "Pass It On," "Have You Seen Jesus My Lord?" even some Jim Croce and Kate Wolf. Crickets sang and garden critters joined along with their own joyful cadence.

Eventually, the words and music fell off into a silence sweet as simple syrup, and we sat back, heads upturned to the stars, and soaked it all in.

"You okay, Comfort?" Mama asked.

"Yes ... I am." Comfort didn't look too sure of her words.

"What is it?" Solly asked, taking her hand.

"It's just … Don't stop coming around. I've got a long row to hoe still, and I'm afraid."

"Afraid of what, child?"

Comfort's face fell into a too-familiar sadness. "Afraid of falling. Afraid of failing. Afraid of silence and the darkness I gotta push through to get well."

"Second Corinthians 1:6 says, 'If we are distressed, it is for your comfort and salvation,'" Ernestine said. "We're here to help you carry your distress, child. You're not alone in your journey."

Solly set his guitar in his lap again, and began to strum.

> Now I've been happy lately
> Thinking about the good things to come.
> And I believe it could be
> Something good has begun
> Oh I've been smiling lately …

At that line, Comfort grinned and began to sing along softly. Then Mama and I joined, and then all of us calling on the peace train.

> Now come and join the living
> It's not so far from you
> And it's getting nearer
> Soon it will all be true …

> Cause out on the edge of darkness
> There rides a peace train

Oh peace train take this country
Come take me home again

"Cat Stevens is great," said Solly. "But I'd like to play one last song. A song that can be a prayer for Comfort. A prayer for us all." He thumped a more gentle rhythm on the back end of his guitar, and soon his fingers fluttered and floated across the strings.

Amazing grace

His voice, a whisper, drifted back into the notes of the strings he played for a few beautiful moments before moving on . . .

How sweet the sound

A sound like a far-off train whistle came closer, from back behind us in the orchards. The closer it came, the more the whistling sounded like a sad song. The more I realized it *was* a song.

A growl rolled deep and long in Molly's throat, and the fur on her back stiffened. Solly stopped a moment, and we all listened for the notes, blending perfect and taking over where Solly left off.

A harmonica.

And a boy.

I realized even before the light shone on his shadowy features it was Jed.

Amazing grace.

How sweet the sound.

For wretches and the wounded, for the good and for those doing the best they can with what they have.

Jed sauntered over to behind where I sat. "Heard there was a homecoming today."

"*Oui*, Jed. Come join the celebration." Ernestine patted her hand on the empty chair between her and me, and Jed obliged.

"Welcome home, Miss Comfort," he said, then held the harmonica back to his lips and kept playing the chords of the old hymn as Solly kept on strumming. None of us uttered a word as Jed slid the metal piece back and forth along his lips, bending the sounds, until we couldn't contain ourselves any longer.

Solly added some chords to the somber notes, and Jed picked up time in response. I handed Ernestine the *frottoir*, and she kicked things up a notch again, until we had "Amazing Grace" going like it'd never gone before. We sang more under the trees with the crickets and night sounds, and the clicking dance of ripening pecans. Didn't matter that some of us sang flat, some of us sang sharp, some of us played out of time.

We made music, the six of us, the likes of which the bay never heard before and might not hear again.

> We've no less days to sing God's praise
> Than when we'd first begun

Si li se Bondye menm ki voye ou,
Li pral peya depans ou yo.
"If it is God who sends you, He'll pay your expenses."

CHAPTER 42

Comfort

There are some things the dark suitor can never have.

I hear Abba as my bedroom is bathed with the ombré of a new day, and I try to believe that parts of me in the deepest places are unscarred. That no matter how great the injustice, how far death digs, it cannot reach the sacred places of my soul.

I ponder these promises, culling my heart for places of me long forgotten—places that hold some semblance of hallowed hope.

Perhaps like pricks of green on the ends of spring pecans, vestal places do bide time within me until the sun warms them enough to bloom.

I want to be who God says I can be.

More than the dance that led me toward death, I want to be free.

It is safe to come out now. No one can hurt you like that or steal from you again.

I hear You. But how, Abba? How?

I'll hold your hand like you held Anni's on the beach when she was a little girl. Remember? I'll keep the waves from reaching you. I'll keep the foam from your feet.

I'm too ruined, Lord.

No, your life is a genesis. Something brand new. A beginning.

I can't, Lord.

You already have. You walked through the fire they said you'd never survive. I have rebuilt you, and I will restore you. Still.

I peek through the transom and see Solly, pale with tiny drops of sweat popping out on his forehead. Before the music faded last night, he asked if he could pay me a visit today.

I open the door, silencing the persistent knocks.

He tips his hat. "Comfort."

"Solly."

"It's good to see you."

"Good to see you, too."

"You—you look good, Comfort. Really good."

I focus on my bare toes and stand aside so he can come in.

"You know, the Moonlight and Magnolias Music Festival's coming up. Always was your favorite," he presses, turning his ball cap around and around in his hands

"Yes, yes it was—is."

"I'll be playing this year. A couple of acts in front of Alabama."

"Solly, that's a dream come true for you!"

"Just got the call this morning. Somebody backed out and they needed a filler act. I'd thrown in an application and auditioned a long time ago, never thinking anything would come of it. Almost forgot about it, really. I'm only playing a handful of cover songs. Nothin' fancy."

"You deserve that. You really do."

"Well, we could go together, stay on the outskirts, or I could find a spot for you to watch from backstage ..." His voice trails off.

I fix my eyes hard upon him, feeling the burn of want returning slow and sweet deep inside me. "Would you care to take a walk?" It's the first thing I've initiated between us in nearly a year.

"I'd like that."

He offers me his arm, and we head toward the orchards, where nuts press against their shells, waiting for time to ripen them enough to unfurl for harvest. Though we don't exchange words, we exchange a knowing that comes from loving someone for years, a silence that speaks much more than utterances breathed simply to fill the space between strangers. Each step along the unswerving rows brings the shivering ambivalence of wide-open space and the heart-cradling surety that God provided me with the chance to walk between them with Solly at my side again. When I wanted to give up, no one else did. When I thought I was alone, I had more company than I ever knew.

You can do this, Abba says.

I can try, I answer Him.

"Okay," I say as Solly and I face each other back on my front porch.

"Okay?"

"Okay. I'll go to the festival with you."

"Okay then. Pick you up at 7:30 Saturday night." He starts to leave.

"Solly?"

"Yeah?"

"No expectations. No guarantees."

He takes a moment to think on that before he replies. "Darlin', I'm your friend. First, foremost, and always, I'm your friend."

I feel my cheeks pink and click the door closed as he walks down the front porch steps.

Maybe You're right, Abba.

Maybe You're right.

Pawòl gen zèl.
"Words have wings."

CHAPTER 43

Anniston

Heat bore down on us that first weekend in September, leaving our skin constantly wet and sticky. Thankfully, time spent in the orchards with Jed again, along with the buzz of the Moonlight and Magnolias Music Festival, kept our spirits bobbing above the muggy days like a buoy.

"Come to the festival with me, Anni," Jed whispered in my ear the night of Comfort's homecoming.

And so I found myself strolling next to him along the decked-out streets of Bay Spring. My favorite time of the year in town, the Moonlight and Magnolias Festival brought some of the best bands, food, and artists in the state to our streets. This year would be better than ever with Solly playing. Banners announcing the festival stretched across intersections. Newly planted flowers in hanging baskets decked with ribbons applauded from their seats high on light posts lining the streets. Food and drink vendors unfolded their plain, square box trailers into pop-up parties of lights and sugar and puffs of smoky flavor that made it near impossible to walk by without ordering something: shaved-ice lemonade, smoked turkey legs, shrimp baskets, sausage, corn dogs, hamburgers, hot dogs, funnel cakes, fried oysters, chicken on a stick, barbeque pork and beef, popcorn, pickles, and fried okra, of course.

"We gotta get some taffy." Jed stopped in front of the creaking, pulling, stretching mechanical arms inside the taffy trailer. Lined up like a collection of his rocks or a stretch of seashells shaped by high tide, the waxed-paper–wrapped taffy practically jumped into his empty box. We stuffed it until the box barely closed. I watched the taffy puller as Jed paid, wondering how the candy kept from snapping like a rubber band against all that yanking. But it didn't. It kept stretching thinner and smoother, thinner and smoother, thinner and smoother like the pull of pain on a broken heart.

Jed put the box in his backpack, and we weaved in and out and down the row of food vendors, trying not to trip on all the extension cords burping life into them.

"So why'd you come back?"

He pushed his hands deep in his jeans pockets before he answered. "I didn't leave."

"Maybe not Bay Spring, but you sure left me." As glad as I was to be with him again, these questions pushed hard against my heart.

"I got a lot to figure out. A lot I don't want to drag you through."

I kicked a pop-top that went flying, clanging against the side of the corn-dog booth. "Why doesn't anyone let me decide for myself what I want to be drug through?"

Jed stopped, put his hands on my shoulders, and looked hard into my eyes. "I can't explain it, 'kay? I just can't right now. I'm sorry."

I thought about arguing back, pushing him to tell me about the scars on his chest. What he'd been doing all this time. What he intended to do now. Instead, I punched him in the shoulder and took off running. "You're forgiven. If you can catch me!"

I ran through the food carts and artist tents, my smallness making up for his quickness, the whole time both of us laughing and laughing and laughing.

Until one food booth made me stop quick. "Here, Jed! Over here!"

"Gotcha!" He grabbed my waist.

"Ever tried one of these?"

"Cajun pistols?" he read the flashing lights. "Can't say I ever have."

"You been missing out, then." I paid the vendor, who handed me two steaming, foil-wrapped packages the size of baseballs. "Here. Eat up. But you might need a lemon shake-up to chase it back. They're hot!"

We sat on a bench outside the Curly Q and peeled the foil back from the flaky, dough-covered delicacy.

"What's in it?"

"Only everything good in the world. Cheese, crab, crawdaddies. And hot sauce, of course."

Jed swallowed a bite and licked cheese off his fingers. "You're right. These are awesome!"

We roamed through the crowds—him happy to be forgiven, and me happy to not be alone. Kids juggled cotton candy like bouffant wigs on sticks; fat men sucked down Italian sausages; mamas divvied out pieces of sparkling elephant ears that flopped over the sides of greasy plates. Soon the food vendors gave way to artist tents lining sidewalks down to the city park and pier. The smell of hot wood shavings and leather floated up from where artisans carved monogrammed wood toys and gifts. Folks pressed in tight around cases full of silver jewelry and jars of jams and jellies. Kids begged their parents for balloon animals, airbrushed T-shirts, and nickel trinkets.

"Let's find Ernestine's tent." I grabbed Jed's hand and pulled him along. He pulled me back, causing me to turn around and face him. For the first time, I noticed his eyes were blue with flecks of gold and green, like the sun setting over the ocean. Right then, I knew Jed's eye was crooked so he could keep one eye on heaven.

Then he kissed me. His kiss felt like a thousand steps down a road lined with bright red roses. It tasted like a hundred pieces of soft vanilla taffy. And when I opened my eyes, I thought my knees were gonna wobble right out from under me. "Jed Manon!"

He held my hand tighter. "Couldn't help it. Been thinking about doing that for a long time now."

"You have?" My face was so hot it was like I'd been standing too long in front of a bonfire.

"Yes, I have." He smiled as big as I ever seen him smile. Then he let go of my hand. "C'mon, I'll race you to the docks!"

Racing a boy who limps might not seem fair, but when he ran, he left his limp behind. By the time we got down to the docks, I coughed from laughing and breathing so hard. "Jed, wait up!"

The white sails of the boats cut pure, pointed holes in the blue summer sky. We walked among them, their shadows bowing and shielding us from the sun and salty spray of the choppy bay and motoring boats. We talked about living on one of those yachts, with nothing to do but travel from port to port and soak in the sun. We let the taffy melt on our tongues and pressed it between our teeth and against the insides of our cheeks until we'd eaten nearly half the box by the time we reached Ernestine's tent full of pecan pies, boxes of Harlan pecans, and other pecan confections.

"*Gade! Ou se yon je wè.* Y'all are a sight to behold!" Ernestine laughed and offered us wet paper towels for our sticky mouths and hands. I felt different, kissed for the first time, and wondered if Ernestine could tell. If I looked any different, she kept silent about it.

"Sold many pies?" I plucked a piece from the samples laid out on a glass cake stand on the makeshift checkout counter, which consisted of several wooden shipping crates stacked on top of each other.

"*Piti piti.* Sold a few. Better than none." Ernestine waved a festival brochure, folded like a fan, in front of her neck. "He, on the other hand, can't make 'em fast enough." She nodded toward the booth across from her, where a man used a machine to cut people's names into key chains and signs and great big belt buckles.

"That's not right."

"What's not right is you two lollygagging around this old woman instead of getting on with yourselves and having a good time. *Ale gen plezi!*"

After getting a lemon shake-up for Ernestine and one for each of us, we rode every ride we could and then rode them again. We stuck our feet in the sand at the public beach, finished off our taffy, and ran to the end of the pier, where we sat and watched the sun set over the bay. The first couple of bands had already played, but we were happy to let fish nibble at us as we twirled water with our toes.

"You know, they're selling oyster skiffs over near Apalachicola, over in Florida. Couple hundred bucks. Some less. But I could fix one up." Jed stared out at an oysterman tonging along the shallow edge of the bay. "Word is, they need more tongers. Cullers, too. I could start out culling until I get my boat fixed up—"

"You leaving Bay Spring?" Surely not. Surely he didn't come back in my life to leave again.

"I'm sixteen. I can do anything I want now." He skipped a shell across the water. It bounced seven times. "I've been reading in the papers—there's thousands of acres of oyster bars over in Apalachicola, on account of the river meeting the ocean there. Winter bars open October first. I could even catch the tail end of some of the summer bars before they close 'em up end of September."

He caught a wisp of my hair and tucked it behind my ear. He left his hand on the side of my neck and looked right through me with his eyes, a whole mix of browns, greens, and golds. "I don't want to leave you, Anni."

"Then don't."

"It's not that simple. All my life, I been put places I don't belong. Places I'm not a part of. Places that stick to parts of me, whether I want 'em to or not. Been told I'm not good enough, not smart enough, not wanted enough. Been told I'm too expensive, too much a bother, too much a mess to ever matter. Hettie and John, they don't want me, either. I'm just their little sidekick who makes money for his booze and gambling and her cigarettes."

I didn't like where this conversation was headed.

"If something comes up that gives me the chance to make a life of my own, I gotta take it."

A hot tear rolled down my face, down the side of my neck, all the way down to my heart. "I suppose you do."

We sat there a while longer, watching the green and red lights of incoming and outgoing boats as the sun set on the far side of the bay. Across the way, the announcer introduced another featured band as the last sliver fell under the water, and while I didn't want to miss Solly playing, I didn't want to miss out on this night with Jed, either. I grabbed his hand, and we raced back to the rides. We rode all of them again—the Skymaster and the Looper, the Rok 'n' Rol and the Ramba Zamba, the Scat and the Hustler. Around and around we flew, up and down. Gravity yanked at our souls. Lights in our eyes rivaled those on the sides of the rides that held us in, straps and bars keeping our bodies and hearts from swinging away, out of control, into the night.

Dizzy and alive, so fully alive, we soaked it all in, every last bit of the day, like it was the last one of our lives.

Gratitid frè pa gen anyen.
"Thanks costs nothing."

CHAPTER 44

Comfort

Chartreuse husks, pregnant with the fruit of summer months, don't let on that eventually they'll pull away from the pecans, their hard, brown inner shells clicking in the wind, eager to catch a first glimpse of the world. A John Denver song plays on the radio as I pick at a hangnail. Blood seeps around the half-moon of white at the base of my fingernail, and I wrap it in my T-shirt to make it stop.

Solly grips the wheel of his truck with one hand and changes the station with the other as he steers us toward the festival along the highway that parallels Mobile Bay. He settles on Waylon Jennings as we drive by the golden, dappled water of the bay. Pelicans tuck their beaks under their wings and hunker down on barren pilings, remnants of docks blown away by Hurricane Frederic. Cars park bumper to bumper on both sides of the highway as we get closer to town, and I feel a knot pull tight inside my gut. *Doing nails at the Curly Q's one thing. Why did I ever agree to this?*

As if reading my mind, Solly reassures me. "I'll find us a spot to park away from this mess of traffic."

The sun hangs above the sea, reluctant to meet the imminent kiss of the horizon, and I am grateful we can hide ourselves in the protection of twilight. The truck shudders to a stop in the lot behind the Methodist church, three blocks away from the center of all the festivities. Only a half a dozen other cars are parked there. Solly opens my door, and side by side, our steps crunch along the crushed cover of oyster shells. Guy McGovern, one of the church ushers, comes toward us across the lot.

"Hey, Guy, how's the festival?"

"Oh, same old, same old," Guy replies. His eyes move up and down my body, real slow, like he's checking out jewelry beneath the glass cases at the Walmart. His lip turns up in a sneer when he meets my stare, but Solly doesn't notice.

I drop my head.

This, Solly notices, and he grabs my hand as Guy passes us by. "You okay? We don't have to do this."

"I'm fine."

"He say something to you?" Solly cranes his neck to watch Guy get in his car and tear out of the lot, spewing the dust of broken oyster shells up behind him.

"No, nothin'. Let's keep goin'."

I focus on the distant music of one of the folk bands and wonder if Solly's as nervous as I am—him with reason to be, and me just a mess. The soothing, familiar chorus of "Smokey Mountain Rain" by Ronnie Milsap spills over the crowd and helps calm my thumping heart. *I can do this.*

Yes, with My help, you can.

Solly and I walk around to the back of the stage, where various bands sort instruments, amplifiers, cords, and microphones. Roadies stack and unstack black trunks trimmed in steel, covered in stickers of venues, political statements, and destination cities.

"You can stay back here and listen if you'd like," Solly encourages me.

"Sure. I'll be fine." My voice sounds braver, more upbeat, than I feel, and I am glad thoughts are invisible things. A throng of people gather around the guys from the band Alabama, from Fort Payne, who've been getting airtime on national radio stations. I hover close to the shadows in back of the stage and am relieved I do not see any locals I recognize.

"It's almost time." Solly takes a deep breath, trying to inhale confidence, and puts his arm around my shoulder. I am relieved by his touch.

"You'll do great." I smile up at him, and his blue eyes overwhelm me with their unbridled adoration.

The audience looks to be at least a couple hundred people, many of them moving the folding chairs to the side of the streets to make room for dancing. They clap and holler as the band onstage finishes an original song that sounds a lot like Don McClean. Solly tunes his guitar for at least the tenth time, pick in his mouth as he concentrates on the chords and makes final turns to the tuning pegs.

The announcer, Frank Streeter, editor in chief of the *Bay Spring Banner Sentinel*, croons Solly's name into the microphone, welcoming him to the stage. Solly kisses me, then runs on stage, plugging in his acoustic guitar and sitting on a high stool.

"Thanks for having me, y'all. I'm Solly Daniels."

Several in the audience applaud.

"I hope to treat y'all with some songs you know, and a couple you don't that I wrote myself. But I'll teach ya the chorus, so together we can all have a good time with this."

I sit on the edge of an unused riser backstage and smile at the way Solly brings even a crowd of people so easily under his wing. I close my eyes and let his voice and the movement of his fingers upon the strings of his beloved guitar soothe my frayed and fragile nerves. Folks sing along to the familiar chords of some of his favorite James Taylor, Jim Croce, and Cat Stevens songs, and they do join in on a couple of the songs he wrote himself. Emotion overwhelms me as I ache to delight easily in these moments with him again someday. And as he comes offstage, I reach for him first, embracing him, feeling the soft curls of hair on the back of his neck, taking in the solid scent of him. He rests his guitar against the risers and holds me back, until a whole slew of dance troupes crowd us off.

Frank Streeter introduces them—The Pecanettes—a conglomeration of high school dancers from across the region, dressed in black-and-gold lamé-skirted dance costumes. In the front row, the twelve-and-under version of the Pecanettes, called the Pralines, mimic the cheers.

Muddy and the Flaps, preparing to go onstage next, pass us and congratulate Solly as he puts his guitar away.

"Great job there, Daniels," says the lead singer.

"Thanks, man!"

"Anytime you wanna join us, you let us know. We could use an extra guitar whenever you can spare the time."

"Will do. Thanks a lot!"

Solly and I stroll through and follow the crowd, much of which dissipates back into the temporary community of white-tented craft booths and the screaming lights of the carnival. We share a funnel cake. We listen to the lore of artisans in tents glowing golden against the cloud-laden twilight sky.

"I think the crowd really liked you."

"Yeah?"

"Yeah."

He pulls me close, and I don't shy away.

I spy her first, the tiny girl wandering in the empty, cockeyed rows of tents and folding chairs. She cannot see over the tops of them, and I hear her wimpering, "Mama!" She stops and sits, defeated, on the concrete curb. Her hair, in ringlets and tied with a pink, grosgrain ribbon, falls around her perfectly round face, still chubby with the remnants of toddlerhood.

"Jenny? Jenny Davies?" I call to her.

"Where you goin', Comfort?" Solly stops talking to the stranger next to him he befriended in the craft booth where we're stopped.

"It's Minnie Davies's girl. I think she's lost. So busy with all those others, she probably doesn't even know Jenny's missing yet." Wasn't two weeks ago little Jenny sat on the floor of the Curly Q playing with curlers and clips while her mama got her hair done.

I crouch down so I'm eye to eye with her. "Are you lost, Miss Jenny?"

Well, that's more than Jenny can stand. She bursts into tears and wails, rivers of tears pouring down her cheeks. I pick her up and hold her close, hot tears and snot soaking through my shirt.

"Let's go find your mama, darlin'." Solly pats her on the back, and she presses her face harder into my shoulder. We push through the craft tents toward the booth the state police have set up for precisely such an emergency.

"Comfort! Solly! *Vin isit la?*" I see Ernestine waving to us from her booth.

"Minnie Davies's girl, Jenny. She's lost," I explain.

"Ain't never lost." Ernestine pulls out a handkerchief and wipes Jenny's wet face. "You is found, always found, if you have Jesus."

Jenny stops crying as Mandy Appleton, Bay Spring County Fair Queen, and a few girls from her court, whir by on the back of a golf cart. Mandy sees us and Jenny with her tear-stained face and asks the driver to stop. Jenny regards her like she's Cinderella, especially when Mandy places a plastic tiara on her head. Mandy and I make eye contact for a knowing moment, and Jenny's rosebud lips turn up in a shy smile, and she reaches up to touch the tiara with both of her pudgy-knuckled hands, even as Minnie Davies arrives, frantic, on another golf cart driven by a sheriff. Minnie pulls Jenny from my arms, holds her close, and mouths the words *Thank you* to me through tears.

"Let's head back, Solly."

He takes my hand, and we work our way back toward the stage, where a country-western band performs, and the church beyond, where his truck is parked. The gentle twang of the tail end of Willie Nelson's "Help Me Make It Through the Night" floats through the amps.

"Care to dance?" Solly asks, kissing my hand.

"I'd love to," I say, as truthfully as I've ever been able to since the tragedy. He interlocks his fingers with mine and rests his other hand on the small of my back as the female lead singer begins the next song.

I'll always remember the song they were playin'
The first time we danced and I knew

Raindrops, first a few, then many, plunk around us, catching the light like falling stars.

As we swayed to the music and held to each other
I fell in love with you

A story from the Bible comes to mind, when God asked Hosea to love his wife even though she was wild and wicked and ruined. "Love her as the Lord loves ..." At least I think that's how the scripture reads. I kick off my flip-flops and feel the now-puddles of rainwater splash up onto my legs, baptizing me again into the love of this man, this moment, this life.

Could I have this dance for the rest of my life?
Would you be my partner every night?
When we're together, it feels so right.
Could I have this dance for the rest of my life?

Solly, locks of curls soaked and sticking to the sides of his face, pulls away from me and reaches into his back pocket. He places the engagement ring I sent back to him on my finger.

"How'd you know—"

"Shhhh." He presses a calloused finger to my lips, then holds my face, like Ernestine held Jenny's, in his hands.

"I'll never give up on you. Never did. Never will."

I shake my head in disagreement.

"Don't you argue now. You're my girl. Can't no one or no thing ever take you away from me."

He puts his lips to mine, and they are soft and sweet like the funnel cake we devoured.

Rain pours over us now, heavier than any rain I can remember.

The band plays on.

And still we dance.

We dance.

We dance.

We dance.

Si bòt a twò sere pou ou, mache pye atè.
"If your boot is too tight, walk barefoot."

CHAPTER 45

Anniston

Happens when folks are least expecting it, a jubilee.

The rain passed, leaving the empty, festival-lined streets of Bay Spring glazed with glory under the moon. A soft, eastern breeze helped dry our drizzle-laden hair.

We'd all hidden in artist tents and storefronts until the downpour let up, and so we hardly believed the bell ringing and can-banging had to do with anything besides some of the usual, late-night, midway riffraff living it up before the dazzling lights shut down their fun for the night.

That's when we realized the hollering came from every direction.

"Jubilee!"

"Jubilee!"

"Jubilee!"

Pickup trucks rumbled toward the bay. People ran from every direction carrying old tin buckets and washtubs. And Homer Chastain hurried to reopen his bait shop so he could pass out gigs, spears, nets, and ropes.

"What the heck is going on?" Jed stared, giddy and confused, at the craziness.

I pulled him out from under the lemonade shake-up stand. "C'mon! You'll see! It's a jubilee!"

The moon shone over the slick water of Mobile Bay, which looked smooth enough to skate on. All along the shore, folks waded in with their equipment. Three shirtless men in old army hats hauled washtubs full of crabs into the beds of their pickups, which they'd backed up to the edge of the incoming tide, now lapping at their tires. A weathered group of black women, skirts tucked up between their legs to make shorts, pulled in a net full of groggy-looking flounder and shrimp. A toothless man, in overalls, and his wife, dressed in her nightgown and curlers, had already gigged and strung up a six-foot line of flounder, flapping in the wind like a bunch of wet laundry.

"I ain't never seen anything like it," said Jed. Next to him, a bunch of blue crabs scrambled up a tree stump.

"Only happens a couple of times a year. Here in Bay Spring, up toward Fairhope and Daphne, these parts are the only place in the world this ever happens. Eddie Prince, who thinks he's Einstein, says it happens over in Pakistan or someplace like that, but even if he's right, that's the only other place."

We stood ankle-deep in the water along the shore and watched as folks sang and cheered, flashed their lanterns and flashlights across the water, rang bells, and clanged their gigs and spears on the bottoms of buckets to celebrate.

Jed bent down and picked up a flounder with his bare hands. "What's wrong with them? They ain't moving or trying to get away." Dozens more floated in the water around us, barely bothering to move.

"Maybe they're drunk on moonshine." I picked up a crab that didn't even lift a claw to protest. "The creatures always act this way during a jubilee. That's why it's so easy to catch trucks full of seafood. They swarm the beaches and act all out of their minds, practically swimming right into the buckets and nets."

"Look at those eels." Jed pointed behind us where at least a dozen eels buried their bodies in the shallow water, their heads the only things sticking out and swaying with the gentle roll of the tide. "Their mouths are hanging open like they're starving for air."

"They are." Larry waded over to where we stood, a string of crabs flung over his shoulder, and a bucket full of flounder stacked up like pancakes at his side.

"What's wrong with them?"

"Ran out of oxygen out in the deep. They'll disappear as fast as they came in 'fore too long. Soon as they can breathe again."

A pickup truck already full to overflowing with shrimp pulled away from the frenzy, and other folks with strings overpacked with crab and flounder packed up to get their catch home to clean and freeze.

"Wanna catch some?" Larry offered Jed a gig and rope.

"I can't say that I do. Something's not right about celebrating creatures forced to shore because they can't breathe out in the deep where they're s'posed to. They swim up here, crazed out of their minds and suffocating, and then we all celebrate and stab 'em and string 'em up?"

"It's not such a bad thing. Most folks look at it as a gift from the sea." Larry nodded toward a mother and father, surrounded by at least a half dozen kids, the sort of skin-and-bones that comes from eating gas-station beef jerky and RC Cola all day, and most of 'em needing haircuts or baths or both. An older boy threw two lines of flounder over his shoulders, and each of the younger kids filled buckets with crab. Next to them, a group of older teenagers threw beer cans at the dopey crabs and shrimp floating near the top of the water.

"Maybe." Jed looked Larry straight in the eye. "What else is there to do when you can't breathe but try to swim for shore?"

Larry put a hand on Jed's shoulder. "Swim for shore, or don't be afraid to swim out deeper." He shook him hard and knowing-like.

The Bay Spring Catholic Church bells rang at two a.m., just before the creatures came back to life, like the Lord breathing into Adam. Soon, they all flipped and flopped their way back out to the moonlit sea. The time had passed without us realizing it, and I figured I'd be in a whole mess of trouble for staying up so late until I spied Comfort and Solly tying up Ernestine's tent. They'd stayed to watch the hullabaloo too.

"Be back in a minute!" I called to them.

"We'll wait." Solly winked.

Jed and I walked as far as the library.

"So you'd never heard of the jubilee before tonight?" I asked him.

"Nope. 'Cept for the one in the Bible you told me about. Never heard of this one."

"Pretty crazy, huh?"

"Pretty crazy."

I searched my brain for something else to say besides good-bye, half-afraid and half-hoping the silence that fell between us would bring another kiss. "God's gonna give you a jubilee of your own, Jed. You wait and see. Like He did for Larry. Like Daddy said He did for all those Israelites in Leviticus. God gives second chances. You don't have to leave town. He'll give one to you, too."

"The only second chance I want is this one." He held my face between his hands and kissed me. A second time. A third time. And a fourth. After that I quit counting.

He stepped back, and by the time I opened my eyes, he was gone.

LATE OCTOBER, 1980

Sonje lapli a ki te fè mayi ou grandi.
"Remember the rain that made your corn grow."

CHAPTER 46

Anniston

Vaughn moved the cows out to the far pasture so they wouldn't trample the nuts beginning to fall. Trimmers, mowers, and gatherers worked as many hours a day as they could now that the nuts were really falling. Everyone hoped for a great crop to make up for everything Hurricane Frederic stole, and we used every contraption available to scoop up, pick up, and rake up nuts as they fell from their withering husks.

The good part about harvest was seeing Jed most every day after school when he'd come to work with us, huddling under one of the makeshift, tin-roofed storage sheds that dotted the hills and rows when it rained. Inside, it sounded like popcorn exploding and overflowing Ernestine's old Bromwell popper with the holes in the lid.

The bad part about harvest was seeing him most every day with no time to search the creek beds or lie on our backs, hidden behind an overgrown row of trees, watching the clouds roll past. Too much work to do.

One Friday afternoon, a day an Indian summer sun nearly baked our skin to a crisp, Jed came and found me up at the house before he left for the day. "Meet me at the library tomorrow around noon. We'll go down to Point Clear Creek where it dumps into the bay. I bet a lot of stuff's washed up there after all the cat-and-dog rains we've been having."

"'Kay, but wait for me if I'm running late."

I packed my towel and pulled on my favorite terrycloth shorts over my blue polka-dot swimsuit. "Hey, Molly, I'll be back soon. Then I'll walk ya. Promise." Molly looked up at me from her curled-up spot on the floor, the whites of her eyes hanging like sad smiles. I snuggled my nose into one of her floppy white ears and hugged her good-bye.

"Awww, don't give me that face, girl. It's not like I'm going away forever."

I found Ernestine in the laundry room. "Ernestine? Jed and I are going down to the creek."

"Be careful, and call me if we need to come get you if it's after dark."

By the time I got to the library, Jed wasn't there yet, so I sat on the steps to wait for him. Noon turned into quarter past, then half past, and by then I was getting all riled up.

Where could he be?

I took the chance of running into Mr. and Mrs. Devine to see if he was home. Maybe he was snoozing. Maybe he forgot. I had to find out. The whole trailer rattled when I knocked, and at first, not a sound answered me back.

I knocked again.

A rumble in the far back end grew into loud thumps as it came closer.

A hand pulled the makeshift curtain aside, and the face of a wild man, who I figured was Mr. Devine, greeted me. I tried to calm myself, figuring John the Baptist mighta looked much the same, with a scraggly beard and hair poking up in dreads all over his head. Folks in the Bible thought he looked right crazy, too, but he wasn't. He was the cousin of Jesus, after all.

"What do you want?" he bellowed, and the smell of alcohol nearly knocked me off the rickety steps.

This was no cousin of Jesus.

"Um, afternoon, sir. I'm looking for Jed? Jed Manon?"

"He ain't here. Ain't been here for days, the little rat. Living off us and coming and going as he pleases. S'posed to get us our money. S'posed to got paid yesterday. You ain't come to deliver his pay, have ya?"

"John? Who is it?" Mrs. Devine, whom I recognized from the night she took me home from the cotillion, peeked over his shoulder. She blew out a plume of smoke that rose like a cloud-shaped halo over her head.

Lord, I shoulda listened to Jed and never come here.

"'Scuse me, ma'am. I'm looking for Jed."

Mrs. Devine pushed her husband aside, who was happy to back away and collapse onto the vinyl couch behind her. "You're that friend of his, ain't ya? What's your name? Anni?"

"Anniston, ma'am."

"That's right. Anniston." She looked me over a minute, took another draw of her cigarette, which was nearly down to the stub, and scratched at the rollers in her hair. "I ain't seen him. Not for a few days. Hangs out at that crazy library all the time. Don't know why. So stupid I doubt he can even read. You find him, you tell him he owes us that paycheck, hear?"

"Yes, ma'am. Sorry to bother y'all."

She slammed the door before I even finished my sentence.

Days? They hadn't seen him for days? Where had he been stayin' then? And where was he now?

I checked the library first. I was glad Jed got me going there again. Used to love when Daddy took me there for reading time when I was little. We made crafts and listened to the singsong voice of the librarian as she read us the latest adventure from Frog and Toad or a Shel Silverstein poem. The rows of shelves loomed high over my head, stacked with old books, new books, books covered in plastic, frayed on the spines from so many checkouts, stained from so many wondering, searching fingers. Hundreds of books, but no sign of Jed.

The sun stung my shoulders as I rode my bike down past the docks, down the path that led to where we liked to wade, where Point Clear Creek meets the bay. Maybe I hadn't heard him right. Maybe he'd said to meet him there.

The water crept higher than I'd ever seen it. I hardly recognized the place, and so little shore remained left to walk along. I parked my bike against the overlook railing next to Jed's. His backpack and water bottle were still there, which meant he probably started wading already. I hurried down the trail that led to the creek. Jed's shoes and socks sat like bullfrogs on top of a boulder.

"Je-ed! Hey, Jed!" I didn't hear anything except water running fast over nearby rocks and over an old tree halfsunk, giant roots whittled away to nubs by the currents.

I kicked off my flip-flops and waded in to my knees, surprised by how hard the water pulled toward the bay.

"Jed! Je-ed, where are you?" I wished he'd waited. Irritation melted into a fear at the bottom of my backbone, creeping around to my stomach and making my chest burn.

"Jed, come on! This isn't funny!" It wasn't like him to play a joke.

I waded in farther, and my whole body throbbed with panic. I remembered how he said he wasn't a good swimmer, that I shouldn't count on him to save me, back on that day we took Larry's boat out onto the bay. If Jed dove or even if he waded too far in, he wouldn't have known about the current. He wouldn't have known about the strength of the undertow. He wouldn't have had anything to grab when he came up for air.

If he came up.

I ran back up the trail, tripping over thick, bare roots jutting up out of the ground, washed bare by all the recent rain. I peered down once more from the overlook to see if I could see Jed anywhere.

The roads and trails blurred around me. I pedaled fast. My legs burned. My heart hurt. I had to get help. Tears stung my eyes.

"Help me.

"Help Jed!

"Someone!"

A policeman passed, slowed down, and backed up when he saw me. I tried to tell him. My words got all mixed up. I choked on the dreadful thoughts trying to push their way out of me, about what happened—

No. I would not think of him as gone.

The back of the police car felt refrigerator cold. The chemical-like smell of vinyl and the commotion of lights and sirens shot a wave of vomit into my throat.

Police boats trolled, and I worried a motor might cut him, there beneath the surface.

Police dogs barked and sniffed in crazy-making circles down by the river.

Divers bobbed up and down, empty armed every time they surfaced.

More lights and cars arrived.

Mama.

Ernestine.

Vaughn.

Solly and Comfort, too.

Someone put a towel around me. Ernestine covered me with her shawl. I shook and trembled despite the still-ninety-degree heat.

The sun disappeared into the bay, and the world turned gray.

People tried to convince me to go, but I couldn't.

Wouldn't.

"We won't be able to find anything more tonight," the officer said, badge glaring at me from the center of his chest.

"You can't stop looking!" I screamed. Vaughn held me back before I could take a swing at him. I swung anyway, clawing at the soupy air.

Mama pulled me closer, held me, helped me to the car.

"Wait!" I tore myself from her grip and ran to Jed's bike and clutched his orange tackle box full of fossils to my chest. Detectives or somebody had already taken his backpack, but at least I could save his collection.

Our collection.

Vaughn talked softly to the officer I'd tried to clobber and to a couple of dripping-wet police divers before driving us home. It was the first time I remembered Vaughn driving me anywhere, ever, as I sat in the back, leaning into the wide, soft folds of Ernestine's side.

Vaughn handed me a wet piece of fabric. "Here, darlin'. One of the divers found this bandana."

It was the bandana Jed handed me the day we'd taken Larry's skiff out onto the bay.

I avoided Vaughn's eyes as he searched for mine in the rearview mirror.

I was sure I already knew the rest of the truth he wanted to say.

Quand prend trop boucoup, li glisse.
"Grab for too much, and it slips away from you."

CHAPTER 47

Anniston

I am lost. Gone. Wandering through a graveyard. Tangled in moss hanging, tendrils reaching, tapping me on the shoulder. Teasing. Making me think someone is there. But the blackness reminds me.

He's gone.

I woke up to a still-black world. Felt like morning, but I couldn't tell. Maybe I'd slept through the day. Maybe yesterday was a dream. But I saw the double brooksella on my nightstand, and I knew. I pulled my covers up tighter and curled into a ball. If I could make myself small enough, maybe the hurt would squeeze out and away like toothpaste down a drain. Washed far away. To the river. To the ocean. To Jed.

"Anni." Mama knocked soft and weak against my solid wood door. "Anni, may I come in?"

"Did they find somethin'?"

She opened the door and shook her head. "No. Nothin' yet."

I groaned, and she came and sat on the bed beside me. I saw her hand rubbing my leg, but I felt nothing. Nothing to feel.

"It's not morning yet, but I couldn't sleep. Figured maybe you couldn't either. You okay?"

"What time is it?"

"'Bout five."

I rolled away from her.

She lay down behind me like a spoon and rubbed my back for a little while, like she used to before we moved here. Before Daddy died. Before any of this mess.

"I'm sorry, Anni. About everything. And now this. This is too much for anyone to bear."

I didn't know what to say about that.

It was too much.

Way too much.

Later that morning, the sun woke me up like a glaring smack of fire. I patted the side of the bed, and Molly stretched herself out, long and alive. She jumped up, circled three times, then curled her back up against me.

What was I supposed to do with all this death?

I shoved my feet into my slippers and shuffled to the kitchen. I sorta hoped to be alone, but Mama and Ernestine were already up and dressed, drinking their coffee.

I felt their eyes on me as I pulled open the refrigerator to find something that would make the ache in my belly stop.

"Quit," I said into the open refrigerator.

"What's that, child?"

"Quit staring at me!" I spun around and felt right then that I hated them both very much—a new and mighty and wild, wild feeling. "Quit staring at me! Make all of this quit!"

"Baby girl—"

"I'm not a baby! He kissed me, you know. I'm not a baby anymore, because he kissed me!" I ran back to my room and nearly caught Molly's tail in the door when I slammed it shut. I crawled under my desk and cried. Hard, heaving crying, like giant hiccups, one after the other.

Ernestine knocked on my door this time. "Can I come in, child?"

I sniffed and wiped the snot off my face.

She perched herself on the edge of my bed. "What you got there?"

I turned the fossil over in my hand. "He found this."

She waited, patient as ever, for me to keep talking.

"Jed found this and gave it to me. Two fossils. Brooksella fossils. Connected. Hardly anyone ever finds two of 'em connected like this. But he found it and gave it to me soon after we met."

"It's beautiful. Like they's holding hands."

"They are holding hands. Because something awful and fierce made them stick together. Me and Jed, we were stuck together by everything around spinning us, and now we're unstuck. Broke apart. And I don't know what I'm gonna do." I searched her eyes for help. "What am I supposed to do?"

She turned and gazed outside the window. "You supposed to look, child. God don't let a person precious as Jed leave without leaving his friends who loved him with ladders."

I rolled my eyes and didn't feel guilty that she saw me.

"*Nechel.* Angels coming down to take away your pain, and angels coming down to replace that pain with life. One tiny ladder, one small rung to climb. One small rung at a time."

"Humph." No good in that advice. And no angels scooping away any of my pain. Besides, whatever pain they scooped out would fill right back up again, like digging a hole at the beach. Dig too far, and you hit water, and the hole fills right back up, no matter how much or how fast you keep digging.

Ernestine interrupted my thoughts. "Don't you think Jed would look for *nechel?*"

He would.

I knew he would.

And sure enough, a ladder came down that evening.

"What else can you tell us about Jed's home life?" the detective asked me. He sat across the dining room table from me, gold badge glinting from the light of the chandelier above us. Made me nervous knowing a gun rested in his holster. Reminded me of the night Daddy died. This was the same officer Vaughn had talked to before we left the park Saturday night. The same man I tried to punch in the chest for saying they had to call off the search for the night.

"Nothin'. He never let me come near his house—the trailer where he lived." It didn't feel right to tell him about the cigarette burns. Or the beatings. Or the fact that the Devines made Jed turn over all his hard-earned money to them.

"Miss Anniston." He got up real close, too close, probably to make sure I was aware of the seriousness of his questioning. "We have reason to believe Hettie and John ... well ... that the Devines shoulda never been allowed to provide a home for a foster child. That they've been dishonest with the law."

"What's this have to do with Jed? You're still looking for him, aren't you? Well, aren't you?"

He looked over at Mama, as if he needed permission to tell me the truth. I felt like I might be sick and covered my mouth.

"We have reason to believe—"

I couldn't listen. I stood, ready to run outta there as fast as I could into the orchards, down to the creek—

"Anni, sit down, child." Ernestine, who'd been sitting next to me, tugged at my hand.

"We have reason to believe your friend Jed is a runaway. And as he's a ward of the state, we have the responsibility to find him."

"A runaway? Jed? He wouldn't run away without telling me." But as soon as I said the words, I knew this was one of the ladders Ernestine said would come. Relief fell over me like rain over parched summer orchards, and I knew.

Jed was alive.

As sure as I was sitting there breathing, Jed was surely alive.

Sonje lapli ki leve mayi.
"Remember the rain that made your corn grow."

CHAPTER 48

Comfort

Alive.

I lie in my bed, exhausted by a day in the orchards, and for the first time I can remember, I feel alive. Blood pulses warm through my withered veins. My heart thumps, feral, against the center of my chest. The skin of my arms, my legs, tingle from a day spent soaking up currents of air, of indigo sky. Joy immerses me, unsettles me, like a body hurtling off a barren cliff, slicing through water, then floating in the depths, suspended, whole.

I admit I wait like Cinderella for another midnight to arrive—and still I do not feel I have escaped its doomed chime—but for now, I feel what God intended unfurling within me. Released from darkness at last, I taste the essence of hope pushing, shy but intent on release.

Is this how God heals? Slow enough to feel the slough of pain, but quick enough to press me deeper into Him? Is this how God binds up wounds, salving them with the trembling assurance of a lover, binding them with the gauze of peace?

Freedom proclaims its truth. My bones near rattle with the rhythm of its ringing.

I am awash in ashes transformed into a tiara of astonishment. I am draped in an array of applause directed at me from the One who not only made me, but who is making me still.

I pull the old, worn burlap pecan bags off every mirror in my house, permitting myself to see reflections of places long devastated and letting my heart roam ancient ruins. Not without fear, but with possibility. Not without shame, but with the advent of a double portion of joy.

Even as the pecans drop all around the trees, I am sure there will be a spring—as sure as I am that the branches will once again display the splendor of their journey through rock-laden soil and torrents of storms because of the beckoning sun. Because of the rains that soak them. Because of the hands that turn the soil.

The phone rings as the sun grazes the tree-laden hills with a final caress, and I answer, sure it is Solly. But there is silence on the other end. "Hello? Who's there?"

A sob, more like a choke, is muffled, but even that much is familiar. "Mama?"

"I'm so sorry." Her words come slurred, but they come, just the same, before the connection breaks.

In the morning, I open the front door and find a rose, red and wilted, on the step.

The stem is broken, but care has been taken to see that the thorns are trimmed off.

I hold it to my cheek and weep.

Yon manman pa janm mòde pitit li nan zo a.
"A mother never bites her child to the bone."

CHAPTER 49

Anniston

More ladders fell from heaven after that. The first couple came when October stretched into November, and I'd grown tired of waiting for a word from Jed. The pain of him running away without saying good-bye and not being 100 percent certain he was alive mixed together in my heart. I couldn't figure out whether to hope or to grieve. Loneliness and relief fought for a place in my head, which didn't have room for the both of them. At school, words blurred across my textbook pages. I tried to focus on all the work there was to do in preparing hundreds of holiday pecan orders, but the annual routine provided little comfort. Sally Roberts and her friends invited me to sit at their table at lunch again, but I knew they only felt sorry for me. So I refused, choosing instead to keep company with an empty seat at the table where Jed and I had sat all last spring.

The only break in the days came from working at the Curly Q on Saturdays. On one particular afternoon, I waited for Comfort to finish up with Lila Roberts, Sally's mother.

Lila left no doubt in my mind that snooty was a genetic trait. "Oh, it feels so scrumptious to have my nails done. Three days overdue does nothing but make me panic. Think of how folks have seen my falling-apart nails every time I go to pay for something at the cash registers, taking money out of my wallet with cracked and chipped-up nails."

"You can't tell, Lila. They always look fabulous when you come in. Like you just had 'em done."

"Comfort, you are too kind."

"'Scuse me, Mrs. Roberts. Comfort, may I run to the library for a bit? I'm almost done with *Song of the Lark* and want to see if there's something else I can take home to read."

"Sure. Go on over, and I'll meet you there after I finish here."

I took my time moseying down Main Street. Mrs. Bixley's Shell Seeker gift-store window held mirrors framed with sand dollars and even one of Comfort's brand-new shell mosaic end tables. An electric train weaved its way through mountain passes and tunnels in the window of the toy store. I stopped to tap the glass at the puppies in the pet-store window, and as I did, I saw Mr. Morgan, the owner, hand a cage holding a bright yellow canary to a girl and her mother.

I burst through the door, jolting all the puppies and kittens in the front window out of their slumber. "Where'd you get that canary, sir?"

Mr. Morgan, a mostly bald, gray-headed man, adjusted his bright red suspenders, which matched his bow tie. "Oh, I'm sorry, but I don't have any more, young lady."

"I don't want to buy one. I just wondered how you came upon him."

He massaged his chin and considered me for a moment. "Funny you should ask. I don't carry birds too often. Not much of a demand for them. But a boy a little older than yourself brought him to me a few weeks ago. Said he'd found him in the wild. Nursed him back to health. Wondered if I could find him a good, safe home."

"Thanks, Mr. Morgan. That's what I thought." Before he could ask me anything more, I skipped out of the store. I don't think I stopped grinning until I reached the library, where a blast of air-conditioning greeted me when I walked into the one-hundred-year-old building. A librarian stacked new arrivals on a rolling cart, and I picked up one called *Sophie's Choice*, by William Styron. The unbent spine creaked open, and I sank my nose into the paper, which smelled like tree pulp and ink still drying on the pages, then set it down next to another new arrival called *The Thorn Birds*.

I made my way to the back corner of the first floor, where the scent of people's fingers and homes blended together and soaked in the paper, which made the library smell a little like the Goodwill over in Foley. I thumbed through the young adult books like *Are You There God? It's Me, Margaret*; *Confessions of a Teenage Baboon*; and *Flowers in the Attic*, which Mama said was not appropriate for me yet. Girls like Sally carried around a new one from this section every week, and I tried to find one that looked interesting there. But I always ended up in the literature section.

This time, though, I headed to the paleontology, rocks, and minerals section of the library. I knew from Jed and a little help from the card catalog that most were in the 500s section. Sure enough, I found *Exploring and Understanding Rocks and Minerals*, by Robinson; *Rocks, Minerals, and Crystals*, by Almond and Whitten; *An Introduction to the Practical Study of Crystals, Minerals, and Rocks*, by Cox; and *A Field Guide to Rocks and Minerals*, by Frederick H. Pough.

Close by, I found *The Bone Hunters*, by Lanham; *Late Canadian Cephalopod Faunas from Southwestern United States*, by Flower, Hayner, and Hook; *Let's Go Fossil Shark Tooth Hunting*, by Cartmell; and *Collecting Fossils*, by Major.

Stuck in the middle were four books that were definitely out of place: *Experimental Oyster Transplanting in Louisiana*, by Tarver and Dugas; *The Oyster Thief*, by Devine; *A Survey of the Oyster and Oyster Shell Resources of Alabama*, by May; *Experiments to Re-establish Historical Oyster Seed Grounds and to Control the Southern Oyster Drill*, by Pollard. Strange, but not if Jed spent lots of time there. I doubt the librarians sorted these books much.

I tilted my head sideways, reading more titles, when I noticed *I Know Why the Caged Bird Sings*, by Maya Angelou, squashed far back between *The Weekend Fossil Hunter*, by LaPlante, and *Microspores from the Fredericksburg Group of the Southern United States*, by Srivastava. Last year, Mrs. Nowlan mentioned Ms. Angelou's book in English class as a very important work of literature we'd study later in high school. Literature was definitely a lot of rows away from rocks and fossils.

As I picked up the book, an envelope fell out.

Anni

My hands jittered as I opened the seal.

From between the folds of paper, red rose petals fell, hitting the floor without a sound.

Dear Anni,

If you find this letter, the first thing I need to say is I'm sorry. Again. Sorry for leaving the way I did. Sorry for making you think I was dead. But it was the only way I could think of to escape.

You've always been the brave one, the one who faces things head-on. I guess that makes me a coward, 'cause I couldn't face another day caught in the cage of other folks making my life into what they wanted. I had to go when I had the chance. I had to do this, to make a life for myself so that someday, Lord willing, I can make a life with someone like you. Maybe, someday, with you.

I thought maybe you'd find your way to this section of the library. That maybe, when things settled down, you'd wonder about me enough to wonder about fossils and minerals and the stuff of the earth human hands can't hurt. That maybe, you'd find this out-of-place book like you found out-of-place me last spring and find the treasure inside.

If you're reading this, you found me. I'm free like the canary we found last spring. I won't say where I went, in case someone besides you finds this, but you'll know when I tell you I saved up the money I needed to for things longed for, and I'm not far beyond the distant hill.

Yours,

Jed

"You ready to go home, little bookworm?" I nearly jumped a mile when Comfort rounded the corner into the aisle where I sat, dried red rose petals scattered all around me.

All I could do was hold the letter out to her, along with a string of leather holding a single bead of hematite rose.

As Comfort read the letter, tears spilled out of her eyes too.

"Is this what Ernestine means about God bringing us ladders like He brought one to Jacob, out in the middle of the desert?"

"It is, Anni. It surely is."

The next ladder fell that same night. Didn't start out that way, though. After supper, the bedroom grew dark as I reread Comfort's notes and poems, and I tucked the letter from Jed into the shoe box along with them under my bed. When I rolled over, Princella stood in my doorway, the light shining behind her in a way that reminded me of the line of framed silhouettes in the front hall.

"Mama never took care of me." Whiskey sloshed out of her glass as she took a step toward the bed where I lay. "Took to her bed in a dark room every evening, dark like this room now." She closed her eyes and turned in a circle, as if held by some invisible dance partner.

Was she telling me about her growing up? Why now?

"After St. Augustine's—" She took a gulp of her drink, then wiped a drip off the side of the sweaty glass. "Cole was the first good thing came out of my life up 'til then. The only good thing."

"I don't—I don't understand."

"Hush." The word slid out of her mouth, and she stumbled, reaching toward me to put a finger over my lips. "Let me finish. My daddy—he raped me. My brother raped me. Mama's boyfriends raped me. Like someone painted a bull's-eye right here."

She cackled those last two words in my face, and I nearly vomited as the acrid smell of whiskey tumbled out with the rot of grief in her story. She drew an imaginary circle on her forehead like she was tracing a bull's-eye. Reminded me of the circles of grass cuttings around the base of all the pecan trees.

"Guess green eyes aren't the only thing I passed down to Comfort, now are they?"

I searched my heart for something to tell her she'd done right, fighting back the feeling of having to be sick at the thought of her raped over and over and over again, as a child, a baby, as a girl like me who shoulda had no other worries than running wild and free down red, red roads and into the arms of a daddy like mine. "But ... you had Daddy."

"I did have your daddy. Messed that up too."

I pushed myself up tight against the head of Comfort's canopy bed, grabbed a pillow, and clutched it hard against my chest. My heart thumped like a wild rabbit thrashing around inside. I studied my fingernails, afraid to look at her. Afraid to hear what she might say next. And what she said next was the last thing I ever thought I'd hear from her.

"I'm trying to tell you I'm sorry. Sorry for what I done and what I have not done. Sorry for what I am and sorry for what I ain't. Sorry I chose to hate instead of forgive, when forgive is all folks around me ever did for me." The rest of the whiskey disappeared down her throat as she threw the glass back. "All those things that was done to me, I wanted someone to *pay* for all that. Someone shoulda paid. Don't you think? Can you understand that?"

Her spittle sprayed into my eyes as her tongue, thick from the drink, struggled to get the words out. I tried to wipe it away with the corner of the bedsheet without her noticing.

"Yes, ma'am."

"You do? You understand?" She turned her face up toward the ceiling, arms outstretched, toward God, I supposed. "You hear that? My granddaughter says she understands. She understands I never intended those someones to be my own sons. Never intended my own daughter ... what it cost my beautiful daughter ... cost her the same as all it cost me." She slowly turned, then wobbled out of the room, pausing to grab hold of the doorframe for one last moment. "I'm going to do better. Starting tomorrow. I promise."

That might not have sounded like a ladder, but the angels, they brought down hope and took away pain, floating down on their silvery wings even as I fought to fall into a fitful sleep. Faceless shadows of Princella's family I'd never met haunted me, running after me. Then sirens came, like the same ones that screamed Daddy's departure from the earth—sirens I soon realized were not a dream, but real. Too real. Again.

Every light in the house was on when I stumbled down the stairs. By the time I got to the den, the medics had already pulled the white sheet over Princella's head, her body stretched out straight and flat on the gurney.

"Mama!"

"Oh, Anni, come here, baby girl." Mama held me in her arms, covered, like the night Daddy died, in her thick pink bathrobe. Her hair smelled like freesia shampoo, and everything felt the same except no puddles of blood spread all over the floor.

"What happened?"

"It was the drink. She had too much. Her heart plain stopped beatin'. Broken as it was, I'm s'prised she lasted this long." Ernestine dusted off a framed picture lying facedown on the floor. "She was holdin' this picture of Cole to her chest when Mr. Vaughn found her. She was already gone."

Wòch nan dlo pa konn doulè wòch nan solèy.
"The stone in the water does not know the pain of the stone in the sun."

CHAPTER 50

Comfort

Mama. Her name is a statement. A fact. A truth.

She is my mama. She was my mama. Now she lies still, unable to argue. Unable to chastise. Unable to correct.

I think of the broken rose.

I consider her broken road.

Her skin is pale, but not the gray or white I expect as I pull the sheet down to take one last look at her. More the color of the champagne. Or porcelain. Or of grace—the secret abandon of one who has finally found peace.

I press my lips against her cold cheek, rosy only from the tear-smeared rouge.

"I forgive you."

And I do.

"Fly away, Mama. Fly away free."

And somehow, I know she does.

SUMMER 1981

Bondye Bon.
"God is good."

CHAPTER 51

Anniston

After Princella died, Harlan Pecan Company filled Christmas orders just in time for the holidays. Ronald Reagan took office just in time for the hostages to be released in Iran. The Daughters of the Confederacy Cotillion and Bay Spring Auxiliary Auction crowned Sally Roberts as their 1981 princess just in time for me to never attend another cotillion again. Mama and I got our very own house in town where we hung Granddaddy Harlan's sword above the mantel. Grass grew over the three deep graves. I learned enough chords on Daddy's old guitar that I could play a song or two. Bells rang, and the town went hog wild over an early June jubilee.

And in the midst of all that good, Comfort and Solly got married.

As he'd promised, Vaughn made sure the ceremony and celebration held nothing back for his daughter, the bride, and her groom. Handkerchiefs came out all over when Vaughn walked Comfort down the aisle, his arm entwined with his only living child's. His only daughter, surrounded and battered by troubles, but not demoralized. Terrorized, but held up by the love of family and Jesus. Thrown down, but unbroken.

Comfort wore a string of asters braided into her hair. And it was clear as Vaughn, his face wet with tears, lifted her veil and kissed her cheek, that this day brought with it a new beginning for us all.

A grand *Cochon de Lait* followed the ceremony, bringing the most fun the Harlan plantation had ever seen in its hills. Felt like springtime coming to Narnia, the worst of things melting into the best. We roasted a suckling pig over hickory, and most of the town came, even Mrs. Reed, the organist, and her husband, who only came out for Friday-night bingo. Muddy and the Flaps rocked the reception and received several requests—including several asking them specifically to bring Solly along with 'em—to play at other upcoming venues in town, and Shirley O'Day never printed another nasty word about them in her social column.

Late in the evening, when the music of Muddy and the Flaps switched from rock and roll to ballads, couples slow-danced down our red-ribboned driveway to their cars. Husbands put their arms around wives, and wives put theirs around their husbands.

The wire fence separating Comfort's yard from the cemetery was covered with the blossoms of bright-orange trumpet-vine flowers. The shadow of Daddy's, Cole's, and Princella's gravestones stood tall as the last rays of the sun stretched out. I took the double brooksella out of my dress pocket and traced the places where the arms of the stars blended together.

I pulled the letter and photo out of my pocket next, edges of both yellowed from all the times I'd held them. In the picture, Jed stands shirtless on top of his brand-new oysterin' skiff, hands on his hips, chest stuck out like a rooster.

Dear Anni,
You were right.
    God gives second chances.
    I hope He gives one to us someday too.

                            Jed

I could almost hear the water sloshing against the hull of that steely gray boat, against the letters standing tall in fresh black paint.

JUBILEE

I turned to watch Comfort and Solly dancing under a canopy of white lights and wisteria, and walked over to join them while Muddy and the Flaps played on.

... a little more ...

When a delightful concert comes to an end,

the orchestra might offer an encore.

When a fine meal comes to an end,

it's always nice to savor a bit of dessert.

When a great story comes to an end,

we think you may want to linger.

And so, we offer ...

AfterWords—just a little something more after you

have finished a David C Cook novel.

We invite you to stay awhile in the story.

Thanks for reading!

Turn the page for ...

- A Word about Tamar and Survivors
- Book Club Questions
- Author Interview
- Recipes from Bay Spring and the
  Harlan Family and Friends

A WORD ABOUT TAMAR
AND SURVIVORS

Writing a novel about sexual abuse might lead folks to believe the story of Comfort is a parallel to my own journey of abuse and healing. As with most writers, words strung from the heart to the page cannot exist without a certain degree of autobiography, for as artists, our calling is to create from what we know and feel most deeply.

On the contrary, however, the intricacies of what I went through as a child differ greatly from the path and inspiration of this novel. I prefer to let the perpetrators wrestle with their own misdeeds and perversions in private. They and I know precisely what they did, and that is enough.

Instead, *How Sweet the Sound* is inspired by the story of King David's daughter Tamar, whose story is written in 2 Samuel 13. After her brother, Amnon, raped her, what happened next is possibly worse than the rape:

> Her brother Absalom said to her, "Has your brother
> Amnon had his way with you? Now, my dear sister,
> let's keep it quiet—a family matter. He is, after all,
> your brother. Don't take this so hard." Tamar lived
> in her brother Absalom's home, bitter and desolate.
> (2 Sam. 13:20 MSG)

Rape, incest, and molestation are the silent epidemics of our society. Conservative estimates are that one out of four girls and one out of six boys will suffer such atrocities before the age of eighteen. And the victims are threatened, coerced, and frightened into staying silent. As a result of their silence, most of them battle lifelong mental, spiritual, and even physical illnesses.

As a follower of Christ, I am not satisfied with the ending of Tamar's story. None of us should be. The truth and light shining into the darkest places of our broken, ailing world is what sets people free. And so I wrote this book as a loose, modern-day allegory in hopes that it might challenge and encourage the Tamars of the world, that they might not live bitter and desolate lives, but that they might instead find hope, healing, and freedom.

BOOK CLUB QUESTIONS

1. Overall, how did you feel after reading *How Sweet the Sound?* Renewed? Hopeful? Or depressed? Angry? Perhaps perplexed?

2. Why does Rey shoot Cole? Do you feel his actions are justified? Why or why not?

3. Princella and Comfort react to similar pasts in very different ways. What life events and choices may have shaped the way they chose to live their lives? Did any of their behaviors disturb you, or did you feel sympathy toward them? Why or why not?

4. Anniston begins the book by saying she thought she'd lived through everything. How does her view change by the end of the book? Does she grow and mature?

5. In what ways—if any—does Jed's journey parallel the journeys of Comfort and Princella? How are his reactions to his past different from or similar to Comfort's and Princella's? How does Jed's life teach Anni about her aunt and grandmother?

6. As a figure of goodness and truth, Ernestine provides a voice of reason and encouragement in the novel. As a bystander to most of the tragedies and secrets of the Harlan family, what is the primary

role of her character in the story? Would you have changed anything about her part in the story?

7. What did you think about the two-narrator structure of the book? Did you like being able to see the thoughts of both Anni and Comfort? How might the book have changed if told from only one or the other's viewpoint?

8. Did the plot keep moving you forward? Was it engaging? Too slow? Too fast? Enough details? Too many?

9. What themes are explored in *How Sweet the Sound*? What symbols are used to reinforce these themes?

10. What chapter or passage was the most moving or profound for you and why?

11. Did you feel like the ending was fulfilling? How might you change the ending?

12. How has this novel changed you? Have you learned something new by reading it? If so, what will you do with that new knowledge or insight?

AUTHOR INTERVIEW

What is your schedule like when you're writing?

My writing schedule is a bit unusual, and perhaps unconventional by industry standards. Most experts will tell you that you must write every day. I have tried that, and I have failed every time. Because I am a wife, a mama of three teenage boys, and I work two to three days a week as a registered nurse, I have learned to fit my writing time in while I wait in school pickup lines, during halftimes of lacrosse games, in doctor's office waiting rooms, and on the back patio on those rare, quiet mornings after everyone has gone to work and school.

What would you say is your interesting writing quirk?

Personally, my writing process involves a lot of thinking, and so I often do artistic projects around the house, like reupholstering and refinishing furniture and antiques. This helps me back up and gain a little insight into what I'm writing. If I'm too close to the story, I tend to get "stuck." For me, art truly inspires my art.

Where do you get your information or ideas for your books?

My ideas come from a spring bulb pushing up from the crusty, winter ground; from the pull of an oysterman's tongs across shallow, coastal bay waters; from holding the wrinkled hand, crisscrossed with blue veins, of a dying nonagenarian; from the laughter of my sons; and from the chords and strains and banjos of a rip-roaring worship set at church. My ideas come from my past and my future. From a psalm and a lament. But deep, deep down, I believe my ideas come from love.

What books/authors have influenced your writing?

I love great Southern stories: anything by Kaye Gibbons, Sue Monk Kidd, and Kathryn Stockett; Eudora Welty's short stories; Maya Angelou and Mary Oliver's poems. Recently, I have come to adore Kent Haruf and Chaim Potok. And Brennan Manning, well, he wrecks me every time. I would be remiss if I did not mention that Francine Rivers's book *Redeeming Love* prompted me to seek traditional publication.

Do you ever experience writer's block?

I don't believe there is such a thing as writer's block. I do believe in the luring power of procrastination, and unfortunately I can be found practicing it all too often.

Who is your favorite character from your book and why?

Honestly, Solly is my favorite character in this book. First of all, I imagined him to look like Matthew McConaughey, so what's not to like? But secondly, he reminds me of my husband, who has endless patience and who adores me, though I'm not sure—despite eighteen years together—why.

What was the hardest part of this book for you to write?

Originally, Princella had no redeeming qualities. None. I hated her. But with the wise prompting of my editor, I knew I had to make her more well-rounded. It was painful for me to find ways to pull the beautiful parts out of her. And in the end, I realized my struggle with Princella paralleled her own search for forgiveness. And so Princella and I, we both came a long way together.

Give us an interesting fun fact related to your book.

I've never once eaten pecan pie. Not one bite.

What can we expect from you in the future?

I have a second novel due out about a year from now. It is quite different from *How Sweet the Sound* in that it is set in Michigan and Ukraine. Although it is a very different (and even a bit mysterious) story, readers will enjoy the same strong themes of hope and redemption. Beyond that, I have a couple more stories brewing, and I plan to continue writing novels for as long as I can write them well.

RECIPES FROM BAY SPRING AND THE HARLAN FAMILY AND FRIENDS

You can't have a novel about the South without featuring food. Here are some good recipes for you to try, many of them featured in the novel. And if these aren't enough, you can find more—like Ernestine's cheesy jambalaya and cinnamon rolls, Anni's favorite pecan pancakes, Princella's holiday pecan log, and more—at my author website.

Cajun Pistols from the Moonlight and Magnolia Music Festival

(be sure to have a lemonade shake-up or a cold glass of sweet tea on hand!)

FILLING

½ cup chopped onion

½ cup chopped celery

½ cup butter

Minced garlic

Salt and pepper

½ pound crawfish tails

½ pound crab meat

¼ cup shredded cheddar cheese

¼ cup shredded Swiss cheese or whatever cheese you like

1-½ tablespoons chopped green onion

1-½ tablespoons chopped parsley

A shake or two of ground hot pepper

A shake (or six!) of your favorite hot sauce

DOUGH

2 cups Bisquick

¾ cups water

Vegetable oil for frying

1. Sauté onion and celery in butter until tender.
2. Add garlic, seasoning, and crawfish tails. Simmer 10 minutes or until all liquid evaporates.
3. Set aside and let cool completely.
4. Add cheese, green onions, and parsley.
5. Prepare dough by stirring biscuit mix and water with a fork. On well-floured surface, roll out dough. Cut with 4-inch circle cutter.
6. Place crawfish filling on half of dough.
7. Fold circle in half, seal edges with fork dipped in flour.
8. In deep pot, heat oil to 350 degrees. Fry beignets until golden brown.
9. Serve warm.

Makes about sixteen beignets.

Jed's Favorite Pecan–Crusted Chicken Strips

2 pounds ½-inch chicken strips
1–2 beaten eggs
¼ cup flour
Salt and pepper to taste
1-½ cups finely chopped pecans
¼-inch canola oil for skillet

1. Salt and pepper chicken strips to taste.
2. Dredge lightly in flour, then egg.
3. Roll in chopped pecans. Set aside.
4. Heat oil in pan to medium high.
5. Place coated chicken strips in pan and cook about 2 minutes on each side, until pecans are a nice golden-brown.
6. Place cooked chicken strips on paper towels to drain.

Solly's Hotter-than-Snot Pecan-Stuffed Pickled Jalapeños

Whole pickled jalapeño peppers
Spreadable garlic-and-herb cheese, softened
Chopped toasted pecans

1. Cut peppers in half lengthwise; remove and discard seeds and membranes.
2. Pipe softened cheese into each pepper half.
3. Press peppers, cheese sides down, into chopped toasted pecans.
4. Cover and chill up to one full day.

Captain Larry's Parmesan Oysters

2 dozen oysters, in the shell

¼ cup butter

1 tablespoon lemon juice

1 clove garlic, minced

¼ cup seasoned bread crumbs

1 cup Parmesan cheese, shredded

1. Place oysters (still in the shell) in the bottom of a shallow baking dish.
2. Melt butter and add garlic and lemon juice, pour over oysters.
3. Sprinkle with bread crumbs and Parmesan cheese.
4. Bake at 375 degrees for 15 minutes.
5. Serve warm with hot sauce, of course.

Vaughn's Crawdaddy Pecan Dressing

1 medium onion, chopped

1 rib celery, chopped

1 green bell pepper, chopped

1 red bell pepper, chopped

1 pound ground beef

2 tablespoons cooking oil

2 cloves garlic, minced

2 pounds cooked crawfish tails

1 cup cooked rice

1 cup pecans, toasted and chopped

¼ cup butter

1 small bunch green onions, chopped

2 tablespoons creole seasoning

½ teaspoon black pepper

1. Cook onion, celery, bell peppers, garlic, and ground beef over medium-high heat until beef crumbles and no pink remains.
2. Stir in crawfish, rice, pecans, butter, green onions, creole seasoning, and black pepper.
3. Cook three minutes or until thoroughly heated.
4. Spoon into baking dish lightly greased or sprayed with cooking spray.
5. Bake at 350 degrees for 25 to 30 minutes.

Comfort's Homecoming Peach–Pecan Pie

CRUST

½ a store-bought crust, or use your mama's pie crust recipe

FILLING

3 cups peeled and sliced fresh peaches

1 cup sugar

⅔ cup sour cream

3 egg yolks

2 tablespoons all-purpose flour

Dash of lemon rind

PECAN-CRUMB TOPPING

½ cup (1 stick) cold unsalted butter

½ cup sugar

¼ cup all-purpose flour

½ teaspoon ground cinnamon

¼ teaspoon allspice

½ cup (2 oz.) chopped pecans

FOR FILLING:

1. Scatter peach slices over bottom of pie crust.
2. Using a whisk, combine sugar, sour cream, egg yolks, and flour, and pour over the peaches.
3. Bake at 350 until the custard is set and the crust is golden-brown, approximately 30 minutes.

FOR TOPPING:

1. Combine butter, sugar, flour, and cinnamon in the bowl of a food processor. Pulse until the mixture resembles peas and cornmeal. Stir in the chopped pecans and set aside.
2. Scatter pecan topping over pie.
3. Return pie to oven and bake until the topping is golden-brown, about 10–15 minutes more.
4. Place pie on a cooling rack and let cool to room temperature.
5. Ernestine recommends topping with cinnamon whipped cream.